COLD CASE

A COLD HARBOR NOVEL - BOOK FOUR

SUSAN SLEEMAN

EDGE OF YOUR SEAT BOOKS, INC.

Published by Edge of Your Seat Books, Inc.

Contact the publisher at contact@edgeofyourseatbooks.com

1

Cancel your classes or your computer isn't the only thing that will be DOA.

Eryn Calloway couldn't look away from her computer. Away from the blue screen—the visual known in the computer world as the "blue screen of death," warning of a fatal system error.

But this warning was different. Very different.

It wasn't a Windows error. Not a virus. Her machine hadn't crashed.

Someone was threatening her life. Here. Now. At the annual Policing in the Modern World Conference where she was teaching computer courses as a representative of her team, Blackwell Tactical.

How could this be?

She was smack dab in the middle of a crowd of law enforcement officers mingling in the lobby of The Dunes Resort and someone wanted her dead.

Craziness. She shook her head at the absurdity, but fear had a hold of her stomach and it wouldn't let go.

"Eryn?" Deputy Trey Sawyer's deep voice jolted her.

She whipped around to see him approaching her, weaving through the crowd.

If she hadn't recognized his voice, his red hair would make him easy to find in a crowd. But his voice stood out to her much like a mother instantly picked out her child's voice in a group. Not that Eryn's feelings for him were motherly. Not by any stretch of the imagination.

She filled her lungs with air and connected with his grayish-blue eyes that were often calm and reflective of his easygoing personality. But not today. He looked darkly dangerous and very intimidating.

Every bit of air she'd drawn in whooshed out. She'd never seen this side of him, but man, she liked it equally as well as the laid-back guy.

He ran his gaze over her. "You're as white as a sheet. What's wrong?"

No way she was telling him anything. He was the last guy she wanted to share her problem with.

She reached for the laptop screen to lower it. He shot out a hand and pressed it over hers, halting her movement. His touch amplified the usual tingle of excitement she felt in his presence, and her already stressed-out mind whirled.

She swallowed hard and did her best not to reveal her unease about the hack *and* about seeing him again. They'd danced around their mutual attraction for a year now, and she found him almost impossible to resist. *Almost.* But she managed it so far. The key was to eliminate the time they spent together.

Today was no exception. She would move on as soon as possible, and while he was here, she wouldn't display even a hint of her feelings. Not when she would never let things develop with him. Or any other man for that matter.

He bent forward to stare at the screen and released her

hand. He worked the muscles in his strong jaw for a moment then turned his gaze on her, the intensity there making her gasp. "What in the world is going on, Eryn?"

"It's nothing." She tried to sound casual, but she didn't manage it.

"Right. *Nothing* made all the color drain from your face." He grabbed a chair and turned it to face her. He straddled the seat and rested powerful arms on the chair back.

She took a moment to look at him. Not a good idea, but then she didn't have good ideas around him. He wore black tactical pants much like hers, and an Under Armour tactical shirt in an army green color that fit him like a second set of skin, accentuating his muscular build and broad shoulders.

Her gaze wanted to linger there, but she forced it back to his face. She steeled her expression and her voice. "It's nothing. Leave it alone."

She closed her computer and started to get up.

He rested a hand on her shoulder, effectively stopping her from rising. She held there, midair, and refused to look at him.

"I can't let this go, and you know it." The vehemence in his tone surprised her. Where was the laid-back guy she knew? "Someone is threatening you, and you need help."

Right. *His* help. She shook his hand off and stood up. He was acting like most guys—assuming she wasn't capable of taking care of herself. But as a former FBI agent and cyber-security expert, she was capable. Very capable. She turned to glare at him and walk away, but his eyes were locked on her like a sniper eyeing his target. Leaving without discussing this was pointless. He would trail her and corner her in another location.

She sat back down and lifted her chin. "I can handle this."

His gaze softened, his eyes bluer now, a striking contrast to his rich red hair. "Why do you always think you need to be so tough?"

She *did* have to be tough in the law enforcement world to ensure that men took her seriously. Fortunately, her male teammates at Blackwell Tactical respected her skills and abilities.

She deflected his question with a wave of her hand. "Why do you have to interrogate me? I said I can handle it."

He eyed her but didn't budge.

"Look. I'm a cyber professional and know how to deal with this hack." She leaned closer so they wouldn't be overheard in the crowded lobby. "The guy deployed ransomware. You've likely heard of the software that locks a computer until the owner pays ransom to have it released. Well in this case, he doesn't want money. He probably did it to show off. It likely happened when I logged into the unsecured resort network. I'll restore my machine, trace the hack back to the offender, and turn him over to the authorities. End of story."

Trey shook his head. "That doesn't explain why this hacker wants you to cancel your classes, and he's threatening your life if you don't."

Her gut was twisted in a knot over that very thing, but she ignored Trey's concern. "He's likely just testing my competency."

Trey's eyes hardened to steel. "Or this person really does want you to stop teaching and is going to kill you if you don't."

Eryn sat back, putting a wall up between them. "You've been in law enforcement too long for your own good—seeing a problem where one doesn't exist."

"No." He planted his hands on the table. "I'm seeing

4

what was right in front of my face before you closed your computer."

She didn't know how to respond, so she said nothing.

He made a low sound in his throat like a growl, then shook his head. "Tell me about your classes."

She wanted to rush up to her room to take care of the computer issue. But Trey was tenacious and wouldn't let it go until she explained, so she would get it over as quickly as possible. "I'm teaching two classes. One is about how every cell phone is unique and pictures taken on a cell can be traced back to an individual phone due to these unique characteristics."

He sat up a little higher. "I've never heard of that."

"It's a new discovery and not readily used yet, but I want detectives to start thinking about the possibilities of how to utilize this element in their investigations."

"Explain," he demanded.

At his tone, she thought about refusing, but again, he would keep badgering her until she answered. "Digital cameras are built identically, but manufacturing imperfections create tiny variations in the camera sensors. The variations cause some of the sensors' pixels to project slightly brighter or darker colors than they should—called pattern noise. It's not visible to the naked eye but can be found with deeper examination."

"Very interesting, but worth killing you over?" He shook his head. "I don't get that."

"I agree, which is why it's likely just an attention-grabbing measure."

"Don't be so quick to dismiss it without further thought."

She should've known he would keep after it. She would, too. The minute she reached her room. She shifted to stand.

"And the other class?" he asked, stilling her.

She had to appease him. "It's about the Internet of Things."

"Is that a new term? I've never heard of it."

"Not new, but fairly recent, I guess. IoT devices are those with on and off switches and connect to the Internet and/or to each other. Things like cars, televisions, phones, and refrigerators."

"Yeah, I can see that. Computers have invaded our world. There's a 'smart' *everything* these days."

"I know, isn't it great?" She chuckled.

He frowned. If he couldn't laugh at her joke then he really was upset.

"What are you going to do about the hack?" he asked.

"First, I need to get my PowerPoint presentations up and running on my computer so I can teach my next class."

"Now wait a minute." He sat forward. "You're not going to ignore the warning."

"Wouldn't you?"

He blinked. "Yeah, likely, but—"

"But you're not a helpless girl like me and can protect yourself," she finished for him and crossed her arms.

"Wait, no. I don't think you're helpless."

"But I *do* need protecting."

He rolled his eyes and ran his fingers through his fiery red hair, leaving it in disarray. "I can't win here, can I?"

"Honestly, no. I get tired of the double standards in law enforcement. Either I'm as capable as you are or I'm not."

He clenched his jaw. "You know that's not all it is. I care about you, and when I care about someone I do my best to make sure they're safe. Just like you and the rest of your team have each other's backs. If one of the team members is in danger, the others step up."

He was right, and she couldn't argue. He knew the team well. He was good friends with Eryn's boss, Gage Blackwell who owned Blackwell Tactical. Their friendship went back to their military days when Gage was a SEAL and Trey served as a Green Beret, and they'd worked on a joint team together. And a year ago, Trey helped Blackwell out when someone threatened Gage's wife. That was when Eryn had met Trey. Since then, he'd attended several of their law enforcement trainings at the team compound an hour up the coast in Cold Harbor.

She didn't mind acknowledging the team dynamics, but she wouldn't respond to his comment of caring about her. That would take them through a rabbit hole she didn't want to go down.

"You're right," she said. "We do look after each other and have a strong bond. Maybe stronger than most teams since injuries took us out of our chosen professions. It's a bond we all share. But we don't overreact, and *you're* overreacting, Trey."

He shot her a testy look. "No. I'm stepping up here like the team would. You're not going to stop me, so you might as well quit wasting your effort trying." He jabbed his finger on the table. "You can't teach the classes."

"See? You *are* overreacting." His behavior made her even more stubborn. "I'm not going to back down on that. I'll be teaching my scheduled classes."

He jerked his legs back, the muscles rippling against his pant leg as if he was ready to spring from his chair and fight her foe. He grimaced, but it disappeared as fast as it started. He'd been shot in the leg helping Hannah and still hadn't recovered.

He met her gaze and held it. "You're not teaching if I have anything to say about it."

She worked hard to remain calm and not snap at him. "Why would you have anything to say about it?"

"Because someone has to watch out for you."

"Please," she said and resisted rolling her eyes. "There are five big strapping guys on our team. They're all I need."

"So, you're going to tell them about this, then?"

She hadn't planned on bringing it up. Not when there wasn't proof that this was nothing more than an idle threat. But she wouldn't tell Trey that. Lying went against her Christian beliefs, and she wouldn't start now simply to calm Trey down.

He glared at her. "You tell Gage or I will."

Trey wouldn't hesitate to call his buddy Gage. It would be far better coming from her. "Fine. I'll tell him."

"Today."

She stood and stared down on him. "I'll do it the moment I get my computer up and running."

"How long will that take?"

She rubbed her neck to ease the tension. "If all goes well, a few hours or so."

"Okay, I'll cut you some slack and give you three hours. If you haven't told Gage by then, I will."

She eyed him. "You really are a pain, you know that?"

He smiled, his eyes softening. "A pain who cares about you and doesn't want to see anything bad happen to you."

She blew out a breath. "I appreciate that you care, Trey. I just wish you didn't care so stinkin' much."

Trey didn't like letting Eryn walk away from him when she was irritated with him. For so many reasons it was hard to count. But most of all, he knew she hated it when guys underestimated her abilities. Was one of her pet peeves actually, and he fell prey to it all the time.

At five-foot-seven, he thought of her as petite compared to his six-foot-four height. A petite and very pretty woman. She had long black glossy hair that she usually wore in a ponytail, but today it was free flowing and swung with each step. She wore her usual black tactical pants and a no-nonsense knit shirt revealing upper body muscles that she worked hard to build and maintain.

She looked tough, but at the same time managed to appear so feminine that the combination did a number on him. Couple that with her big brown eyes, delicate eyebrows, and a full bottom lip that he dreamed of kissing for months now, and he was captivated by her. Smitten—if truth be told.

He got up to keep an eye on her, his right thigh aching with the movement. He'd suffered a gunshot wound to the thigh when he was helping apprehend a thug bent on killing Gage's wife, and Trey had been confined to desk duty since then. He was starting to believe it wasn't going to fully heal, and he would never go back to patrol.

Eryn slowly made her way through the sea of officers lingering between classes, and many of them paused to follow her progress across the room. A stab of jealousy bit into him. Not that he thought she would be any more interested in one of them than she was in him.

She lost her husband four years ago and was solely focused on raising her four-year-old daughter Bekah. Trey had once asked Eryn out, and she said she had no time for a man in her life. But then, there were moments when he caught her looking at him with such longing, he couldn't help but hope she would change her mind if he was just persistent. So he had been. Very persistent because she was so worth it.

But now? Now he needed to lay back. His leg wasn't one hundred percent, making his future employment uncertain. Not a good time to start dating, and he wouldn't want to lead her on. He had to get his mind right about his future job before embarking on a relationship.

He sighed out a long breath. Life was so complicated at times, even with God's guidance. He knew God heard his pleas since the injury and would point him in the right direction, but Trey had never been faced with such a big U-turn in life. God would show Trey the way as long as he kept the lines of communication open and didn't step out before the timing was right. But man, he wanted to step out. Wanted to get back to work. Forget the mounds of paper-work and get back to actively helping others.

He shook his head, clearing his mind, and started through the lobby toward the coffee stand in the corner. His leg throbbed with each step, but he tried to ignore it to smile at the barista as he ordered a black cup of coffee. None of that fancy stuff for him.

"Trey," Gage Blackwell's voice came from over Trey's shoulder.

He turned and schooled his expression so he didn't let on about his worry for Eryn. As much as he'd pushed her, he wanted her to have a chance to explain the situation to Gage.

"What's up?" Trey asked.

"I was hoping I'd run into you." Gage clapped Trey on the back. "How about we sit down for a minute?"

"If this is about the job offer, I'm not ready to go there yet." When Trey had been shot, Gage offered Trey a job on the team. Trey wouldn't mind joining Blackwell, but he couldn't be around Eryn every day. Not with the way he felt about her when she didn't return the feelings.

"Leg's getting better then?" Gage asked.

"Nah, but after the latest surgery, I still have a few more weeks of PT so I'm hopeful."

Gage gave him a knowing look, and Trey didn't like it. Gage suffered a permanent arm injury as a SEAL and was faced with riding a desk or leaving the team. Like most men in spec ops, he didn't do desk duty well so he left his team. Everyone on Blackwell Tactical had faced a similar situation. Trey was heading down the same path, but not willingly.

"I hope it works out for you," Gage said. "So this isn't about a job. Got a minute then?"

Trey nodded. "Let's find some place quieter."

He led Gage to the area where he and Eryn had talked. Her face, white against her dark hair, came to mind again, and his gut cramped. He resolved to find a way to get her to agree to let him keep an eye on her until this situation was resolved.

He sat on a plump sofa in a beachy turquoise color and moved around until he eliminated the ache in his leg.

Gage took a seat in a matching plush chair across from him. "Did I mention that I'm looking for a forensic person for the team?"

Trey shook his head.

"Law enforcement training and protection services are still our main focus, but the number of clients needing us to investigate unsolved crimes has grown rapidly. So we need a forensic expert."

Trey took a sip of the rich black coffee. "Makes sense. Especially since you want to collect the evidence in a manner that would make it usable in court."

Gage nodded. "But you also know one of my main purposes of starting Blackwell is to offer injured soldiers or officers a second chance at a job they love."

"So you're looking for a crime scene investigator who's been injured and benched."

"Exactly. And I'm striking out."

"Yeah, not too many CSI's get injured on the job." Trey rested his cup on his knee. "Did you try the Portland Police Bureau? Their criminalists are required to be sworn officers, and they still work patrol jobs for protests and riots."

Gage shook his head. "Do you have any contacts there?"

"Yeah, I have a buddy on the force. I can give him a call to see if he knows anyone who fits the bill."

"Appreciate it, man." Gage sat back and crossed his feet at the ankles. "I'm a little surprised to see you here."

"Why's that?"

"Didn't think you'd need a lot of training for desk duty." Gage chuckled.

Trey forced a smile. He hadn't reached the point where he could joke about his potential loss of career yet. And besides, Trey thought Gage knew exactly why he was here. Why he always signed up for other trainings at Blackwell's compound, too. Shoot, the whole team probably knew he had it bad for Eryn. He doubted he was very subtle about it.

"Seriously, man, if the leg doesn't improve enough to go back on patrol, let me know. I'll always have a job open for you."

"You don't have to feel guilty, you know. Just because I was helping you out when it happened."

"Actually, I credit you with saving Hannah's life and will always be in your debt, but this is business. I'm smart enough to know you'd be a real asset to the team. But don't go telling anyone that. I won't admit to saying it." Gage grinned, but he looked over Trey's shoulder, and his smile vanished.

Trey pivoted to see what had changed Gage's good mood and spotted Eryn storming their way.

"Wonder what's got Eryn so mad?" Gage mused.

Trey didn't know, but he suspected it had to do with the threat and computer issue. Maybe she failed at restoring her computer.

She locked gazes with Trey and stormed straight ahead. Her muscular legs took her through the crowd in seconds. Breathing hard, she came to a stop in front of him. She looked like a fierce lion planning to defend her cub, and the wild beauty in her expression got Trey's heart pumping hard.

"You couldn't wait, could you?" She locked onto his gaze like a Sidewinder missile. "You had to rat me out."

"I didn't—"

"What happened to giving me three hours? It's been less than thirty minutes."

"Like I said, I—"

"I thought you were a man of your word."

"Eryn," Gage said calmly. "Breathe and give the guy a chance to speak."

She fisted her hands on her hips and glared at him. "Well?"

"I didn't tell Gage anything. He asked to talk to me about finding a forensic person for the team."

"Oh." Her anger evaporated from her expression, and she seemed to melt right in front of them.

"I thought..." She shook her head. "I'm sorry, Trey. There was no call for doubting your word."

Gage looked back and forth between them, his gaze

questioning. "But apparently there *is* call for me to wonder what the two of you are keeping from me."

Eryn sank down on the sofa next to Trey. She didn't seem to realize how close she was sitting to him, but he could feel the heat of her leg resting nearby, and he had a hard time focusing on anything but that.

"I got a ransomware notice on my laptop," she said, her breathing under control. "And Trey happened to be passing by and saw it."

"Ransomware?" Gage shook his head. "I can see that happening to others on the team, but you? I can hardly believe it."

"I know, right?" She frowned. "I'm never going to live it down."

"Truer words have never been said." Gage chuckled. "Is that why you didn't want to tell me?"

"Sort of." Eryn glanced at Trey.

He figured her look meant she wanted him to back down about mentioning the warning, but he wasn't about to do so. He opened his mouth to say that when she faced Gage again. "It wasn't your typical ransomware warning."

"How's that?" Gage's eyes widened.

"They didn't ask for payment to release my computer. Not that I would pay it anyway. No point. I back up my machine daily and can restore it with little effort. And this is my travel computer so there's not much on it anyway."

"Travel computer?" Trey asked.

"When I do trainings I often have to access unsecured networks like here at the resort. So I don't want to risk having confidential information on my machine in case I'm hacked."

"But what if you're working an investigation?" Trey asked. "Don't you need access to more information then?"

She nodded. "In that case, I don't access unsecured networks. I use my phone as a hot spot instead."

Trey nodded. He'd heard of using a cell phone like a wireless router, but honestly, he didn't know how it worked.

"I've already traced the ransomware," she continued. "My class files were infected. I was on my way to talk to the conference director about it when I saw you two talking." A sheepish look crossed her face.

"You mentioned this wasn't a typical ransomware warning," Gage said.

She nodded. "The threat actor didn't ask for money or Bitcoins. He wants me to stop teaching my classes."

It often seemed like she spoke another language, and Trey always learned something new when he talked to her. "What's a threat actor?"

"The person or entity responsible for a malicious act. They're often called hackers by laypeople, but in the IT world they're called actors."

"Well this hacker or actor or whatever you want to call him says if you don't cancel your classes he'll kill you," Trey added. "Or at least that's what I thought the warning meant when it said you'd be DOA if you didn't stop."

Gage frowned and locked his gaze on Eryn. "And you didn't want to tell me about this—why?"

"Because of the way you're looking at me."

"And how's that exactly?"

"Like you want to lock me in my room and not let me out until this guy is caught. Or worse, send me back to Cold Harbor for my own protection."

"Neither of those are bad ideas," Trey said.

Eryn fired him an irritated look. "I committed to teaching here, and I *will* follow through on that. The officers only have so much money and time for continuing ed in a year, and I won't make them miss out."

Gage scrunched his dark eyebrows together. "Then we need to be smart about this. I'll assign someone on the team to your protection."

"Who?" she asked. "You, Riley, and Alex are holding classes here. Coop and Jackson are training at the compound. Any change to that would create the same problem."

"I'm free," Trey offered. "And glad to step in."

"Perfect solution," Gage readily agreed.

"No," Eryn said. "No. No way."

"Why not?" Gage asked. "Trey is as capable as anyone on the team."

"It's not that."

"Then what?"

Eryn nipped on her lip, and Trey knew she was trying to come up with anything other than to mention that he had a thing for her.

He could solve that problem for her. "I think she's worried that I've fallen for her and can't keep my hands off her."

"We all know that, but so far you seem to be able to control yourself." Gage grinned.

Eryn frowned. "It's not funny."

"I know," Gage said. "But you've got to admit, it paints a pretty interesting picture."

"Not one I want to paint." She crossed her arms.

"Look," Trey said. "If I promise not to even hint at my interest in you other than to make sure you're safe, will you let me do this for you?"

She frowned and looked like she planned to refuse. Maybe she should. Because even frowning, he wanted to kiss those lips. Still, he couldn't let her off the hook. "If you won't think about yourself, think about Bekah."

She shot him a frustrated look. "Low blow bringing my daughter into this."

"May be low," Gage said. "But he has a point. Your mom and Bekah came along on this trip, so you need to think of them, too."

"I'll send them back to the compound."

"How?" Trey asked. "The compound is an hour down the coast and no one's free to escort them."

"Fine," she said, but crossed her arms, her eyes still locked on Trey. "You can be my bodyguard, but you need to promise to keep things professional between us at all times."

"I promise I'll do my best."

"Glad that's settled." Gage fixed his focus on Eryn. "The guys and I have a three-bedroom suite. We'll move out so you and your family can have it. That way the hacker won't know the exact room where you're staying, and it'll give Trey a room in the same suite, too."

"You're right, *if* the hacker doesn't have her under surveillance," Trey added.

"I can't have you give up such a nice room," Eryn said ignoring Trey's comment.

Gage waved a hand. "I only booked a suite so we'd have a place for the team to meet. We can still meet there, right?"

"Of course."

"Good. Then it's settled. I'll text the others to let them know we're moving."

"Bekah's napping so we'll move our things when she wakes up... if that works for you."

"Sounds good."

She stood. "Thanks, Gage. We can always count on you."

Trey got up, and the jealousy that hit him earlier took a

bite again. He wanted Eryn to think the same thing about him. He was dependable and reliable and would be there for her every minute she needed him. She could count on that.

She glanced at him. "I suppose you'll want to come with me now."

He nodded and chose not to comment on the fact that her expression said she would rather go a few rounds with a rattlesnake than have him accompany her. He would have his work cut out for him, but he was always up for a challenge.

Especially when that challenge was someone as beautiful and captivating as Eryn Calloway.

2

Unbelievable. Just unbelievable.

Trey would be Eryn's shadow for the next three days of the conference or less if they found the actor, and she already wanted to bolt from him. Instead, she headed straight across the lobby to the room assigned to the training company.

Even with a bum thigh, Trey kept up with her. She told him she should be able to find the actor, but the reality was, actors were notoriously hard to trace. She possessed an advanced degree in IT, and in her former job as an FBI agent, she'd worked in the cyber crimes division. Meant she had both experience and training, and it would still be a challenge.

She knocked on the door that held a placard with the name Law Enforcement Network, Inc. Not a minute passed before company owner Martha Green pulled the door open. Eryn pegged Martha at fifty with shoulder length greyish-blond hair in tight corkscrew curls. She had a square face, and her eyebrows were drawn on with a heavy black pencil.

"Eryn, how nice to see you." She looked over Eryn's

shoulder. "Now I know *you're* not a Blackwell Tactical member, but you're in law enforcement. That much I can tell."

Trey stuck out his hand. "Trey Sawyer, Deschutes County Deputy."

"Knew it." She stepped back. "C'mon in."

"This isn't a social call," Eryn said, but entered the suite as she didn't want others to overhear her when she told Martha her company had been hacked.

Martha closed the door. "That sounds ominous."

Eryn didn't bother sitting but turned to face Martha. "I hate to bring you bad news, but your company's network server was hacked."

Martha blanched, and with her already pale complexion, she was nearly as white as the sheet Trey had mentioned earlier. "Say what?"

"Why don't we sit down," Eryn suggested before Martha dropped to the floor.

They took seats at a small round dining table, Trey turning the chair and straddling it again. Did he always have to do that? Made Eryn notice the corded muscles in his arms and wonder how it would feel to be held by them.

Focus, Eryn. It's just muscles. You have them, too. Get a grip.

She shifted to put her entire focus on Martha. "My laptop was compromised this morning—locked up with ransomware. I know I didn't download any malware in the usual ways so—"

"Usual ways?" Martha interrupted.

"Clicking on links in emails. Inserting a flash drive that I found or was given to me. Or falling for social media hoaxes. Things like that. The only files I accessed since arriving here are the forms I had participants fill out, scan, and upload to your server for my IoT class."

Eryn took a breath and gave Martha a moment to process the news before continuing. "I downloaded those files right before the ransomware deployed on my laptop. I should have realized one of the images was a much larger file size and been more cautious, but I thought maybe the participant saved it with greater resolution. I reviewed that file and discovered the ransomware code embedded in it."

"You can embed malware in an image?" Trey asked.

Eryn nodded. "It's called Steganography. It's been used by malicious software writers for quite some time. By embedding code in a file format that looks legitimate, there's a chance the file will pass security software protocols, making it more likely to be accessed."

"So you think someone hacked into LEN's website and altered this file?" Trey asked.

"Either that or the officer who uploaded the file wrote the code, which I doubt."

"Why?"

"As far as coding goes, it's not overly complicated, but for most casual computer users—like those who attend my classes, it would be very advanced.

"But that doesn't necessarily mean my site was hacked, right?" Martha asked. "Couldn't someone have used your login to upload this file?"

Eryn resisted sighing as people were rarely willing to accept their servers were compromised. "My password and login are too secure for anyone to crack without a super computer, which means the actor had to find another way to access the file. And the only other way to do so is to alter the file while it resides on your server. That could only occur if your employees aren't ethical or by hacking."

"Employee singular. There's only one person with permission to alter network files. My administrator, Preston

Hunt. And he wouldn't do something like this." Martha twisted her hands together. "Do you think the hacker modified anything else?"

Eryn wasn't ready to concede that Preston was on the up and up without reviewing the files to see how and by who they were modified. "I can't know about further modifications without full access to your website files and logs. If you'll grant me permission to access them, I can evaluate all files along with trying to trace the actor."

"You'd do that for me?" Martha asked.

"Of course, but you should know I also have a vested interest in locating this actor since he threatened me. I'll also want to look at the class rosters."

Martha grabbed a notepad and pen. "Here's Preston's contact info. I'll call him right away and tell him to grant you full access. Then you can connect with him to get the details."

"Sounds perfect."

Martha gnawed on her lip. "The last thing I need is for law enforcement officers to have to deal with their computers being hacked. Maybe have their confidential data stolen. That could mean the end of my company."

"On that note," Eryn said. "I suggest you have Preston suspend access to any files and go the old-fashioned route and have your instructors print handouts."

"Of course. I'll tell Preston to do that first." She picked at a dot of fuzz on her black slacks and flicked it away, looking very much like she wanted to flick this problem away as easily. "Is there anything else I should do?"

"If you can't get ahold of Preston immediately," Eryn said. "I'd get in touch with instructors for the next few classes and tell them not to download any files and to instruct their students not to do so."

Martha jumped up and grabbed her phone from the desk. "If you don't mind seeing yourselves out, I'll call him now."

Eryn smiled at the older woman in an attempt to ease her mind. "Thanks for being so cooperative, Martha."

She was already dialing her phone and didn't seem to notice when Eryn and Trey headed for the door.

"Preston," Martha breathed out his name in a sigh of relief. "Thank goodness you answered. Our server's been hacked."

Eryn was glad to hear that Martha connected with him as it would make things go much faster if Eryn had file access.

Trey looked at Eryn as they walked down the quiet hallway. "Could it be possible that this hack wasn't about you but was about LEN's network, and the warning was to throw you off target?"

"Could be," she replied. "But I don't yet have proof that anything else was compromised in their files."

"I know hacking is a big business, but is there another reason to hack the network other than for monetary gain?"

"LEN has a database containing officer's information and someone could want access to that. Still, as much as I don't want to, I believe the hack was all about me, not about the site in general."

"Big head much?" He chuckled.

She punched his arm. "You know what I mean."

"Yeah, just had to tease you a little bit." His mouth tipped in a wide grin that she found irresistible. "So, computer pro, what next?"

"We head up to my room to call Preston. Once he has the other logins disabled, he'll set up access for me, and I'll start reviewing the files and logs."

"Sounds like there's nothing I can do to help with that."

"Actually, you could help out with Detective Young. He uploaded the image containing the ransomware code, and you can run a background check on him."

"It didn't sound like you thought an officer uploaded an infected file."

"I don't, but I never leave anything to chance."

She started for the elevator and kept her head on a swivel, looking for anyone who might be watching them. For the most part, she'd been playing down the danger, hoping Trey would relax a bit. She felt the threat was legitimate, but the actor wouldn't have reason to follow through on his threat until after she failed to cancel her classes.

"Too bad you're so good-looking," Trey said out of the blue.

"What?" She gaped at him as she didn't have any idea where he was going with that comment.

"You're drawing attention from many of the men, and I can't tell if they're watching you because they think you're gorgeous or if one of them is our hacker."

She put her hands on her hips. "They're only looking at me because I'm one of the few females in the room."

"Um, Eryn, trust me. That's not the only reason."

But you're biased, she wanted to say, but didn't. She wasn't about to bring up anything personal.

They rode the glass elevator overlooking the luxurious lobby. She should take a moment to enjoy the view. She couldn't afford to stay in such a resort without the generous conference discount, but the tension cutting between her and Trey made it impossible to focus anywhere else. When the doors opened, she led him down the hallway to her room that adjoined her mother's room where Bekah napped.

Eryn's room smelled of baby wipes used to clean sticky hands, a constant thing with Bekah. How one little four-year-old could find so much stickiness, Eryn didn't know, but her daughter excelled at it.

Her mother stepped into the room, and Eryn felt self-conscious about her mother's flowing patchwork maxi skirt, tunic top, and fringed leather vest. She was a beautiful woman and looked great in her throwback hippie fashion, but Eryn experienced years of teasing about her mother being different from other moms. She never knew how someone would react to the unusual attire.

Her mother spotted Trey, and her eyes widened. "We have a guest, I see."

"Mom, this is Trey Sawyer. Trey, this is my mother, Sandra Dawson."

Her mother offered her usual warm smile and shook his hand. "Nice to meet you, Trey."

"Likewise," Trey said sincerely.

Eryn relaxed a notch. "Trey's volunteered to be our bodyguard until I find the actor who deployed the ransomware."

Her mother blinked long false lashes that she wore with heavy blue eye shadow. "Is that really necessary?"

"No," Eryn said.

"Yes," Trey said at the same time.

Eryn rubbed her forehead. "With you and Bekah here, it's better to be safe than sorry. In any event, the actor won't try anything until he figures out I didn't cancel my classes."

Her mother fixed her focus on Trey. "I presume you don't plan to use this as an excuse to stay in Eryn's room."

Trey's mouth dropped open, and Eryn almost snorted. Her mother had many hippie values, but men and women sharing a room before marriage was not one of them.

"Gage offered to give us his suite," Eryn said. "Trey will have his own room."

"Good, good."

Eryn nodded. "Okay, I need to get to work before Bekah wakes up."

"You don't have to look so excited about working." Her mother shook her head. "How I ever had a child who loves computers the way you do, I'll never know."

Eryn faced Trey. "Mom refuses to even get a smartphone. She's a hippie throwback. Needs no electronics in her life at all."

"No one *needs* electronics," Trey said.

"Et tu brute!" Laughing, Eryn clutched her chest and went to the desk in the corner.

"I'm going to like your young man," her mother called after her.

"He's not my—"

"And I know I already like your mother," Trey interrupted.

With her back to the pair, Eryn could imagine them both deviously rubbing their hands together like evil TV villains while conspiring against her.

"Since you're here," her mother said. "I'm going to run out and grab a few things we forgot to bring."

"Maybe Trey should go with you," Eryn called out and sat in the desk chair.

"Nice try," Trey said. "But there's no evidence that Sandra will be in any danger right now. Like you said, you should be okay until you don't cancel those classes."

"Like he said." Her mother chuckled and grabbed her purse embellished with heavy suede fringes on the way out the door.

"Your mom seems real nice." Trey took a seat in a chair in the corner.

Eryn turned to face him. "She's the best. Even if I do tease her about the electronics. For some reason I can't even fathom, ignoring it all works for her."

"I probably should tell you right up front that I don't know much about electronics either. Most of what I know I learned at work."

"Not a video gamer, then?"

"Not really. You?"

"I used to be more of one. I play with the guys sometimes, especially Riley, but as a single mom I really don't have a lot of free time, and I'd rather spend it in other ways." She swiveled back to the desk. "Now I really need to get to work."

She took out her phone to call Preston and hoped Trey would start running the background check on Detective Young. She got Preston on the first ring, and he confirmed that he was now the only person with access to the files. He was working on providing her with read-only credentials so she could look at files but not write to them. They discussed the hack for bit, throwing out ideas, but discussing it was really a waste of time until she looked at the files. He promised she'd have access in a few minutes and provided a login and password before he hung up.

"Seriously, was any of that in English?" Trey joked.

She gave him a fiendish look. "That's how we ensure you all need us. You can't understand the language."

He chuckled, which she was starting to learn he did often, and she had to admit that so far, she didn't dislike having him around. His personality was generally so light-hearted when she tended toward serious. Maybe that's why she felt this overwhelming attraction to him. They balanced each other out.

Her computer signaled the end to reformatting, and she tested the login for LEN's server. *Bingo*. She was in and had access to the files and logs. She wanted to get to work, but she felt Trey watching her as if she was an ant farm he was studying through glass panes.

She took a quiet peek at him over her shoulder. He held his phone, but he was looking at her not the screen. She couldn't work like this. And she couldn't constantly be reminded of his attraction to her. That brought up her interest in him, and then it all snowballed in her mind into a blizzard of emotions she didn't want to feel.

She rolled her desk chair over to face him. "If this is going to work, you need to stop watching me."

"Sorry," he said. "You're much more interesting than my phone." His lips turned up in one of his charming and irresistible grins.

She took a long breath and forced from her mind all emotions the smile evoked. "You promised to keep this professional."

"I said I'd do my best, and I'm trying, but I'm obviously not succeeding."

She watched him for a long moment to gauge his sincerity. "You have to try harder. And honestly, while I'm in my room, you don't even need to be here."

"I get that, but I also know you. You'll be working along and suddenly realize you need to do something." His nose flared as if she'd made him mad. "Will you call me and wait for me to come back? No, you'll go barreling out of the room without thinking about it. And if I'm not here, you'll be alone."

She wished she could argue his point, but it was valid.

"Okay. I might do that. So can you keep busy and stop watching me?"

"You know," he said. "Maybe we should finally talk about this thing between us, and it won't be a big deal anymore."

She wrinkled her nose. "There's nothing going on between us."

"So you're not attracted to me, then?" He seemed genuinely disappointed.

"I didn't say that. You're a very good-looking man, and I'm sure you've had to fend off your share of advances over the years."

"Ditto for you."

"I'm a good-looking man, huh?" She laughed and hoped it would lighten the mood.

"Oh, no, honey. Trust me. You are as far from a man as they come." He winked.

She both loved and hated having him call her *honey*. It'd been too long since a man had used a personal endearment for her, but her dislike for crossing the line from professional won out over the joy of his interest, and she frowned.

"Wait, did I say the wrong thing? I mean you're still as capable as a man." He shook his head. "I seem to have 'open mouth insert foot' syndrome today."

Normally, she would make a joke over his discomfort, but she couldn't get beyond thinking about being thrown together with him for days. They hadn't managed an hour, let alone surviving being in close proximity for days.

"Okay, so I *am* attracted to you. More than a little. Not only your looks, but you, Trey. You're a great guy. Smart. Funny. Compassionate. A real catch."

"But," he said, a vein in his temple throbbing.

"But, when my husband died, something died inside me.

Or, more accurately, something grew inside me. Fear." She paused to pull in a long breath. "Fear that if I let myself get attached to a guy again, I could never survive losing him, too. I just couldn't. So it's far easier to focus on raising Bekah and avoid everything else."

"Don't you miss being married?"

"Miss it? Yeah, I do, but like I said—"

"You're not willing to risk losing someone again." He watched her carefully. "And what about your faith?"

"What about it?"

"Isn't all this worry like saying you don't trust God?"

"Oh, that."

"Yeah, that."

She slumped back. "I hate to admit this, but losing Rich has completely sidetracked my faith."

He opened his mouth as if to say something, then snapped it closed and took a long breath.

"Go ahead," she said, knowing she shouldn't continue this discussion. "Say whatever you were going to say."

"I get it. I mean, not the fear of losing someone close to me. I faced that back when I was a Beret and came through it with my faith intact. I mean about getting sidetracked in faith." He stretched out his leg and rubbed his thigh. "This injury has me questioning, you know? I spent years as a Beret in extremely dangerous situations and came out unscathed. And then I take a pretty routine job that for the most part isn't outrageously dangerous. I step out to help Gage with one thing and take a bullet. And now what? I ride a desk? Makes no sense."

"I thought Gage offered you a job."

"He did, but..." Trey shrugged.

She watched him for a long moment. "You're not turning him down because of me, are you?"

He shrugged again.

She leaned forward and put her hand on his arm, wanting the connection as well as to make things right. "We can work this out. You can take the job. Honest. I'll be more understanding, and we can work together."

A wave of sadness flooded his eyes. "You can't 'understand' away my interest in you, Eryn. It's there, and as far as I can see, it's not going away soon."

3

Well, that discussion didn't clear the air. Totally not, and Trey was even more at a loss on how he was supposed to handle the hours and hours ahead when he'd be cooped up with the woman who could send his senses reeling with a simple look.

Too bad, dude. You asked to be with her. Now man up and get over yourself.

Maybe the answer was to have another person with them as much as possible. He'd be conscious of that and try not to be alone with her.

She turned back to her laptop. "What in the world?"

Her tone had Trey behind her in a second. "What's wrong?"

She pointed at her computer screen. "The actor's taken control of my computer again. Means he's infiltrated LEN's server. I suppose it's not a surprise, but still, I'd hoped it was just the one file."

Trey read the message and wasn't surprised to see the hacker was getting irritated.

What are you waiting for? Cancel the classes. Now! The

screen flashed, and the message disappeared.

"That's crazy." She gaped at her laptop. "He released my computer."

"Why would he do that?"

She looked up at Trey. "I don't know. Maybe the ransomware malfunctioned. Or maybe he wants me to see his code. Or he infected my computer with other malware, and he hopes I wouldn't have thought of that and I'll spread it. I just don't know."

"So what will you do?"

"I need to review his code, but he could lock up the computer again. I need to find it ASAP and put it on a flash drive." Her fingers flew over the keyboard.

A black window with white typing appeared, and she frantically typed what looked like gibberish to him. He was so impressed with her skills and would be happy to stand there watching her work, but she didn't want that, so he took a seat again in the corner. He did watch her for a minute since she was so wrapped up in her work and had no idea his focus was on her. Her intensity right now was over the top, her gaze pinned to the screen. Her delicate hands floated over the keyboard and typed at a rate he couldn't imagine achieving with his bigger chunkier fingers.

She might be far more able to protect herself than many women, but she was still small and vulnerable to a larger enemy. An overwhelming protective urge slid over Trey, and the intensity left him breathing hard. He needed to do everything to make sure the hacker didn't find her.

He picked up the handset for the room phone and dialed the operator.

"Security please," he said when she answered.

"One moment."

Trey thought Eryn might turn to look at him when he spoke, but she didn't even seem to notice.

The security guard answered, and Trey identified himself as a deputy and explained the situation. He felt a bit guilty for letting the guard think he was on official duty, but Trey would do whatever it took to protect Eryn. "I'm hoping there's a back entrance to the room that Ms. Calloway will use for her next class."

"Sure," the man said. "We have a service entrance you can use."

"How will we get access to that entrance?"

"Call my cell about thirty minutes before each class starts, and I'll meet you there." He provided his contact information.

Trey jotted it down on the hotel notepad. He disconnected and entered the guy's name and number into his phone then opened the Internet to begin a background check on Detective Young. Trey knew the guy didn't have a criminal record or he wouldn't be a detective, but that didn't mean he was on the up and up.

Trey entered Young's name in a search box and checked out every link. Time flew, but in the end, each link checked out. Young had received several commendations, and he showed up in his department's newsletter often as an example of exemplary service. Trey had also found the Facebook page for Young's wife, and Trey could only conclude that Young was a solid husband and family man.

Trey shifted his focus in hopes of finding financial issues, especially targeting a bankruptcy. Young came up clean in the limited search, but Trey didn't have access to the guy's actual financial accounts. This was an important part in checking a person's background as debt or the need for money could be motive for getting involved in something nefarious. Still, Trey's gut said the guy wasn't the suspect they were looking for.

So exactly who were they hunting? Was he dangerous or a blowhard making idle threats? If dangerous, Trey needed to take additional precautions.

He got up. "I need to run to my room for a minute. Promise you won't go anywhere."

"Promise," she said absently.

He found her keycard on the entry table and once in his room he grabbed his gun and mounted the holster on his belt. He slipped into a button-down shirt to wear over his other one and hide the fact that he was carrying. He felt more prepared as he settled back in the chair in her room. But the fact of the matter was, if her hacker was an officer attending the conference, he'd be carrying, too, and that made him deadly.

"Mommy, where are you?" A child's high voice filtered through the open door to Eryn's room.

"That's Bekah," Eryn said as she stood.

Interesting. Eryn was so deep in her work she barely heard or saw anything else, but her child called out, and she was instantly aware. God made such a special bond between mothers. He saw it often enough with his sisters and their children, and it always amazed him.

Looking forward to meeting Bekah, he got up. His experience with his nieces and nephews told him kids could be unpredictable, and he had to admit he was a bit nervous.

Eryn sighed. "You don't need to come with me."

"Wasn't planning on it," he said.

"Oh. Sorry. Be right back." She slipped through the doorway.

He went to the window and lifted the drapes to look out. He would rather have the drapes open letting light into the room, but he'd closed them as a security precaution.

He heard Eryn and Bekah talking, then the sound of water running. He'd never really thought of Eryn as a mother. Not that he didn't think she would be an amazing one, but he never got that far in thinking about her. But maybe having a child also explained why she was wary of getting involved with a guy. She wouldn't want to bring men into her daughter's life only for them to leave.

Giggling sounded from the doorway, and he turned to see a child the spitting image of Eryn come barreling into the room. She took one look at Trey and came to a dead stop. Eryn charged in behind her as if they'd been playing tag.

"Hi," he said to Bekah.

She frowned up at him, her lower lip coming out, and she looked like she might cry.

"This is my friend, Trey." Eryn knelt next to Bekah. "I know he looks big and scary, but he's not. He's a real softy, and you don't have to be afraid of him."

Bekah's lip went back in, but her gaze remained wary.

Trey squatted down. "Your mom is right. I'm not scary at all. I have three nieces and four nephews, and we all have a lot of fun."

She looked at her mother. "What's a niece and nephew?"

"Trey has brothers or sisters and he's talking about their children."

Bekah's bright eyes narrowed at Eryn. "You don't have a brother or sister."

"That's right."

"But I do," Trey said. "Two sisters and two brothers."

"I want a brother."

Eryn's eyes went wide. "You do?"

36

"Uh-huh. And maybe a sister, too, but she can't have my toys."

Trey wanted to laugh at the horrified look on Eryn's face, but he knew that wouldn't earn him any brownie points. He reached into his pocket for a quarter and palmed it in one hand then held out the other in a fist. "I have something for you, Bekah."

"You do?"

He nodded and jiggled his empty hand. "Want to see it?"

She rushed over to him and tugged his fingers open. "It's empty."

"Hmm," he said and narrowed his eyes. "I had a quarter in there. I wonder where it went."

He clasped his hands together to transfer the coin then reached his hand up to her ear and came back holding the quarter. "Now how did that get in your ear?"

She touched her ear. "My ear? It was in there?"

He nodded seriously.

She took the quarter and showed it to Eryn. "Did you see, Mommy? This was in my ear."

"I did." Eryn beamed at her daughter.

Wow, just wow. He thought Eryn was beautiful before, but with love for her daughter shining from her eyes, she captivated him in a whole new way. What would it be like to be on the receiving end of one of those smiles? He didn't know, but man, he wanted to find out.

The door lock released, and Trey automatically shot to his feet, his hand going to his sidearm. Bekah jumped back and looked like she might cry.

Sandra entered the room carrying packages, her gaze going between Trey and Bekah. He hadn't noticed when they'd met, but she had the same dark probing gaze as Eryn. That's where the similarities ended. Sandra's hair was a lighter brown and cut below her chin, not over the shoulder like Eryn's. She was trim and fit though, and Trey suspected this was what Eryn might look like when she got older, minus the flowing clothes.

Bekah ran to her grandmother and hugged her leg.

"Sorry I scared you, Bekah," Trey said in the softest tone he could muster, but the damage had been done. Her smile was gone, and she seemed afraid of him again.

"Why don't you tell Gammy about your quarter," Eryn suggested.

"Gammy?" Trey asked.

"Bekah's version of grandma that stuck."

"What's this about a quarter?" Sandra asked.

Bekah shook her head, and her pigtails bobbed. "Trey found one in my ear."

Sandra grinned, her face lighting up and taking ten years from her face. "He did, did he?"

Bekah gave a serious nod. "Do you think there's one in your ear, too?"

"Want me to check?" Trey asked.

"Um..." Bekah glanced at him. "Yes."

Trey walked slowly to Sandra, palming another quarter as he moved.

"Let's see." He lifted his hand to Sandra's ear and let the coin drop to his fingers. "Well would you look at that? She has one, too."

Bekah clapped her hands. "Now, Mommy. Check Mommy's ear."

Trey palmed the quarter and turned to Eryn with an apologetic look for having started this.

She smiled at him. "I'm sure you won't find one there."

"He will," Bekah said, excited enough to burst. "I know he will."

He lifted his hand to Eryn's ear and wished her family was anywhere but here, and he could tuck her hair behind her ear and kiss her instead of faking the whole quarter thing. But for Bekah, he made a big show of finding the coin.

"I knew it, Mommy. I knew it." Bekah jumped up and down and clapped her hands. "Me. Do me again."

"I think one time's enough," Eryn said. "It's time for your snack."

"Can Trey have a snack with me?"

Trey's heart melted at her inclusion.

Eryn opened her mouth.

"I'd love to," he said before Eryn could refuse. "What are we having?"

"Mommy promised we could go to the resraunt to have chicken nuggets."

He loved the way she said restaurant. "That sounds wonderful."

Bekah reached up on tiptoes to grab his hand. "Let's go. You can have nuggets, too. And if you use your best manners maybe Mommy will let you have a treat."

Trey had to work hard not to laugh. She tugged on his hand, and he let her pull him to the door. His heart was warm and overflowing from her attention, but he wouldn't let that distract him from his duty. With this little one to watch over too, he would be even more on guard.

In the casual dining room decorated with seashells, driftwood, and worn oars, Eryn stared across the table at Trey and Bekah. Her daughter had insisted on sitting next to him so they could share nuggets, though to be fair, Eryn ordered several servings. As big as Trey was, she suspected he had a big appetite, and she'd been right.

Bekah gazed up at him with adoring eyes. Eryn wasn't sure how she felt about Bekah warming up to him this easily. Not that it was a surprise. She was outgoing and trusting, in part due to her sheltered life living at Blackwell's super secure compound.

On the bright side, she and Trey were likely to be keeping company for the next few days and if Bekah liked Trey it would be easier, but then when it was time to say goodbye, her heart would be broken. Eryn wanted Bekah to have a male role model in her life, but there were plenty of guys on the team who spoiled her. She didn't need another one.

Bekah swallowed her bite and looked at Eryn. "Can we go swimming in the big pool?"

"Sorry, honey, I have to work." Eryn smiled to cover up her ongoing dislike of water from a childhood incident when their family canoe capsized, and she was caught under it for a few terrifying minutes.

"Aw." Bekah's expression fell, and she shot a look up at Trey. "Can you take me swimming?"

Trey smiled. "I wish I could, but I have to work with your mother."

"Gammy?" Bekah asked next, and Eryn felt bad that her mother was last choice when she was such an amazing grandmother and readily available when Eryn needed her.

Her mother smiled. "That's up to your mother."

"Mommy can I go?"

Eryn didn't want Bekah out of the room without someone on the team or Trey escorting her. "It's best if we wait until after dinner. Then I'll have time to go with you."

Bekah's lower lip came out.

"You know how much I like to do things with my best girl," Eryn said.

"Yes."

"And I can come then, too," Trey added.

Eryn's mind traveled to seeing Trey at the pool. That thought was the last thing she needed to be having right now. "I'm sure one of the guys on the team will want to go tonight."

Trey frowned, and so did Bekah.

"For now," Eryn rushed on before either of them said anything. "We should get back to the room so I can get to work and you and Gammy can watch the Curious George movie."

"Yay, Curious George." Bekah clapped and glanced up at Trey. "Do you like George? You can watch with me."

"I don't know," he said and glanced at Eryn.

"That's great," she said, knowing if he was with Bekah in the other room he wouldn't be watching her while she worked.

Bekah hopped down and grabbed his hand.

"Sorry," Eryn said. "I didn't get a chance to clean her up, and you likely have ketchup all over you now."

"No worries." Trey stood.

He really was an easygoing guy outside of work. At work, though, she'd seen firsthand his fierce protectiveness, and she trusted him to defend her and her family's lives with his own if it came to that. She needed to stop being such a big baby about having to spend time with him and thank him for his help instead.

They started for the elevator. Trey and Bekah in front, her mother by her side.

"Trey seems like a nice guy," her mother said, in her fishing-for-more-information tone.

"He is."

"And he's single. At least he's not wearing a ring."

"Mom," Eryn hissed. "He's gonna hear you."

"And that would be a bad thing why?"

"Because we're colleagues. Nothing more."

"Why? Does he have a significant other?"

"Not that I'm aware of."

"Good, because he's sending you signals left and right."

Her mother worked as a psychologist before she retired and was very in tune with others. Too in tune at times for Eryn's own good.

They piled into the elevator and took it to the third floor. Gage strode down the corridor toward them, duffel bag in hand.

"Oh, no," Eryn said. "I forgot about Gage swapping rooms with us. We should be packed up and ready to go. How could I have forgotten?"

"Hmm," her mother said. "Stress. A hacker threatening your life. A very handsome man doting on your every word. Take your pick."

She swatted her hand at her mother.

"Want me to pack while you work?" her mother asked.

"That would be great so I can do more searching for the actor." She joined Gage. "We're not ready to change rooms yet. Sorry."

He shrugged off her apology. "No worries. Neither are the others. I have a class to teach so wanted to drop off my bag and a key to the room."

Bekah dragged Trey over to Gage and peered up at him. "I have a new friend. His name is Trey."

Gage smiled. "Trey's been my friend for years, too."

"I like him. He can find quarters in your ear. Want him to try?"

Gage appraised Trey, who blushed a bright red. Eryn thought it was so very sweet that she felt a bit of the wall around her heart melting.

"Wish I had time, sweetheart," Gage said to Bekah. "But I have to drop my bag and go."

"Maybe you can come swimming with us after dinner, and he can find your quarter, too."

"Maybe."

Eryn unlocked the door before her daughter blurted out anything else.

"C'mon, Trey." Bekah towed Trey into the room like one of her stuffed animals. "Let's watch George."

Gage dropped his bag inside the door and cast a questioning look at Eryn.

"Bekah's taken a real liking to Trey," she said.

"And what about you?"

"Seriously? I can't even believe you asked me that."

"Sorry. I had to. When I call Hannah tonight she'll want to know how you're handling this, and you know how I hate disappointing her."

Eryn snorted and shooed Gage toward the door.

"Okay, I'm going." He looked back at her. "No other sign of the hacker?"

She shook her head. "Mom will pack us up while I work on tracing him. And I'd appreciate it if we could have a team brainstorming session after dinner."

"Sounds like we'll have to do it without Trey. What with the full social schedule Bekah has planned for him." Chuckling, Gage stepped out the door.

If he looked back he would catch Eryn rolling her eyes, but he didn't, so she closed the door and headed for the desk. She opened her laptop and settled in to work, but Trey entered the room taking her attention.

"How in the world did you escape the clutches of my daughter?" Eryn smiled up at him.

"I promised to come right back." He grinned and plopped onto the corner of one of the beds. "She's really something, isn't she? Reminds me a lot of you."

"So I'm crazy adorable, then?" she joked.

He nodded with a mock serious expression. "And maybe a little pushy and someone who likes to have her way at all costs."

She knew he was joking, but there was truth in his words. "I'm sorry about being such a grump when you're only trying to help us. I appreciate it. I do. It's just..." She shrugged as she didn't want to talk about their mutual attraction again.

"It's okay. I get it."

She watched him for a moment, liking very much what she was seeing. "You really are a nice guy, Trey Sawyer."

"Was that ever in doubt? 'Cause if it was, don't tell my mom or she'll have my hide. She raised me to be a gentleman."

Okay, mentioning his mom was even sweeter than his finding the quarters trick.

All she wanted to do was keep looking into eyes more blue than gray right now, but she dragged her focus away and gestured at her computer. "I should get to work."

"And I'll let you, but..." His voice fell off so she glanced back at him. "I've done as much digging on Young as I can. He seems squeaky clean by the way. But I was wondering if there was anything you wanted me to do while I *watch* George with Bekah." He did air quotes around the word watch.

"You can't help with the technical details I'm working

on, but it would be great if you searched the Internet for any big ransomware incidents this week."

He arched a brow. "Do you think this is bigger than you?"

"I'm not sure." She started to turn back then said, "Oh, and I asked Gage to gather the team for an after-dinner meeting tonight."

"What about swimming?" Trey grinned again.

She noticed for the first time that his smile was a bit lopsided, and his nose ever-so-slightly crooked. When he worked patrol, he was clean-shaven, but now he'd grown a close-cut beard, and she wanted to stroke the whiskers to see if they were soft or prickly.

"I don't want to let the little pipsqueak down," he added, bringing Eryn back to the conversation.

"We'll make it quick at the pool." She forced herself to quit staring at him so her heartbeat would return to normal. "You're really good with Bekah."

"Guess it's all those nieces and nephews."

"Do you want kids of your own?" she asked, and immediately regretted the personal question when she was the one who asked him to be professional.

"Absolutely. Four or five."

"Wow. That's specific."

"I come from a big family and liked growing up with brothers and a sister. Well, maybe not the sisters so much back then, but now I love them to death."

"I was an only child. I liked that, too, but there were times I wanted a sibling."

"The more the merrier, I say."

She didn't necessarily agree. If she ever had that many children, she would want to quit her job. As it was, there were days when she much preferred to be at home with

Bekah than to be working. Not that she didn't love her job. She did, but being a stay-at-home mom was always the plan before a car crash took Rich's life.

She came out of her thoughts to find Trey watching her as usual. Why was she letting him get to her like this?

"My work." She quickly swiveled her chair before she spent more time talking about things they had no need to discuss.

"I'll be in the other room if you need me."

"Thanks," she said but didn't look up before she was sucked back into his pleasant smile and easy personality.

He was so different than other men she'd worked with in law enforcement. They were often intense and driven. Her teammates proved that, but Trey didn't seem to fit the mold. And he was different from Rich, too. He'd worked in finance, and despite being introverted, he was driven to succeed in his job and had worked his way up to his company's chief financial officer position. They'd led a busy life that didn't end when she became a single mom. But going to work with Blackwell simplified so many things for her.

Funny how things turned out. She suffered a serious injury at the FBI which ended her job there. It was devastating to leave the work she loved and excelled at, especially when she didn't know what else she would do with her life. But being forced to leave the high-pressure Bureau job and take a less all-encompassing job with Gage worked out to be unexpectedly freeing, as well as rewarding. Gage gave her flexibility in her schedule, and whenever possible, she worked nights so she could be with Bekah during the day.

What would life be like with Trey? Filled with kids if he had his way. She was surprised to find that the thought didn't horrify her. Thinking about it did, however.

She sighed and clicked the log from LEN's server. When

actors wanted to hack into a computer network, they usually started with a scan to gather intel on the network in much the same way her team would do reconnaissance on a target. If the actor was an amateur, he or she might not do a stealth scan, and the network's intrusion detection system would pick up the scan, log it, and notify the network administrator. If the actor who threatened her was experienced or talented, he would've used a stealth scan that wouldn't be picked up at the network level, and she wouldn't expect to find any obvious evidence of the intrusion.

She worked through the log for the past month, line by line, and found nothing readily apparent. The actor could have been planning the hack for a longer timeframe and might've made the initial scan sooner, so she worked her way back through earlier logs.

Nothing again.

So fine. It wasn't going to be easy. It usually wasn't.

The image had only been uploaded yesterday, but the actor could have found a way into the network sooner and was lying in wait, ready to act. In fact, that was the biggest problem facing companies today. Actors penetrate a network not to mess with the company files or create havoc, but to hang around and quietly steal proprietary data. Many network administrators were too busy watching only for intrusions not packets of data leaving the network.

She didn't locate any modified files, and she couldn't account for that. It was going to take further study. She set her mind to digging deeper. When she found that the network had a gaping security hole, she knew how the actor got into the file.

"Time for dinner," her mother announced as she stepped over to Eryn.

Eryn looked at the clock on her computer, surprised to see hours had passed.

"And swimming." Bekah patted her swimming tote hanging over her shoulder.

Eryn stretched. "We can come back for your bag, sweetie."

"Nuh-uh. I want to bring it so I'm ready."

"Okay," Eryn said, knowing this wasn't a battle worth fighting. "But I'll have to come back for my things."

"K." Bekah jutted out her hip and held tight to her bag.

Perhaps this was what Eryn looked like to Trey when she was being stubborn about her independence.

She got up and saw their suitcases sitting at the door. "And we still have to move into the new suite."

"About that," Trey said from the chair in the corner where she totally forgot he had moved to after the movie had ended. "I asked Gage if the guys could swap things while we're at dinner. I figured if your friend was keeping tabs on you he would know you went to dinner and not be looking at the room."

"What friend, Mommy?" Bekah flashed her gaze to Eryn. "Is he coming swimming with us, too?"

Eryn shook her head and was so thankful Trey had referred to the actor as a friend.

"So where to for dinner?" Trey asked.

"Mommy said we can have pizza." Bekah gazed at Trey, her eyes alight with excitement. "Do you like pizza?"

"Do I ever." He stood, his shoulders back, looking like the fierce warrior he was.

"Then let's get going." Eryn's mother started for the door.

Was this what life would've been like if Rich had lived? Their small family headed out for a meal together. A deep aching sadness Eryn hadn't experienced in a long time threatened to bring tears to the surface. She looked away and blinked hard to stem them.

Trey rushed past her to the door. "Give me a minute to check things out."

Right. This wasn't a little family outing. Far from it. Trey was with them for one reason and one reason only. To make sure none of them came to any harm.

4

Trey waited in the suite's living area with several of the Blackwell Tactical team members while Eryn tucked Bekah in bed. The atmosphere was relaxed and the guys treated Trey like he was one of the incredible fearless warriors on the team. Of course, he'd known Gage for years, but had connected with the others this past year and they made him feel like part of their group.

Team sniper, Riley Glenn, sat across from Trey on the couch. Riley had served as a sniper for the Portland Police Bureau, and law enforcement experience gave them something in common. Riley was also the peacemaker or mediator of the group, a role Trey often held in his big boisterous family so he totally related to that, too.

Sitting next to Riley was Alex Hamilton who had served as a recon marine. Trey had the military in common with him, but Alex was harder to get to know. He liked to joke around a lot, on the surface looking like an easygoing guy, but Trey caught an undercurrent that Alex was covering up.

Trey's thigh started aching, and he moved in his chair to get more comfortable. He wanted to massage the muscle, but he wouldn't do so in front the team. Would only draw attention to his weaknesses, and he never wanted to do that. Ever. With anyone.

Eryn stepped into the room, and all eyes followed her. He once wondered if she was involved with any of the guys on the team, but as he got to know them, he realized she was like a kid sister who they all looked out for and teased.

She sat between Riley and Alex on the sofa, the ebony color of her hair so different from Riley's blond coloring. It was closer to Alex's deep brown, but her hair was much more intensely saturated.

"Sorry that took longer than expected." She smiled. "Bekah's prayers are taking longer with you big lugs to pray for."

"And we need all the prayers we can get." Alex chuckled.

"You said it." Eryn grinned. "I have a long night ahead of me so we should get started."

"We thought about starting without you," Alex said. "But then none of us understand any of the hacking stuff so we had to wait."

"Hey, speak for yourself," Riley said with a hint of humor. "Seems to me since this involves computer hacking, we must be looking for someone with top-notch computer skills."

Eryn tipped her head, and Trey saw where Bekah got her cute curious little tilt of the head when she didn't understand something.

"You'd think so," Eryn said. "But not necessarily. I got far enough to see that LEN's hack wasn't all that difficult. They had a glaring security hole that most people with strong programming knowledge could have walked through."

"But what about the ransomware?" Gage sat forward and rested his arms on his knees. "That must take some skill."

"Again, you'd think so, but there isn't actually much skill involved in deploying ransomware. The software isn't very sophisticated. It can be quickly created and successfully deployed without much effort. And these days, actors don't even have to create their own ransomware. Vendors on the darknet offer do-it-yourself hacking kits. These often include pre-developed malware and a set of instructions for using it."

"You're kidding, right?" Trey asked.

She shook her head. "It's similar to buying any other software, like Windows. Many of the vendors offer customer service. Some products even come with money-back guarantees."

Trey couldn't believe what he was hearing. "That's just crazy."

She nodded. "Even more surprising is that a lot of the ransomware vendors also offer call-in or email services for the victims. They tell them how to make payment and decrypt the ransomware, so the actor doesn't have to deal with it. I know of one product that offers customer service via live chat."

"Seriously." Gage shook his head. "How do you know all of this anyway?"

"Back in my days at the Bureau, I infiltrated a malware organization and worked as one of their employees."

Trey knew she must have some very interesting stories to tell. He could imagine sitting in front of a roaring fire with her as they grew old together, listening to her recount those stories. A pipe dream at this point. "How do you even get into a group like that?"

"It's actually not that hard, believe it or not." She sat back, looking completely comfortable in her element. "The money these organizations are making is so good they are looking to expand. They want a bigger payout and need more people. So they form groups and sell their products together. And that means they need to hire additional workers."

"How do they go about that?" Alex asked with a smirk. "Hold a job fair?"

"Not quite, but they're like regular companies in that you apply with a resume and go through an online interview process. And as soon as they've vetted and trust you, they'll share all the new tools they are coming out with and who they're going after." She took a long breath. "I played a big part in bringing down a large group this way and many of the actors went away to serve serious time."

"Could this ransomware attack be payback for that?" Trey asked.

She tapped her chin, a long slender finger beating in time with the overhead ceiling fan's rotations. "I suppose they could be hoping I don't backup on a regular basis and would lose all of my information." She scoffed. "Honestly, though, they should know better. And, if they *are* seeking revenge, there would be so many better ways to do it."

"Like what?" Trey asked, now totally interested in her story.

"Like stealing my money. That would be a lot more devastating than stopping me from teaching a few classes."

"About that," Alex said. "Who would gain from cancelling the classes?"

"Seems to me like we might first need to ask who knows about me teaching these classes and how they know."

"Exactly what are you teaching?" Alex asked. "And can we have it in plain English please, not your famous computerese?"

She swatted a hand at his knee and that jealousy

returned, swirling in Trey's insides. He got that she wasn't romantically involved with her teammates, but he was jealous of the ease she had with them while tension permeated the room when the two of them were alone together.

"I have two classes," she said. "The first is about recognizing unknown security threats via the Internet of Things."

"Internet of Things?" Riley asked.

She got up and went to a box on the table. She dug out and held up a black plastic traffic light that was about six inches tall. It had a USB hub at the base and a cord attached. She brought it to the table and handed it to Gage. "Go ahead and pass this around. On the first day of class I hand out this stoplight that's powered by a computer USB port. It's a USB hub, meaning you can plug in multiple USB devices at one time."

"So it lights up like a regular stoplight?" Trey clarified.

"Exactly. Each color is connected to one of the ports and when you plug in a USB device, a light glows. Something I thought officers could relate to. So when I tell them to plug it into a computer that night and report back on how it works, I have a good chance they'll do it."

"I'd have plugged it in," Trey said.

"Not sure I would," Riley said.

"But you're always the teacher's pet, so you don't have to do what's required and that doesn't count," Alex grumbled good-naturedly.

"I know right?" Riley laughed. "Must be because I'm so charming."

"And the stoplight is important, why?" Gage said, drawing them back to the topic.

"This is going to be a little technical, but here goes." She held up the stoplight. "I modified this light to make it a spy gadget that can intercept electrical signals leaking from adjacent USB ports. This leakage is technically called channel-to-channel crosstalk leakage."

"I need more of an explanation than that," Trey said, not at all embarrassed that he didn't understand a word.

"Okay, so think of plumbing. Water flows through pipes and can leak out. Electricity flows the same way and voltage fluctuates. These fluctuations of a USB port's data results in leakage that can be monitored by the adjacent ports. That means sensitive information like keystrokes showing passwords or other private information can be captured and easily stolen by the spy device."

"So you had your students plug in the stoplight, and you recorded their keyboard keystrokes as the participants typed?" Trey asked.

She nodded. "If this was used in a real application, passwords, bank account information, etc. could be stolen through the USB crosstalk."

Alex's eyes widened. "That's crazy."

"Yes, and it can also gather information from USB credit card and fingerprint readers. I don't have to tell you the implications here. Now, before you think this is commonplace, don't. I simply use this to point out to the officers that security threats come in all shapes and sizes. I tell them I recorded their keystrokes from the prior night and can play it back to them. In reality, I don't even check to see if something recorded, but if they ever called me on it, I could provide the data."

Riley's eyes widened. "Do you think you may have recorded something that someone didn't expect you to record?"

"Possible, I suppose," she said and drummed her fingers on her knee as if thinking. "But in that case, why stop me from teaching additional classes? Why not come after me to get the information?"

"Let's table that thought for now," Gage said. "Tell us about the other class."

"Okay," she replied. "That one is far less complicated. Basically, I show them how pictures taken on a cell phone are traceable back to the cell phone they were taken on."

"So if we each used our own phones to take your picture right now, you could tell us which pictures came from which phone?" Gage asked.

She nodded. "Think of smartphones like fingerprints. No two are the same. No matter the manufacturer or make, each phone can be identified through a pattern of microscopic imaging flaws that are present in every picture. We're all familiar with how you can match a bullet to a gun, right?"

Everyone nodded.

"This is basically the same. Each gun has the slightest of differences created in the manufacturing process and so do phones. The problem centers on an obscure flaw in digital imaging called photo-response non-uniformity or PRNU. So here we're matching photos to a smartphone camera, not a bullet to a rifle."

"That could be huge in solving crimes, right?" Gage asked.

"Totally," Trey said, impressed that Eryn was so up to date with technology.

"Again, this is not used yet, but I want officers to know that it's coming and to be on the lookout for it as it's going to be key in investigations *and* successful prosecutions." She planted her hands on her knees. "So that's the basics of both classes."

"I'm guessing that your class participants are all geeks," Alex said.

"Honestly, no. I talked with a couple of guys yesterday who don't have any real computer skills or even much interest. They're both working investigations that this photo technology could help crack, and they wanted to connect with me and put me in touch with their tech people."

"Like Eryn mentioned a few minutes ago," Riley said. "It would help if we could figure out who knows about these classes other than the attendees. People who wouldn't want this information shared."

Eryn turned her focus on Trey. "How did you hear about the class?"

He couldn't very well tell her he kept up with the team's training schedules so he could see her, but his department had also gotten a flyer, so he would go with that. "My LT got an email from LEN, which I'm assuming was sent to departments across the state."

"So officers in these departments would be notified," Gage said. "Maybe even tech people."

"Then there's word of mouth," Alex added. "We're talking about a large group here."

"Yeah, and Martha told me that we also got press coverage," Eryn said. "Not positive press, but EPR was troubled by my training content."

"Seriously, not them again," Alex mumbled.

Trey didn't like Alex's response, but Trey didn't know who ERP was. "Exactly who is EPR?"

"Electronic Privacy Rights," Eryn responded. "They're a local watchdog group who hunt for any chance to protest the way electronic communication is violating our privacy rights or is too 'big brother' for their liking."

Alex rolled his eyes. "They think everything is too 'big brother'."

Eryn nodded. "And their protests are always so unique that they often get good media coverage. But in this case, they don't have a leg to stand on. Officers will follow strict protocols when they use the techniques I teach, and no one's privacy will be illegally compromised."

Gage frowned. "If it hit the news, then the general public would know about the classes."

"Could EPR be behind the ransomware?" Trey asked.

"I wouldn't put it past them," Eryn said. "Their leader is skilled in IT, which is why it riled him. Let me do an Internet search tonight to see what I can find on their recent actions."

"Speaking of Internet," Trey said. "I completed the background check on Detective Young. At least as far as I can without access to his financial information, and we need to interview him."

Eryn looked at her watch. "Why don't we try to find him when we're done here?"

"Did I miss something?" Riley asked. "Who's Detective Young?"

"He uploaded the image that contained the ransomware code," she explained.

"Why did you have them do that anyway?" Alex asked.

"In my IoT class, I give the participants surveys to fill out, and I instruct them to scan the form and upload it to my folder on LEN's server. It's a practical exercise I use to teach them that many devices have memory, not only computers."

"Scanners can remember what you've scanned?" Riley asked.

"Some can, at least until they're unplugged. And a commercial machine like the one used here at the resort or in many offices have hard drives, and they almost all store files in memory."

"So I could come up to the scanner after you used it and see what you scanned?" Gage asked.

"Exactly."

Riley shook his head. "Seriously, there's so much to know about electronics safety."

"Which is why everyone needs me." Eryn chuckled.

Trey smiled along with her, but the others rolled their eyes, again reminding Trey how close these guys were too her and how outside her world he was.

Eryn suddenly sobered and sat forward. "Here's something I didn't think of before. I randomly take pictures of class participants' phones for a slideshow I do on day two of my phone class. Maybe I caught something in a picture that I shouldn't have. I'll need to review those tonight."

"What if someone who took your class has ulterior motives?" Trey asked. "Maybe he's extorting someone. Then he hears about how pictures can be tracked, he doesn't want others in his department to learn about it."

"Sounds possible," Gage said.

"Or what if someone in the class took a picture of an officer doing something illegal, and they're extorting them," Riley suggested. "I mean I hate to point a finger at an officer, but there are bad ones out there."

"But how would this relate to the class?" Eryn asked.

"The conference has been covered on TV. What if the person who took the picture saw the story on the local news and wants to stop the officer from learning that they can trace the picture back to them?"

"It's clear that there could be many motives," Gage said. "Maybe questioning class participants—both ones who've taken the class and future participants—will make things clearer."

"We can split up the list and interview them," Eryn said. "But don't mention the hack as I want to keep that under wraps for now. Just get an idea why they're taking the class, and if they have fellow officers here with them. Oh, and ask about their phone so if I do find something when I review the pictures tonight, we'll know who to go to."

"I'll grab the participant list." Trey went to the desk to get the names they'd printed that afternoon.

Gage stood. "We can talk to as many participants as possible tonight, and then regroup in the morning."

"One thing to remember," Riley said. "We're dealing with officers here—a suspicious lot at best. They'll try to turn the questioning back on you. You'll need to keep that in mind so you don't give away any information that might make things worse for Eryn."

Gage faced Eryn. "When is your next class scheduled?"

"Thursday at two."

"Okay, then we have less than forty-eight hours to figure this out." He ran his gaze over the group, stopping at each person and giving them a pointed look. "Let's get after it and nail this guy before he makes good on his threat."

5

The team filed out of the suite, and Eryn sat back to prioritize her tasks. In addition to reviewing the ransomware code she'd located on her computer, she also had to review the stoplight files and study the cell phone photos. Then she also needed to talk to Detective Young. All before she got any sleep tonight.

Trey twisted the deadbolt on the door. "You look deep in thought."

"Just prioritizing." She glanced at the clock on the kitchenette microwave. "It's getting late. We should talk to Young first, and I'll review the other files later. Let me tell Mom I'm leaving." She crossed the suite living area to one of the three bedrooms and knocked on the door.

"Come in," her mother called out.

Eryn opened the door and poked her head in. Her mom was sitting on the bed already in flowery silk pajamas. She held a book in her hands, and Eryn was suddenly struck by how much she took her mother for granted and didn't thank her often enough.

She crossed the room and gave her a big hug.

"What was that for?" her mother asked.

"For all you do for me and Bekah. You're always there when I need you, and you never complain about anything. Ever."

"That's what mothers do. You do the same thing for Bekah." She smiled, her eyes lighting up. "And besides, I love spending time with Bekah."

"In that case, Trey and I want to interview one of my class participants. Can you watch her?"

"Of course." She frowned. "Be careful, honey, okay?"

"I always am."

Her mother looked like she was debating adding something else but clamped down on her lips.

Eryn didn't really want to hear what her mother had to say, but it looked like she was almost exploding by holding it inside. "Go ahead. Say it."

"If you insist." She wrinkled her nose the way Eryn knew she often did. "You're careful. I know that. But you're also such an adventurer that you may step into danger without thinking about it."

Eryn sat back. "I'm a thirty-two-year old woman who can—"

"Take care of herself." Her mom smiled. "Yeah, I know. You've told me often enough. But to me you're still that five-year-old who climbed the tree in the back yard only to fall out and break your arm."

Eryn got that. Even as Bekah got older, Eryn wanted to protect her like she did when Bekah was a toddler. Eryn had to force herself to relax and let Bekah discover who she was. Within boundaries, of course. She knew it would only get more difficult as her baby got older.

"I'll be careful, and Trey will be with me." Eryn stood.

"I like him," her mom said. "And I think you do to."

Eryn wasn't going there. "I shouldn't be gone for more than an hour."

"Take your time. Enjoy his company."

"Mom, please."

Her mother chuckled, and Eryn closed the door before her mother said anything else about Trey. She found him leaning on the wall outside the door.

"FYI, I like your mom. You, too." He grinned, that adorable lopsided smile that tugged at her heartstrings.

She didn't respond. There was no point. She headed for the door. Trey caught up and passed her to step into the hallway first. As much as she wanted to protest, she also had to admit it felt good to have a guy looking out for her best interests again. She wasn't one of those women who *had* to do everything herself, but she did like to be consulted and not taken for granted.

She looked out where he stood tall and strong in the hallway surveying the lobby and open walkways, his dark gaze deadly intense. He'd put on a loose-fitting shirt when he'd gone to his room, and she knew it was because he was hiding his gun. She'd done the same thing after tucking Bekah in bed, and Eryn suspected her teammates had followed suit before heading out to conduct their interviews, too. You could never be too careful, as she'd told her mother.

Trey turned, his gaze unwavering. "We're clear."

She stepped out and instantly felt vulnerable. She wasn't afraid, but apprehensive.

"Mind walking near the doors, and I'll take the outer edge?" he asked.

"Don't mind at all." She was so thankful he asked that she smiled up at him.

He sucked in a breath and jerked his gaze away. She didn't think smiling was being too personal, but she wasn't about to go there. They had to focus solely on their mission. They traveled along the walkway that circled and overlooked the lobby. When they reached Young's room, she knocked.

The door was soon opened by a tall, thin detective with a studious gaze. She pegged him in his late fifties, and he had the look of a career police officer. Wary. Inquisitive. But then a genuine smile broke out. "Ms. Calloway. To what do I owe the pleasure of a visit?"

If he was behind the ransomware, he was doing an impressive job as appearing innocent, and Eryn had to watch for any telltale signs of lying. "I have a few questions for you regarding the survey you uploaded for me."

"Sure. Want to come in? Or there's a sitting area right down the way."

Eryn remembered seeing the protected alcove. "The spot down the hall sounds good."

He held out his hand. "Then, after you."

In the little alcove, she settled into a chair. Young sat next to her, but Trey stood sentry, and once again she was thankful for his care.

"Tell me about filling out the survey," she said, reverting back to her FBI training and making sure to use open-ended statements to not lead Young.

"What's to tell? I answered the questions, scanned it in the resort's business office like you said, and uploaded the image."

"Do you remember when you completed it?"

"Right after the class got out. I did it then so I wouldn't forget." A wry smile crossed his face. "I teach classes for my department, and I hate it when officers don't return things I ask for. So I wanted to make sure I wasn't one of *those* people."

"Thank you," she said and meant it. "Did you try to change the image after that?"

"How could I? I'd have to redo it and upload it again, right?"

"That's one way."

His eyes narrowed in confusion. "It's the only way I know how to change it."

"Tell me about your computer skills and why you took my class."

"Skills? If you count reading and sending email as skills, then I have mad skills." He laughed. "Oh, and I can fill out reports at work, too."

"Then why take my class?"

"Just because I don't know how to do something doesn't mean I don't recognize the need to be informed. Electronics in case investigations is becoming more and more prevalent, and I need to at least know what's possible."

"Well, said." She admired his desire to keep up on technology when many detectives his age might avoid it.

His gaze turned suspicious. "What's this about, Ms. Calloway?"

"I'm really not at liberty to discuss it."

"So this is what it feels like to be on the other side of an investigation, huh?" He chuckled.

"I didn't say I was investigating anything."

"You didn't have to. Your FBI roots are showing." He shifted as if ready to rise. "Whatever you think I might have done, I didn't do it. Just scanned and uploaded the form like you asked." He stood and looked down at her. "But I'm always glad to help you out with whatever you need, so let me know if I can help."

"Thank you," she said, and he departed.

Trey looked at her. "You think he's telling the truth."

"I do," Eryn said, but she also knew as a career officer he'd seen plenty and could easily lie to her. "I'll put him on the back burner for now but won't forget about him. He can be sure of that."

∾

Trey had no idea how Eryn could sit behind a computer screen for so many hours. He was all for computers and what they did to make life easier, but spend an entire day looking at one? No way. And he'd never want to look through all the computer gibberish that she'd reviewed since they returned to the suite.

He got up to stretch his leg before the stiffness set in and pain followed. "Don't take this the wrong way, but you seem like a really active person. How did you get involved with computers?"

She swiveled to face him, her ponytail swinging, and she looked unhappy about the interruption. "First, it's a stereo-type that all computer geeks do nothing but spend every waking hour with their computer."

"I get that." He settled back on the sofa so he wasn't towering over her. "But stereotypes come about because they are in large part true."

"Yeah, but I don't like to perpetuate them." She cast him a disappointed look.

He'd offended her. "Sorry. Like I said, I didn't want you to take it the wrong way. Your mom said you're this big adventurer so I thought it was a valid question."

"No, I'm the one who's sorry. I really am." She exhaled loudly and rubbed her neck. "This ransomware has me more freaked out than I care to admit. As each hour ticks by and I haven't made much progress, I'm getting cranky.

Overly touchy, too."

"Maybe you should take a break," he suggested.

"You're probably right." She stood and stretched her arms over her head, and he was powerless to look away from her sleek profile. Her clothes hugged all her curves, and her glossy ponytail slid over her shoulders to rest on her back. She twisted and turned, moving fluidly like a dancer.

She lowered her arms. "What I'd really like to do is go outside for a walk. We spend a lot of time outside at the compound, and I miss it."

He wasn't about to encourage a walk, but with her mood she would probably fight him nixing the idea. He'd redirect the conversation instead. "All the team members live at the compound, right?"

"Yes, but that will likely change when they get married and start having kids. Our cabins aren't big enough for raising a family."

Trey hadn't heard about any marriage plans. "Who's getting married?"

"Coop and Kiera are next month. Jackson is engaged, too, but hasn't set the date." She plopped onto the couch next to Trey and rested her head back.

He followed the long arch of her neck and had the urge to plant a kiss in the hollow of her throat.

"What about you? Do you want more space in your cabin?" he asked quickly to change his focus.

"Nah, I'm good with our place. When we joined the team, we each designed and built our own cabins. I made sure mine fits our needs, and it still does. Might be a different story when Bekah gets older though."

"So at the risk of offending you, I'm gonna ask again... how *did* you get involved in computers?"

She swiveled to face him, and he'd never been this close

to her before. If he had been, he would've noticed that the chestnut coloring of her eyes also held striations of warm honey. How could any man ignore those eyes? How could he?

"Actually, it was because of my adventurous side that I discovered computers," she said, totally oblivious to his warring thoughts. "I was riding a dirt bike at a friend's farm in middle school, and I crashed. Broke my leg and was in a full leg cast. It was awful at first. I spent all my day sitting around. I'm a type A personality and it was pure torture. My salvation was a laptop computer that one of my teachers loaned me. It was this big brick of a thing compared to today's laptops."

A fond look crossed her face, and she chuckled. "Anyway, the Internet was just becoming mainstream then. We didn't have an account, and we didn't have the money to buy many games. But my curiosity about how this computer worked got the best of me, and I had to figure it out. The more I learned, the more I wanted to know, and it totally sucked me in."

"And is sounds like it never let you go."

She laughed joyfully, and he loved the way her eyes sparkled, and her whole face came alive. It took everything he was made of not to reach out and touch her.

Her smile suddenly faded. "And when criminals started messing around with the thing I loved so much, I knew I had to work in cyber crimes. There was no better place to do that than at the FBI."

"What ended your career as an agent, if you don't mind me asking?"

She flattened her left hand on her knee and trailed her finger along a scar running the width of her hand. "Being in the FBI isn't like being a deputy. The job's really nothing like you see on TV. Not a lot of field work and no big shootouts. It mostly involves sitting behind a desk, pushing paper, and doing analysis. Of course, it's even more so in cyber crimes. So when an opportunity came up for agents to get out in the field, we jumped at it. Especially when it involved breaking down doors and hauling people in."

"Yeah, I get that part," he said. "I don't much like people having to go to jail, but the adrenaline rush is there when you make the collar."

"Exactly. So one day I had the chance to serve an arrest warrant on a fairly high-level cyber criminal. The guy answered the door, but as soon as I identified myself, he started to slam the door in my face. I instinctually reached out to stop him. Problem was, I grabbed the edge of the door when I should have palmed it. He slammed the door on my hand and it suffered some pretty serious damage."

She lifted her left hand and stared at it. "I don't have the ability to clench my fist or grasp an object very well. The FBI wouldn't risk the potential liability such an injury raises, so they benched me as an agent. I could've taken an analyst job, but I wanted at least the hope of some adventure. So I left, and in a lot of ways, I'm glad I did."

"How so?" he asked as he couldn't see anything positive about his own injury.

"At the Bureau, it often took a long time to see that I was making a difference. With Blackwell, I see on a daily basis how I'm helping others. The job also gives me a lot of flexibility with my work schedule, and that's great for being a single mom."

"Sounds like you're handling it well." He prayed he would eventually embrace such a positive outlook if it came down to losing his job.

"I didn't at first. Blamed God. But gradually, He let me

see it was a blessing in disguise. So now, for the most part, I do okay with it. Don't get me wrong. I still have my moments when I wish I could do things that the guys can do. Like fast roping from the helo. Man, my adventurous side would love to do that." She grinned, looking exactly like Bekah when she'd jumped into the pool without a care.

Trey could easily imagine Eryn grabbing the rope, dangling from a helicopter, and sliding down. She'd have that fierce determined look on her face, and she'd give it her all to make sure she landed on target. If his leg didn't improve, he wouldn't be doing that either, and if he joined Blackwell, he'd be watching the other guys from the sidelines, so he could totally understand her frustration.

He met her gaze. "I'm sorry about your hand. I'm just starting to understand the struggle and limitations of having a chronic injury."

She looked down at his leg. "Your leg isn't getting any better, then?"

He wanted to sigh but kept it to himself. "I keep pretending it is, but nah. After several surgeries and more physical therapy than I can count, the doc still won't clear me to return to patrol. So I'm riding a desk, which is too frustrating and confining for me. I need to be involved and active. Like today. I'm sorry this guy is threatening you, but man, for the first time in a long time, I enjoyed my day."

Her eyes softened in understanding, and she reached out to take his hand. The touch of her fingers raced along his nerves, and he sucked in a quick breath.

"And I've been such a bear to you," she said. "I really do appreciate everything you're doing, and I hate that you're missing out on your classes because of me."

"Trust me. I'd take protective detail over sitting in a classroom any day. Especially when it's you I'm protecting."

He rested his other hand over hers, boldly met her gaze, and held it, transmitting his interest.

Her eyes widened, and she jerked back.

"And of course, your little Bekah," he added to play down the intensity of his feelings. "She's a lot of fun. Especially when she says something you don't want her to say."

Eryn pulled her hand back, feigning offense at his last comment, but the underlying unease she had with him was still obvious and that hurt. Hurt a lot. More than he should let it when he had no business getting involved with her.

"I should get back to work." She got up.

Right. Back to business. Exactly what they both needed, but he didn't want her to run from him. "Have you found anything in the stoplight data?"

"Not yet, and honestly, it's a long shot, so I'm going to move on to the cell phone pictures which I think are a more viable lead. You want to help me review them?"

"Sure," he replied, surprised she asked.

"Let me grab my laptop, and we can look at the files here where we can both sit."

"I don't mind standing." He jumped up, drawing her careful scrutiny, but he didn't let that deter him. He moved over to the desk and stood behind the chair. It was far better for him to be looking over her shoulder than having her sit close enough to share the computer screen with him. Sure, he would have liked her at his side, but it would be pure torture, and he doubted he would be able to focus on the work.

She slid into the chair, and he caught a whiff of her fresh citrusy scent that made him think of the laundry his mom hung on clotheslines in the backyard. Eryn was like a breath of fresh air in his life so it was appropriate, but still, he didn't need to be thinking about it.

She opened a folder on the screen, enlarged the pictures, and then started scrolling through them.

"I'm not even sure what we're looking for," he said.

"Watch the ones with dark screens for reflections. The others, a suspicious text. Email. Or even an unusual app."

He wouldn't know an unusual app if it jumped off the screen and bit him, but he devoted all of his attention to the computer and hoped he could be of help.

Two hours later, his thigh burning and eyes strained, he wished he'd been sitting down. He hadn't contributed anything, and after scrutinizing every last photo, Eryn admitted that there didn't appear to be anything unusual. They'd struck out on finding that one lead they needed to propel their investigation forward before this guy could make good on his threat.

6

Eryn woke to chants outside her window. She shot out of bed to look outside. A small group of protestors with placards stood near the resort's drop-off area. They were marching in a circle and waving large signs that were in the shape of a laptop computer broadcasting STOP MASS SURVEILLANCE!

A tall, muscular man wearing biker clothes with stringy long hair the color of an eggplant stomped out from under the awing and raised his arms to incite the crowd. His shoulder-length hair in the deep purple color was a dead giveaway to his and the group's identity—ERP. He was none other than group leader, Chuck Coker. And a real jerk with a capital J.

Eryn never expected them to come all the way from Portland for this. Surely, they had better things to do with their time then to protest her little classes. Maybe it had to do with a recent altercation the police had with Coker. He probably hoped protesting her class would stick it to the police at the same time.

A male guest exited a sedan in the parking lot and

headed for the door. Coker stepped out and tried to stop the guest from entering. He moved past Coker who exaggerated falling back to make it look like the guy accosted him, when from Eryn's point of view, the guest didn't even touch Coker.

Disgusted, Eryn let the drapes fall and checked to make sure Bekah was still asleep on her rollaway bed. She was curled on her side, her thumb resting near her mouth, her favorite blanket clutched in her hand. An overwhelming wave of protectiveness washed over Eryn. She didn't want her baby to learn about people like Coker. Eryn was all for the right to protest, but Coker often used underhanded methods to get his point across.

Shaking her head, Eryn went to the shower in her adjoining bathroom. She put all her frustration in frothing up a big lather of shampoo and scrubbing her scalp harder than was necessary. It helped eliminate some of her frustration so by the time she was dry and dressed, she'd let most of it go, and left it there even when she heard ERP continue to chant outside the window.

She opened the suite door to go make coffee, but the moment she pulled it open, the nutty scent of a fresh brewed pot greeted her. Trey stood in the kitchen filling a mug. He turned and smiled at her, and she forgot about everything else and let the warmth of his greeting wrap around her like a warm hug.

He wore another body-hugging shirt, this one navy blue, and paired it with khaki tactical pants. His gun was holstered at his side, and he hadn't covered it with a shirt, but one lay on the back of the sofa.

He held up his mug. "Want one?"

"Yes, please."

She crossed over to the kitchenette.

"ERT wake you, too?"

She nodded. "Coker seems to be in rare form."

He handed her the cup. "Coker?"

"Chuck Coker. Their fearless leader."

"I'm not familiar with their group at all."

"I wish I wasn't, but they make the news in the technology world all the time. He does some pretty devious things to get their message across." Eryn took a sip of the coffee and groaned over the goodness. "You can make me coffee anytime."

His eyes widened, and she knew he was putting more into her comment than she intended. She was really flattered by his interest, but despite enjoying spending time with him, she couldn't consider anything personal with him. Not even if she wanted to press down a damp lock of hair that was curling in the wrong direction.

He leaned against the counter and crossed his ankles. "Do you really think Coker could be behind the ransomware?"

She set her mug on the counter and gave it some thought. "He's a software engineer. Means he has the skills for hacking, and this hack was so rudimentary he surely could've done it."

"So if he did it, how do we figure that out?"

"I need to talk to him to get a feel for if he knows about the hack. Second, I'll check with my law enforcement contacts to see if he's suspected of any hacks. If he is, I'll get that code and compare it to the current code I'm reviewing to look for a signature."

Trey took a long sip of his coffee. "Hacker's sign their work?"

One corner of her mouth quirked up. "Not a signature like you think of it. More of a pattern of work that is consistent."

"I'll pretend to understand." He grinned.

It was too early in the morning to be faced with such a potent smile. She flashed him a quick one then headed for the sofa and out of the realm of his influence. A big mistake. He came across the room, slipped into his shirt, and sat next to her. She tried not to scoot away, but her instinct to protect herself was stronger than her desire not to offend him. He watched her carefully, but if he was disappointed or felt slighted, it didn't show in his expression.

Put him out of your mind. Do your work. You can always work. This is no different.

Email. She would start with her email. She took a long drink of the coffee then grabbed her phone. No way would she use the resort's unsecured network. She handled business needing immediate attention, and as she signed off, Bekah came padding out of the bedroom. She looked adorable in her jammies covered in pink dinosaurs that she'd named. She rubbed her sleepy eyes and climbed on Eryn's lap.

She kissed her daughter's soft hair. "Morning, pumpkin."

"People are yelling outside." Her eyes narrowed. "Are they mad?"

"It sounds like it," Eryn said but decided to quickly change the subject. "What do you want to do today?"

Bekah turned, her eyes wide now. "Go to the playground with Trey. He was fun at the pool. I like him."

Eryn marveled at the innocence of a child's comment. Trey was sitting right next to them, and Bekah talked about him like he wasn't in the room, much less next to her. And she revealed her feelings for him—just like that—when Eryn fought to hide hers.

She hated to step all over her daughter's desires, but it

had to be done. "Trey and I have to work really hard today, and I don't know if we'll have time. But if we can't go this afternoon, we can do it tomorrow."

She frowned. "Wanna go today."

"I know, pumpkin, but sometimes we have to be patient for the things we want."

"Amen to that," Trey said under his breath and caught Eryn's attention. His pointed expression left no doubt in her mind as to his meaning.

"Let's order breakfast from room service," Eryn moved on. "I know how much you like those little bottles of syrup that come with the French toast."

"Yippee!" Bekah clapped her hands.

Eryn wished she could change her mood so quickly. She rose and settled Bekah on the sofa. Bekah quickly climbed up on Trey's lap and laid her head against his chest. His eyes melted with contentment, and Eryn couldn't look at him. Not when he was the very image of someone she would love to have in her life, and someone that her daughter deserved, too.

Was she doing wrong by Bekah by refusing to get involved with a man again? Something she hadn't really given much thought to. She couldn't think about that now, or she would never get her day started. She handed a room service menu to Trey.

"Decide what you want. After I check with Mom, I'll place the order." She quickly found out what her mother wanted and then ordered meals for all of them.

"Yippee, French toast," Bekah announced, which wasn't a surprise. "It's so yummy. My tummy loves it. I love it, too. So does Trey. He said so."

Eryn didn't know where her daughter got to be such a chatterbox, but now that Eryn thought about it, her mother did like to chat a lot. Bekah probably picked it up from her. "Then let's get you cleaned up and dressed."

"Don't wanna." Bekah settled back, a pout on her face.

Eryn nearly had to pry her from Trey's lap, but she got her wiggle worm into the bathroom, washed up, brushed, and dressed. The protestors continued to shout outside, raising a few questions from Bekah, but Eryn managed to redirect her to other things including last night at the pool.

"It was the bestest," Bekah said. "I wanna swim today, too. And have a tea party. A big one. With cakes and cookies. And my dolls. And I'll invite Trey. He'll be the prince. My dolls will be the princesses who like him, too."

Eryn hadn't realized that the impression Trey had made on her daughter went this deep. It's not like there was a shortage of males in her life, with the guys on the team around all the time. But she never gushed about any of them like she did with Trey. Maybe it was because he devoted his full attention to her. Or maybe he stood out in her mind due to his red hair. Or his kindness. Or his gentleness.

"Stop. Just stop already."

Bekah looked up from tugging up her jeans. "Stop what, Mommy?"

"Nothing, sweetie. I was talking to myself," Eryn said and snapped Bekah's pants.

A knock sounded on the suite door.

"That will be our breakfast."

Bekah bolted from the bedroom, but Eryn took a moment to tidy up the room and make the bed. She wouldn't request maid service for the day except to get extra towels, and she liked things neat.

By the time she got to the table, everyone was seated. Trey was next to Bekah, and he was cutting her French toast.

She looked up at him in awe as if he were doing something she'd never seen before.

Eryn resisted groaning. She couldn't encourage this attachment that Bekah was forming to Trey. Maybe she should talk with him and explain how it wasn't good for Bekah when he wouldn't be in their life beyond this trip.

She took the seat next to her mother and outlined the day so her mom knew what to expect. "We'll start with a team meeting here. I know Bekah would love to watch *Dora the Explorer*."

"Yes, please!" Bekah looked at Trey. "Can you watch with me?"

He tweaked her nose. "Sorry. I have to work with your mom."

Bekah looked crestfallen, but she shoved a bite of French toast in her mouth and didn't ask again.

"Depending on the outcome of that meeting, I'll be away from the room doing interviews," Eryn continued. "I'll try to get back for lunch, but if not, can you order room service again?"

"Sure," her mother replied. "We'll spend our morning on letters, numbers, and cutting skills."

"You're the best, Mom."

Her mother smiled and patted Eryn's hand. "I want the very best for both my girls."

A knock sounded on the door, startling Eryn. She wasn't usually a jumpy person, but the stress was getting to her. "That'll be the team."

"I'll answer it." Trey strode across the room, his rigid law enforcement persona firmly in place. He looked out the peephole then opened the door and stepped back.

Eryn's teammates spilled into the room like water bursting through a dam. They never did anything halfway but put their all into their work—and even their play. They joked around while they greeted her mother and Bekah, then took their seats.

"C'mon, Bekah." Her mother stood and pulled out Bekah's chair. "Let's get the sticky washed off you."

Bekah hopped down and ran across the room to grab onto Trey's leg. Eryn cringed, not only from the fact that Trey would now likely have syrup on his pants, but because of Bekah's reaction to him.

"Don't forget the playground," she said.

"Of course not." He ruffled her hair. "It'll be the highlight of my day."

She pushed off his leg and ran toward her Gammy's room.

"Sorry if you got all sticky," Eryn said to Trey as they joined the others.

"That happened a long time ago at the table." He pulled out his sleeve.

She saw the shiny mark from the syrup, but it was the flexing of his muscles that really held her interest.

"Let's get going," Gage announced.

Eryn grabbed her files from the desk, then took a seat as far from Trey as possible and felt like everyone figured out what she was doing and was watching her to see what she did next. She knew that was only in her head, but she felt so self-conscious she hardly knew where to start.

"I suppose you know that's ERT outside protesting your class," Alex said.

"Yeah. I plan to have a talk with Coker."

Gage met her gaze. "As volatile as he is, do you think that's a good idea?"

"If it was only the protest, no. But he has the skills to

have pulled off the hack, so I absolutely need to question him."

Gage worked his jaw for a moment. "Be careful you don't give him more ammunition to use."

She was known for flying off the handle when she was passionate about something, and Gage's advice was solid. She nodded, then turned to the group. "Anyone have anything to report from the interviews last night?"

"I can report that all the guys I talked to said you're a good teacher," Alex said. "But then, they may have been too captivated by that pretty face and might not have been listening."

Eryn gave him the stink eye. "Let me clarify my question. Did anyone learn anything helpful to our case?"

Riley shifted in his chair. "I talked to a Detective Ivan Petrov whose partner is taking your next class. Her name is Gail Rudd. I got this really bad vibe from Petrov, but he could simply be a jerk. Still, I know you'll want to talk to him."

"Thanks." Eryn circled Rudd's name on her upcoming class roster and Petrov's name on the prior session. "Anyone else."

"No one for me," Gage said. "But I did get everyone's cell phone make and model like you asked."

"Unfortunately, I struck out on finding anything in the phone pictures, but you can all email the phone info to me in case it's needed later." She paused and looked around the group. "I'll run preliminary background checks on the names you've mentioned."

"Do you want help with that?" Trey asked.

"Due to the technology involved, I feel like I'm the best one to handle it." She closed her folder. "But before I do anything about these men, I plan to rattle Coker's cage to see if anything falls out."

"Good luck with that," Alex said. "I don't envy you at all."

"So if that's it, we'll adjourn and get back together tonight for a quick update."

"No!" Trey's voice shot out like a bullet drawing everyone's focus.

"Sorry," he said. "I didn't want you all to take off before we discussed security for Eryn's class tomorrow afternoon."

"What about it?" Eryn tried to hide her surprise.

"I'm glad to take care of clearing the room and standing watch for the class," Trey replied. "But it would be better to have an extra set of eyes."

"I'm teaching then," Gage said.

"Me too," Alex said.

"I'm free and glad to be there," Riley offered. "Just tell me when and where."

"Meeting room 10a." Trey looked at Eryn. "What time do you want to set up for your class?"

"One forty-five should be fine."

Trey changed his focus to Riley. "I'd like you to clear the room right before that and stand watch at the entrance. Don't let anyone in and text me so I know it's safe for Eryn to enter."

"Give me your cell number, and I'm on it." Riley took out his phone, and they exchanged numbers.

Trey shoved his phone into his pocket. "I've arranged with security to bring Eryn in through the staff entrance in the back of the room so she won't have to come in the main door."

"When did you do that?" Eryn asked.

"When you were so deep in code that a bomb could've

gone off next to you, and you wouldn't have noticed." Trey grinned.

"I wasn't—"

Alex held up a hand. "Don't even try to deny it. We've all seen you like that more than once."

Nods of agreement traveled around the room. Eryn knew she got involved, but that deeply? Clearly, she needed to accept that she became obsessively lost in her work, but she didn't want the team to dwell on it.

She cleared her throat. "Thank you for arranging the security measures, Trey."

He responded with a quick nod, but she could see he was pleased that she recognized his extra effort on her behalf. "And I also called my contact at PPB, Gage. He gave me the name and number for a Samantha Willis for your forensic job. I'll text it to you."

"Oh, goodie, another girl on the team." Alex wiggled his eyebrows.

Eryn groaned. "Okay, now can we get going before Alex says anything else?"

"Yes, ma'am." Trey gave a mock salute.

She stood, and as the team filed out, she faced him. "Let me tell Mom I'm leaving, and we'll start with Coker."

Trey nodded his agreement but worry darkened his eyes into a solid wall of gray.

"What's wrong?" she asked.

"I watched some videos of Coker while you checked your email, and I'm not eager for you to be in the same universe with him, much less getting in his face."

"I can handle myself."

"You're like this fierce former agent, but still..." He clenched and unclenched his fists.

She pressed her good hand on his arm. "It'll be okay."

"I know—I'll be there." he said.

She squeezed his arm. "I'll be right back."

She planned on making quick work of saying goodbye to her mother, but the moment Eryn saw Bekah sitting on the bed with a giant picture book, a sudden need to hug her washed over Eryn. Why, she didn't know. Maybe she was buying into Trey's warnings a bit too much.

She scooped Bekah into her arms and held her tight.

"Ouch, Mommy." Bekah squirmed. "You're squishing me."

"Sorry, pumpkin. I needed an extra big hug today."

"Sometimes I like extra big hugs, too." Bekah frowned. "When I'm hurt. Or sad. Or someone is mean. Or I don't want to go to bed. Are you sad, Mommy? Or hurt?"

Eryn tapped the tip of Bekah's button nose. "Nope. Just needed to hug my girl."

Eryn squeezed and tickled her until Bekah was laughing again, and then she set her down. Eryn caught her mother's attention. "I'll keep you updated."

"Stay safe, sweetheart."

"Always," Eryn replied and stepped back into the main room.

Trey waited at the door for her. He was staring at his phone, and she heard Coker's outraged voice echo from his speaker.

"Thought I'd look at another Coker video while I waited."

"You're going to make yourself crazy if you keep watching him."

"Maybe, but I like to be prepared. Especially when it comes to your safety."

Perhaps Trey was right, and she needed to be a bit more careful when approaching Coker. She took a moment to say a prayer of thanks to God for bringing Trey into her life when she needed a bit of extra protection. And to ask God to keep them both safe.

Trey reached for the doorknob but paused to look at her. "You're sure you still want to talk to him?"

She nodded. "He's outside in the public eye right now, and the place is swarming with officers, so he won't likely hurt me. At least not physically."

"Still, you're going to get an earful."

"Won't be the first time."

"And he seems pretty unstable, which means he could lose his cool and forget all about the officers around him. So I need you to promise to be careful. If I ask you to walk away —walk away. Got it?"

She wanted to protest, but Trey looked so fierce that she nodded.

He went out to check the hallway. Once satisfied, he quirked his finger, and they took the elevator to the lobby. He stuck closer to her today, and she knew his concern was elevated, which in turn made her anxious. As they wound their way through the officers, the protests grew louder. She caught conversations with the officers complaining about Coker.

Near the door, Trey reached out for her arm and drew her even closer. She didn't mind since hearing Coker's tone rattled her. Trey abruptly came to a stop, and Eryn almost barreled into him.

"Look at that." He pointed at a display monitor listing the classes for the day.

Eryn stepped closer and stared at the line item he indicated. "Cancelled. What? Who cancelled my classes?"

"Maybe Coker put pressure on Martha, and she did it to appease him."

"But she would've told me. I need to talk to her." Eryn spun and wove through the officers to get to Martha's room. Eryn pounded on the door, the sound echoing through the hallway.

Martha opened the door. "You'll wake the dead with all that racket."

"Did you cancel my classes?" Eryn demanded.

"No. Why would you think that?"

"The lobby monitor has them listed as cancelled."

"Impossible." Martha turned and strode to the desk. "I'll log into the resort scheduling software and see what's up."

Eryn moved to stand behind her, and Trey stepped to Eryn's side.

"Okay." Martha bent closer to the screen. "It says cancelled. But that's impossible. I'm the only one who can change this, and I didn't do it."

"Nothing's impossible with computers." Eryn wished she had a dollar for every time she told someone this. She'd have a nice little nest egg by now.

"I'll change it." Martha clicked on the field and typed in the room number, but when she saved the record, it reverted back to cancelled. "That's odd."

"Mind if I take a look?" Eryn asked.

"Not at all." Martha slid out of her chair.

"These entries are listed in a database and should be changeable." Eryn sat and first tried to change the record on the screen by highlighting it and hitting delete. Nothing happened.

"Interesting." Eryn created a new record using the name of her class and got the same results. Cancelled. She made up a new class title and entered it. That record worked fine. "Looks like someone hacked the software and targeted the name of my class."

"But who?"

"Likely the same person who hacked your company server."

"And the guy who warned you off teaching anymore classes," Trey added.

Eryn had to admit she forgot that Trey was even with them. She looked up at him. "The best thing for me to do now is to talk to the resort's IT person so I can get access to the database logs. It should show me when and who changed the record."

"Couldn't he delete any records that prove he made changes?" Trey asked.

"Yes, but there are a number of places he would have to hide the changes, and odds are good he wouldn't get all of them. Anyway, I don't think he cares if we see that he's been in the database. In fact, this seems to be his way of flaunting it and telling me that he can get to me."

"But can't you track who he is from the changes?" Martha asked.

"It all depends on how good he is at hacking." Which was better than she first thought, and she realized she was facing a more worthy adversary.

7

After the latest hack, Trey wanted to demand that Eryn cancel her remaining classes, but she would stubbornly refuse. There was no point in asking. It would only upset her, and she was already tense as it was. He couldn't convince her to stay out of sight, so he'd keep his eyes open, and if danger appeared, then he'd insist.

Right now she was safe in the small office of Denise Frazier, the resort's computer professional. For the last two hours, Eryn had been sitting with shoulders hunched over the computer next to Denise who seemed in awe of Eryn's skills.

Eryn pushed her chair back. "I've traced the hack to an Internet service provider. Now I need to call in a favor, and hopefully I'll have the physical address of the computer used for hacking."

She stood and looked at Denise. "If I need anything else after I review the files, I hope you'll give me access to your network again."

"Of course."

Eryn jotted numbers down on a sticky note and handed

it to Denise. "You'll want to block this IP address. And make sure you get one of the intrusion programs we talked about in place today. That way, if this happens again, you'll be aware of it."

Denise's face colored. "I should have done more, shouldn't I?"

"Hey, don't feel bad." Eryn smiled. "I've worked with bigger companies who have less in place than you do."

"Really?"

Eryn's expression turned serious. "Absolutely, but now that you know, don't be caught unaware again. You have guests to protect. You may warn them when they log into the Internet that they're accessing an unsecured network, but they still have expectations that you are doing everything you can to protect their electronic data while they're staying with you."

"Thank you." Denise vigorously shook hands with Eryn.

Eryn pulled a business card from her pocket. "If you have any questions about the intrusion programs or any questions at all, call me. I'm always available to help you."

Denise blew out a long breath. "Thank you for being so understanding."

Eryn nodded and made a beeline to the door.

In the hallway, Trey caught her attention. "You're a very nice person, Eryn."

She looked up at him. "What prompted that?"

"A lot of people would have made Denise feel bad in there. Instead, you taught her something and left her with her dignity intact."

"You can thank my mother for that. And the FBI. She taught me the basics, but I learned how important it is when I joined the Bureau."

"That honestly surprises me. I always see these pushy

agents who are hard to work with on TV and in the movies. They're even rude to local officers."

"That's not reality. Maybe many years ago, but not today. You won't meet a more cooperative and uplifting group who are dedicated to helping people than FBI agents."

He held up his hand at the lobby door to take a long look before letting her enter. "Tell me about the intrusion software that you asked Denise to install."

"It acts much like an alarm system on a house. It monitors specific areas of their network and sends an alert if an unauthorized person tries to access sensitive parts of their system, as well as if they succeed at it. It also detects unusually high traffic. When the program spots any of these scenarios, it sends the administrator a message."

His respect for Eryn's knowledge grew exponentially with each hour he spent with her. "And you're sure the contact you mentioned will give you the address we need for this guy?"

"Pretty sure. And once I have that, I'll do a little digging on his name. If it looks like we have a valid lead, then we'll pay him a visit."

"Are you going to do that or talk to Coker first?"

"The guy who hacked the hotel's network could disappear, so he has to come first." She made her way through the lobby.

Back at the suite, Trey felt the tension flood from his body. He hadn't realized how tense he'd been, but he was on high alert with her being in the middle of a crowd where anything could happen.

"Trey!" Bekah jumped up from the couch where she sat with Sandra and came running across the room. "Is it playground time?"

He hated to be the one to burst her bubble. "Sorry. Not yet."

Her smiled drooped into such an adorable pout that he picked her up to comfort her. "Don't worry. We'll make time for the playground."

Her lip jutted out more. "Mommy has to work."

"Yes, she does."

"We could go without her."

"I'm sure your mom wants to have fun, too."

Bekah squirmed free and charged over to Eryn. "I'm being patient, Mommy. Like you said. Can we go now?"

Sandra snorted, and Eryn looked like she wanted to laugh. Trey had a hard time holding his laughter back, but he managed it.

Eryn knelt in front of her daughter. "Being patient means not asking every time you see me."

"Oh." Bekah seemed to think that over, then put her hands on her hips. "I don't like patience."

Eryn stood and stroked her daughter's hair. "I know it's hard, pumpkin, but you can do it. I know you can."

Bekah spun and came running back to Trey. She took his hand. "Show you my cutting. I did good today. Gammy said so. I cut kitties. And puppies. And a tree. And I did my numbers and letters. I'm good at that, too. Gammy tells me all the time. I like numbers better than letters, don't you? They're more fun." She drew in a deep breath, and Trey waited for her to go on.

On her way to the desk, Eryn mouthed, "I'm sorry."

He waved her off as he was actually enjoying Bekah. She helped alleviate the stress generated by protecting a strong stubborn woman who could at any moment go running off, leaving him to chase after her.

He heard her on the phone asking about the IP address,

but Bekah held out a puppy dog that was cut from blue lines on paper, taking his focus. She'd cut off the ears and tail, but basically followed the lines for the body.

"You did do a very good job," Trey said with sincerity.

"Gammy said it's my bestest."

"I did, at that." Sandra smiled at her granddaughter.

"I have an address and a name," Eryn announced. "Quick, Trey. Compare it to the class participants while I start a background check on the guy."

"Your mom needs me to work now," Trey said.

"I'm going to write your name. You can see it when I'm done." Bekah plopped down on the carpet and picked up a big pencil. "Gammy, how do you spell Trey?"

If he wasn't so eager to find the hacker and keep Eryn safe, he would gladly sit and watch Bekah. But finding the hacker came first. He joined Eryn at the desk.

She pointed at the class rosters without taking her focus from her screen. "Guy's name is Rodrick Newton. Lives nearby."

Trey picked up the list and perched on the corner of the desk. On page three, he found a local detective named William Newton listed in her afternoon class. Trey pointed at the entry for Eryn.

"Let me see if I can find a relationship connection." Her fingers flew across the keyboard, and he knew for that moment he ceased to exist for her.

She was exactly like computer professionals he knew, and yet different in so many ways. She was outgoing, confident. Personable. And she was a really nice person, too. He almost wished she was mean to Denise, then he could've found something he didn't like about her. Other than the fact that she didn't want to have anything to do with him romantically.

He should take a page out of her playbook. Until he figured out how his leg situation would resolve, he should fight his attraction more. What if he messed things up with her and then he wanted to work with Blackwell? That would be so uncomfortable, maybe impossible, and he knew he could never find another job like Gage was offering. Not in a million years. So he needed to do a better job of cooling things off for both of their sakes.

She looked up at him. "I found William. I don't see any connection to Rodrick, but then William doesn't have much online. Not unusual for a law enforcement officer. We all try to avoid putting personal information on the Internet."

Trey glanced at the clock on her computer. "We have time to talk to William and still have a late lunch."

"No. Rodrick first." She grabbed her phone and tapped the screen. "I'm calling Gage to get the team ready to head to Rodrick's house."

"Shouldn't you leave that for the sheriff?"

She shook her head hard. "He'll have to get a warrant before doing anything other than talk to Rodrick, and that will take time we don't have. If Rodrick is our actor, he could already be dismantling his equipment and moving on."

She stood and turned her attention to the phone. "Gage, good. Glad I got you. Assemble the team. We have a hacker to visit."

Trey stood back while Gage opened the rear door of his SUV. To avoid an altercation with Coker, Gage had brought his vehicle to the back entrance. Four tote bags labeled with each team member's name were stacked in a neat pile and secured with bungee cords. He jerked them out and passed them to the rightful owners.

Trey had to think these were similar to his "Go Bag" that he'd grabbed from the trunk of his car. His contained a tactical ballistic vest, extra ammo, flexi-cuffs, a flashlight, and other tools a deputy might need. If they ran into any issues with the hacker, they'd be prepared.

Everyone donned their vests then piled into the vehicle. Gage took the wheel and tore out of the resort parking lot.

Eryn laid out a map she printed from the Internet. She tapped an X she'd marked in red. "This is our target's home. ETA five minutes."

"Are you positive this is the hacker?" Trey asked. He was used to quick tactical maneuvers while in the army, but as a deputy he had to be more cautious and follow the laws he swore to uphold. Racing in like this with the potential to subdue someone without due process left him a bit uneasy.

"Not positive, no," she said. "Our actor could've routed the hack through an innocent victim's device to make it look like this person performed the hack. We'll have to be cognizant of that and know whoever answers the door may not be the actor."

"If he's really the talented hacker you say he is, would he really make it this easy to find him?" Trey asked.

"It may have looked easy as you stood and watched me, but it wasn't. And he could very well want us to find this address to taunt me."

"Or to set a trap," Trey grumbled.

"Hence our protective gear," Alex said and gave him a *chill out* look.

Trey took a long breath, but he still didn't like the speed that this op was moving. Sure, this team knew how to act quickly, but it increased the danger to them all, and he'd promised to protect Eryn. Not let her run headlong into danger.

Eryn looked down at the map, and Trey forced down his unease to study it so he'd be prepared to act when they arrived at the tiny neighborhood. An industrial area sat across their target street in the center of this midsized coastal town.

"The best I can tell, the house only has two exits," Eryn said. "But we can't rule out our suspect bailing out a window. Since a threat was made to my life, and we can't know if this is a trap, we'll drop Riley off, and he'll be on overwatch on the roof here." She pressed her index finger on the map touching a two-story building just down the street from the house.

Trey had to admit she seemed to be thinking clearly, and he uncrossed his arms.

"Alex and I'll take the front door," she continued. "Gage the rear exit."

"I'm with you at the front," Trey said.

She looked at him. "I appreciate your offer of assistance, but we're like this well-oiled machine, and an extra person could interfere with our rhythm."

"I'm going to the front door with you, and there'll be no discussion." Trey locked onto her gaze and held it, but he could feel Riley and Alex watching him. Maybe Gage, too, in the rearview mirror.

"Fine," she finally relented. "But you stack to the rear and *stay* in the rear if we have to go in."

He nodded but wasn't promising anything. If the hacker was carrying and he threatened Eryn's life, Trey would instantly shield her. Not because she was a woman —he served with very capable women in the army and on the job now, and he had no trouble letting them do their jobs. But this was Eryn, and he'd risk his life for her in a second.

"Okay, so that's it. A basic touch and go. Any questions?"

"Yeah," Trey said. "What's a touch and go?"

"Team lingo for interview the suspect, but if something seems hinky, be prepared to act." She dug in her bag and pulled out a portable communication unit and handed it to him. "This serves as our main source of communication in an op, but we've developed plenty of hand signals, too, and you won't be familiar with them. So remember to stay in the rear and take lead from us."

He nodded before settling the earbud in his ear and putting the microphone around his neck. The team members did the same, and when they reached the location where they were to drop Riley, Gage put his on, and they performed a basic sound check.

"Okay." Eryn looked at Riley, excitement burning in her eyes. "Report in after you do a quick recon."

"Roger that." Riley hopped out of the vehicle and darted across the street. He carried his rifle in a soft case and made his way to a fire escape. Gage had already contacted the business owner and received permission for the op. Gage warned them all to stay inside, and the workers from the machine shop stood peering out a big window facing the street.

Trey could only imagine their thoughts. Or maybe he couldn't, as he'd been in the military or law enforcement long enough that this kind of operation was second nature to him. Not that he ever let his guard down, but the tactical response was pretty much the same. The interesting part came in how the suspect responded.

"In position," Riley's voice came over Trey's earbud. "No vehicles at the house. No movement either. Front has a small porch, door, and two windows. Back is fenced with a south side entrance. And there's a For Rent sign on the front lawn."

"For rent," she muttered. "Could mean the place is vacant and our actor set up a router there for just that reason."

"Any sign of a threat, Riley?" Gage asked.

"Negative."

"Then we're moving into place," Eryn said.

"Roger that," Riley replied.

Gage didn't waste a second but had the vehicle moving down the road to a small, well-kept bungalow painted bright white with a front porch exactly as Riley described. Gage parked across the street.

The vehicle hadn't quit rocking before Eryn whipped open the door. "Okay, people. We're a go. Be careful out there."

8

Adrenaline rushed through Eryn's veins as she jumped down from the SUV. She'd barely taken a step when she felt Trey hot on her heels. She appreciated his help and support, she really did, but with Riley on overwatch and the rest of the team in position, she felt safe enough.

They rushed toward the house. On the porch, she noticed both window blinds were closed, and the door didn't have a window. Unable to determine their exposure level, she took a safe position to the side of the door. She really doubted their actor would be armed and fire at them, but she didn't want to be caught unaware with a bullet through the door. Alex took a similar position on the other side and thankfully, Trey listened and stacked behind her.

She stood tapping her foot, waiting for Gage to report in from the back.

"In position," he said.

She pounded on the door, and then stepped back again, memories of the day she'd lost full use of her hand coming back. She'd been in similar positions with the team since then, but she hadn't taken lead like this.

No one answered the door.

"Police," she yelled, using the universal name that all law enforcement used regardless of their agency affiliations when approaching a potentially dangerous subject. It was something the subject could easily understand and react appropriately. She pounded harder. "Rodrick Newton, I need to talk to you."

She started counting. One one thousand. Two one thousand. Three one thousand. When she hit sixty, she sighed. "Any movement in the rear, Gage?"

"Nothing, and the patio door and window blinds are all closed. But let me check the windows on the other side of the house."

Her adrenaline was nearly propelling her to wrench open the front door, but they couldn't very well break it down.

"You seeing anything in the scope, Riley?" she asked, though she knew if he had seen something he would report.

"Negative," he responded.

"I struck out, too," Gage said. "All windows locked and blinds closed."

"I'm going to call the rental company on the sign." She stepped back far enough to see the phone number and plugged it into her phone.

A woman answered on the second ring. "Seaview Cove Realty. Owner Felicia Quaker speaking."

"I'm at your property on 5th street. I see it's for rent. Is it available now?"

"Yes, are you interested in renting it?"

Eryn explained their situation. "I'm sure you don't want your rental property to be used to commit a crime. Is there any way someone could let us in to check for the equipment?"

"Yes, of course. I'm five minutes away, and I'll head out now."

Eryn disconnected and stowed her phone. "Property owner on the way. ETA five minutes."

"Don't anyone let their guard down," Gage said. "We're not clear yet."

"Well said," Trey replied.

Eryn could feel the tension rolling off his body like heat from a hot summer sidewalk. Her gut was tight with emotion, too, but she wasn't going to let it get to her. Instead, she kept her focus fixed on the doorknob, her ear toward the house, listening for any movement inside.

But silence reigned in the neighborhood with only a lawnmower down the block cutting through the stillness. Time ticked by slowly until finally a car with a clinging sign on the side announcing Seaview Cove Realty pulled to the curb.

A middle-aged woman with spiked gray hair and turquoise glasses large enough to cover her cheekbones stepped from the car. She wore jeans, red high heels, a black knit shirt, and a necklace of large colorful beads.

She hurried toward them, a ring of keys jingling, and her gaze going between all of them. "So this is really serious, then? I mean with the vests and guns and all it has to be, right?"

Eryn smiled to alleviate her concern. "We always like to err on the side of caution. I suggest you give me the key and allow us to clear the house before you enter."

She took a step back and held out the ring.

"Perhaps you could sit in your car," Eryn suggested.

She nodded and quickly retreated back down the steps, her heels clicking on the concrete.

Eryn waited for her to be seated then inserted the key. "Entering. Riley, keep an eye on the owner."

"Roger that," his voice came sure and strong over Eryn's earbud.

She pushed open the door but quickly stepped back to avoid a bullet. She called out, "Police. Rodrick Newton, we're coming in, and we're armed."

She stepped into the small living room and searched the space. Empty. White walls, fireplace, mirror above, wood floors. No furniture.

"Clear," she said and moved into a hallway. A stairway was dead ahead, the kitchen was to the left, bedrooms and bathroom to the right. "I'll go right. Alex left. Trey up the stairs."

She didn't know if Trey would listen, but she hoped he would. She eased down the hall, gun outstretched. She checked the bathroom with black and white hexagon tiles. The tub held a shower but no curtain so she quickly cleared that space and moved on to the first bedroom.

On the floor sat a wireless router and modem plugged into an electrical outlet. The modem was connected to a cable jack, but no computer or other devices. She checked the closet then moved on to the other bedrooms before returning to the hallway. Alex and Gage entered from the other side.

"Clear," she said.

"Ditto," Gage said.

Footsteps sounded on the stairway. She readied her weapon again, but Trey poked his head out. "Second floor clear."

"I also cleared the garage," Gage said.

"Okay, so our suspect is long gone, but I found a router

and modem in the bedroom." She lowered her weapon. "Riley can you hang in there a bit longer in case the suspect is in the area watching us."

"Roger that."

"So is this a case of the hacker routing the transmission through here?" Gage asked.

"Could be. Or he may have set up the network, hacked the resort, and split. Best bet now is to interview Felicia about the prior tenant and ask if she knows anything about this Internet connection. Then I'll check the router log to see if it contains the IP address that accessed the resort."

"And if it does, does that mean the hacker was physically here?" Trey asked.

"I suppose he could've sent someone else, but yeah, it looks like he's been here."

"In that case," Trey said. "We'll want to report this to Blake so he can get a forensic team out here to process the place."

"I'm not looking forward to telling him about this." Eryn could imagine their county sheriff wouldn't be happy that they didn't call him before heading out on their own.

"I'll handle Blake," Gage offered.

The men had been friends since they played football in high school, so she was glad to let him talk to Blake. The team had a good working relationship with Blake, but he was a stickler for protocol and wouldn't like that he wasn't at least informed of their actions.

Trey moved closer to her. "I'd like you to let one of the guys interview Felicia so you're not exposed outside."

"She could come in here," Eryn suggested.

"Just to the front door, though," Trey said. "If this is a crime scene, we need to minimize any additional contamination."

"That's fine, but I also need my computer to access the router logs."

"I'll grab it," Alex offered.

Eryn waited for Gage and Alex to depart before facing Trey. "Your law enforcement experience is invaluable. I'm sure Riley would be glad to have a fellow former officer on the team."

"Amen to that," Riley said over the comm unit then laughed.

Eryn had forgotten he was still listening but was thankful for the reminder before she said something personal to Trey.

Trey frowned and jammed his gun into his holster. "Don't count me out of my deputy job yet."

"I wouldn't want to do that. Just saying you'd be an asset to the team." She stepped into the living room and waited for Felicia who was climbing the steps with Alex. Gage had gone to the car, likely to call Blake. Trey joined her and stood between her and the door, her guardian once again. Alex took a stand on the porch, looking every bit the defender as Trey.

Felicia entered the room, her gaze flitting around the space as if expecting an attacker to pounce. "You wanted to talk to me?"

Eryn nodded. "How long has this property been vacant?"

"A week now."

"And was Rodrick Newton the prior tenant?"

She nodded.

"Do you have a forwarding address for him?" Eryn asked.

"I do, but it's not something I'm at liberty to share."

"Why did he leave?"

"He bought a house."

"In this area?"

"Yes."

"Was he a responsible tenant?"

Felicia nodded vigorously, her dangling earrings jiggling in rhythm. "He and his family were a delight. They rented the house for five years. Paid on time. Left the place spotless."

Eryn paused for a moment to gather her thoughts as the next questions were very important. "Were you aware that there's still cable equipment here, and that it appears to be connected to an active account?"

She tilted her head in genuine surprise. "It wasn't here when I showed the house two days ago."

Interesting. "Did you give anyone access to the house who might have connected this equipment?"

"No." She shook her head hard. "Definitely not."

"So someone either had to break in or has a key that you don't know about. Did you change the locks after Rodrick moved out?"

"Not yet."

"When we arrived, everything on the first floor was locked up tight, so I'm leaning toward someone possessing a key." Which in Eryn's mind meant they were looking for someone with a connection to Rodrick.

"Let me look for any sign of forced entry." Trey stepped to the front door and studied the lock and doorjamb. "Not here. I'll check the back door and all the windows." He eyed Eryn. "Don't move, okay?"

She nodded and turned her attention back to Felicia. "What does Rodrick do for a living?"

"Computer something. Not sure. But he works at Seaview Cove Computers. That I know."

Eryn was familiar with the IT support company located nearby. They provided technical support to companies and private individuals for the tri-county area. If Rodrick was a support specialist, he would likely have the skills needed to pull off a simple hack. Still, after hearing Felicia rave about him, Eryn doubted he was the actor she sought, but it was possible.

Trey poked his head into the room. "No forced entry at the back door."

He turned, and she heard him jog up the steps as she searched for any other questions she might have for Felicia. Normally, she would ask about Rodrick's finances, but Felicia said he paid on time every month, and he obviously passed close inspection to get a home loan. Unless, of course, he recently came into a large sum of money and paid cash for the house. She doubted anyone would pay him big money to hack her computer or the resort's network, but he could've received some money to do so.

Trey entered the room. "There's a window upstairs in the back unlocked. It was jimmied."

Felicity gasped and pressed her hand against her chest. "Someone broke in here?"

"He'd have needed to bring a ladder to accomplish it," Eryn mused.

"Or there's a tree by that window he could've climbed," Felicia said her hand still flat on her chest.

"We'll bring in the sheriff's department to process this place for leads," Eryn told Felicia. "And with your permission, I want to access the wireless router we found in the bedroom to see if we can learn anything about your intruder."

"Yes, yes, of course."

"Why not go back to your car while we wait for a deputy

or the sheriff to arrive?" Eryn believed Blake would show up if he was available because this involved the team.

Felicia nearly bolted from the house. Alex handed Eryn her computer.

"Will you have Gage call Blake if he hasn't already done so?" she asked.

"You got it." Alex jogged down the stairs behind Felicia.

Eryn turned. "Time to look at that router log."

Trey's forehead furrowed. "Again, I know nothing about this, but aren't there security protocols in place so not just anyone can log in?"

"Usually, but I have the feeling our suspect wants me to know he was here, and I'll get right in. If not, I'll have to figure out the router password."

In the bedroom, she sat down on the floor and crossed her legs to place her computer on her lap. She turned it on and leaned back while waiting for it to boot up.

"Wait," Trey said. "Don't you have to physically connect to the router?"

"It's a wireless router and if I can connect to the network I won't need a hardwired connection."

Trey knelt behind her and looked over her shoulder. She was so aware of his presence that she could barely think straight.

Ignore him. Focus on your computer. On the networks loading on the screen.

She scanned the list of five networks in the immediate area and the closest was called GotchaCalloway.

"We're in the right place," she said as her stomach tightened. She pointed at the unsecured network. "He wants me to find this for sure."

"Can connecting to it hurt your computer?"

"Not unless he's also connected to this network right

now and is waiting to download something to my computer."

"But you'll still connect?"

"Yeah, I'll risk it to see the router logs. Like I said before, this computer can easily be reformatted." She clicked on GotchaCalloway and was immediately connected to the Internet. She typed the standard router IP address in the address bar.

A Wi-Fi router window opened on the Internet. She entered the word *password* into the password field, and the router page opened.

"How did you know to find that page and use that password?" Trey asked.

"Home routers have default private IP addresses. Each manufacturer usually uses the same one for all their devices. I happen to know the addresses for the most common router manufacturers. And the most common passwords used by people are "password" and "123456." Our suspect would know this, and if he wanted me to be able to log in, he would use one of those."

She opened the log window and quickly scanned down.

"So what are we looking at?" Trey asked.

"The fact that only two computers have used this router recently." She pointed at the first device listed. This is my computer. The second one is the IP address that connected to the resort, and the destination URL is the resort."

"So the hacker was here?"

"Again, he could've had someone do this for him, but, yeah, I think he was here. And it seems like he wanted me to come to this house for some reason, too."

Trey's eyebrows drew together. "Then we need to be even more careful leaving."

"Agreed," she said and was already trying to think of a

way to get to the SUV without taking a bullet or falling prey to another attack.

9

Blake marched in the front door in less than thirty minutes. He wore his khaki uniform which made his dark hair look even deeper black. His pointed gaze fixed on Eryn as he crossed the room. Trey watched her stow her phone and frown. Either she got bad news from her cable company friend who she was asking for billing information for this address, or she didn't appreciate Blake's aggressive stance.

Trey didn't mind seeing Blake's attitude. In fact, Trey was glad that they were in Blake's jurisdiction. He was a fine sheriff. Blackwell Tactical worked with him often. Trey had gotten to know him through the team, and he appreciated that the sheriff took the time to show up himself.

"You should've called me, Eryn." He scowled, and Trey could imagine him easily intimidating a suspect.

Not Eryn, though. She pulled back her shoulders. "I couldn't risk the actor taking off."

"I'd have been here as fast as you. Maybe faster."

She lifted her chin. "And then what? If Rodrick was home, you wouldn't have known what to ask him. And he might've clammed up when he saw law enforcement, but it's possible he would've talked to me."

"Why don't we move on," Trey suggested. "This is old news."

Eryn nodded vigorously. "Good idea."

Blake looked less enthused. "Gage brought me up to date on your hacker situation. That crime *also* happened in my jurisdiction, and you should've reported it."

She curled her hands into fists. "I wasn't certain the physical crime took place in your county until coming here. And even if I *did* report it, there's really nothing you could do about the cyber portion."

Blake widened his stance. "Stop splitting hairs, Eryn, or you're going to make me mad."

She looked like she might boil over so Trey stepped in again. "If anything else happens, we'll be sure to involve you."

Eryn gave him a *yeah right* look but quickly erased it. "I *do* want to talk to you about one of your officers."

"Related to this?" Blake eyed her.

"Yes. A Rodrick Newton last rented this house. You have a William Newton on the force who's scheduled to attend my class at the conference."

"And you're thinking there might be a connection." Blake pressed his lips into a fine line. "There are a lot of Newtons in our county."

"Understood, but can it be a coincidence to have an officer named Newton taking my class and a suspect with the same last name?"

"I can see why you want to go there, but you're barking up the wrong tree." Blake fixed a pointed stare on Eryn. "William has been a deputy for over twenty years, and he's a respected member of my team."

"Then you won't mind if we question him."

"I don't mind at all."

"And you won't warn him so I have the element of surprise."

Blake took a breath and let it out. "Feels like I'm selling out one of my guys, but I know he's not involved, so fine. Not a word."

"And Rodrick. I need to talk to him as well. My friend at the cable company told me that he cancelled his cable, but then changed his mind and asked to leave it connected. I can't think of a reason he'd do that unless he was involved in the hack."

Blake opened his mouth to speak, but she quickly held up her hands. "I know you want to interview him, too, but again, I'm the one who knows what to ask. So maybe we can compromise. You bring him in for questioning, and I can attend that interview."

Blake watched her for a long moment and Trey expected she might squirm under the sheriff's intensity, but she held firm.

"I can do that," Blake said.

"Today?" she asked.

"First I have to get his contact information and get ahold of him, so I don't know if I can promise it will happen today."

Irritation flashed in her eyes. "Just search the property tax records for recent sales. His name is unique enough that you should be able to find him."

"I know how to do my job, Eryn." Blake frowned.

"Sorry, I was only trying to help." She took a long breath. "Will you call me as soon as you have a time set up?"

He nodded.

"Then if there's nothing else you need from me, I'd like to get going. I have other interviews to conduct."

"Maybe you should bring me up to speed on who you plan to talk to before you leave."

Her irritation grew, but she gave a sharp nod. "First up is Chuck Coker."

Blake's eyes widened. Obviously, he knew Coker. Not a surprise to Trey as any good sheriff was well aware of troublemakers in the area.

"ERT's Chuck Coker?" Blake asked.

Eryn nodded and gave a concise description of the protest. "He wants me to stop teaching, and he possesses the technical skills to deploy malware."

Blake nodded. "I'd tell you to let me talk to him first, but like you've told me over and over, I don't have any idea what to ask him."

"You're not the only one confused." Trey chuckled to lighten things up. "I've had to ask a ton of questions, but Eryn does a good job of helping me understand it. What if she put together a document for you that explains details in laymen's terms and lists out the suspects she plans to talk to. That way you'll know what's going on and also be more informed."

Blake raised an eyebrow. "You'd be willing to do that?"

Eryn gave a crisp nod. "Sure. I'll have it to you by the morning."

"Good," Blake said and the air cleared between them. "I'll call you if I have any questions."

"Sounds good." All the fight seemed to wash out of her, and her shoulders dipped. "I'm sorry I didn't keep you up to date, Blake. You've always been so helpful to us, and I know you only want to do the right thing. I guess I let this guy's threat cloud my judgement."

"Understandable." He held out his hand, and they shook.

Trey was glad to see them make up. Not only because they didn't need additional stress in their lives, but if Blake's help was needed before they had the hacker behind bars, he was more likely to give it if he wasn't upset with her. And also, his presence, along with a deputy and crime scene team, gave them a way to safely get Eryn out of the house.

"Can we borrow a Tyvek suit?" Trey asked.

"What for?" Eryn asked before Blake could say a word.

Trey met her questioning gaze. "If the hacker's watching the house, and you put on one of the suits with hood up, maybe he'll think you're a tech."

"You think this guy is lying in wait for her?" Blake's voice rose.

"After your arrival, no, but we can never be too careful."

Blake nodded. "Sounds like a good plan. I'll grab a suit for you."

Eryn turned to Trey and ran a hand through her hair. She seemed like she thought he was taking this too far, but he didn't care. His role was to ensure her safety, and he'd do his job to the best of his ability.

The suit was overkill, but Eryn put it on and let the team and Trey circle around her as they headed for the SUV. She kept her head down to hide her identity, and Trey guided her by the arm. Honestly, if the suspect was smart at all, he would know they wouldn't escort a tech to the vehicle like this. But even if he figured that out, he also couldn't prove *she* was wearing the suit, so he wouldn't likely take action.

They all piled in the SUV, Trey keeping his head on a

swivel even after they were seated in the back. Gage got them on the road, and they stopped to pick Riley up.

Gage glanced at her in the rearview mirror. "Run through your plans for the rest of the day for me."

"First up, is interviewing William Newton and Chuck Coker. Then I should finally be able to get to the background checks on Rudd and Petrov, and we can talk to them, if it seems warranted."

"Can someone else on the team help with those checks?" Trey asked.

"We could, but Eryn would double-check our work anyway." Alex grinned. "So why not let her do it from the get-go?"

Eryn wrinkled her nose at Alex. "He's right. I have sources. They don't, and my work will be more thorough, too."

Trey watched her, and she didn't like his skeptical expression. Did he think she was full of herself? She wasn't. She was just realistic about her strengths and the strengths of her teammates.

She held his gaze. "I don't mean to sound conceited. I'm simply better at online research than these guys."

He nodded when she wished he would've said something. Why was his opinion so important anyway? Sure, she was attracted to him, but had she let her feelings go deeper than a physical attraction?

The thought took her aback, and she looked away. She needed to move the discussion forward. "And if Blake locates Rodrick Newton, I'll be interviewing him as well."

Silence descended on the SUV, filling every nook and cranny with tension. The quiet was unnerving because her team liked to laugh and cut up. Especially after an op to release stress. She had to think it meant they were as worried for her safety as Trey. That also meant they would try to baby her, too. She didn't want that and needed to lighten up the mood.

"And of course, most important of all, I have to take Bekah to the playground. You know how she likes to get her way. Wonder where she gets that from." Eryn chuckled, but no one laughed with her.

"Then we'll provide an escort for that and the team is on standby until further notice." Gage eyed her in the mirror. "Text me when you're ready to go."

She nodded, and having failed to change the mood, she sat back for the rest of the drive. She watched out the window and the closer they came to the resort the more overcast the sky turned. They soon drove into a heavy downpour, the driveway slick with water and the lush grass soggy. She rushed into the resort's back door and shook off the rain.

Inside the building, Trey was right next to her, and it took only a few minutes to get to William's room on the third floor. The door was opened by a burly guy who weighed in at a minimum three hundred pounds and stood about six-two. He wore thick glasses that counterbalanced the imminent threat emanating from his overwhelming size.

"William Newton?" Eryn asked and pretended she wasn't the least bit concerned by the way he towered over her.

"Who wants to know?" William growled.

Trey moved closer to her, and she resisted taking a step back from the detective. "I'm Eryn Calloway. I'll be teaching your computer class tomorrow."

"Oh, right." A broad smile spread across his face, revealing a gold tooth. "The one I've been waiting all week to take."

"A fellow geek, huh?" She managed to laugh, though she was still unsettled by his size.

"Geek, me?" He slapped a beefy hand against his chest. "Nah. Just a detective who wants to tell my tech team what to be on the lookout for." He shifted on his feet. "What can I do for you?"

"I was wondering if you're related to a Rodrick Newton."

He tilted his head. "Rodrick, nah. No one by that name in the family. We have a Rodney but not Rodrick."

"Thank you for your time. Sorry to bother you." Eryn gave him another wide smile. "See you in class."

"I'll be in the front row taking notes. But I gotta warn you. It'll be right after lunch so you'll have to work hard to keep me awake." He laughed, a deep belly rumble that shook his whole body as he closed the door.

"So you believe him? Just like that?" Trey asked.

"Yeah, I do. But I'll ask a few more questions in class to see if he really is the computer novice he claims to be."

Trey grimaced. "Then on to Coker."

"Yeah, and I guarantee you that interview won't be nearly as congenial."

10

Coker stood before his tribe, spewing hatred for electronic surveillance of any kind, the words flowing as fast as the cold wind whipping off the ocean. At least the pouring rain had stopped. Looked like Coker's group had been prepared for the unpredictable Oregon coast weather in August. After the downpour and wild winds, it could end up seventy degrees. Hopefully the sun would come out so the protestors would remove their coats. It was hard to keep an eye on everyone, and any of them could be a threat.

Eryn moved closer to Coker, and Trey kept pace with her. He didn't like the anger raging from the group leader. The creep would likely take it out on Eryn. His people didn't seem to be swayed by his speech, though. They looked wet, worn out, and ready to go home. Maybe because of him. At least Trey would be worn out from such venomous intensity all day. Coker's speech appeared to be a ploy to whip them back into the earlier frenzy Trey heard at daybreak. His associates started noticing Eryn, and they gawked at her.

A frizzy blond with an underbite pointed at Eryn. "It's her."

Coker turned slowly, his eyes narrowing to snake eyes. Trey took an instinctual step closer to her, and Coker's hand went to his side. Trey knew that move. The guy clearly had a weapon strapped under his jacket, raising Trey's concern.

Coker sneered. "Well if it isn't electronic super snooper, Eryn Calloway."

"Coker," she said, and Trey didn't know how she could be so civil. "You got a minute?"

"Here to ask us to leave?"

"Nah," she said. "You can stay. It's no skin off my nose."

The jerk's bravado deflated for a moment until he recovered. "Then what do you want and who's your goon?"

"A friend," she said.

Trey appreciated her consideration. The last thing he needed was for his name to end up in the news and get back to his LT.

"I have a couple of questions for you," she continued. "Mind if we step inside where it's a bit warmer and more private?"

"I'm not going to make things easier for you." He widened his stance. "You got questions. Ask them here."

"If that's what you want." She moved closer, and Trey matched her every step.

"Your guard dog is fairly salivating," Coker said.

Trey fisted his hands to keep from decking the guy.

Eryn completely ignored Coker's obnoxious behavior. "Do you know a Rodrick Newton?"

"No. Should I?"

His straightforward answer was odd. At least according to the videos Trey had seen of the guy. He liked to string people along and play with them before answering, and when he *did* answer, it was hard to know if he was telling the truth. But this response seemed almost earnest.

Eryn pulled back her shoulders, giving Trey the first inkling that she was disturbed by Coker's behavior, and she felt a need to appear more confident. "Tell me about your efforts to try to cancel my classes."

"You're looking at them."

"So the protest is all you've done?"

"Look," he said. "If you think I did something, just come out and say it."

"Released any ransomware lately?"

He took a step back, and his gaze darted around as if looking for a reply. Eryn stood patiently waiting when Trey wanted to shake the answer out of the guy.

"You must think I have," he finally said.

"I think it's a good possibility."

"Then I assume you have facts on which to base your accusation." He tipped his head at his team. "Because they're filming this, and I'd hate to take you to court over defamation of character." A snide smile crossed his mouth.

Trey'd had it with this guy. He was going to take him down a peg. He moved toward him.

Eryn held out her hand. He could push past her, but she'd figured out what he planned to do and was stopping him from advancing any closer. Probably a good thing with Coker's associates filming the discussion. As a deputy, if Trey laid hands on Coker, Trey would make the news for sure.

"See, here's the thing, Coker," she said. "I asked you nicely to step inside and talk in private and you chose not to. So the way I see it, you wanted me to tell your people about your activities."

"I didn't say I released any ransomware."

"You also didn't say you didn't."

"I don't have to justify my actions to you." He scowled.

"Now, if that's all your questions, we have important work to do here to stop your teaching of lawless surveillance."

Eryn looked like she wanted to argue with him about her class topics, but that was what he wanted, and she was smart enough not to say anything and let him twist her words in the media.

She spun. Trey knew she had to want to get as far away from Coker as fast as she could, but she took measured steps toward the door. She obviously didn't want Coker to think she was fleeing from him.

Inside, Trey faced her. "Did you notice he was carrying?"

"Yeah, he always does. Says he needs protection from all the crazies out there." Eryn rolled her eyes.

"It took everything I was made of not to deck that guy."

"Me too." She chuckled.

"I've been impressed with the control you've possessed in your interviews. Even laughing with someone like William Newton who could be the hacker."

"Learned that at the FBI."

He grinned. "I would have loved to see you in your agent suit all kamikaze agent."

She laughed. "I don't much wear suits anymore, but I still have them, so I suppose I could start again if I wanted to."

"I won't ask you to, but I'm sure it was a sight to behold. Still." He paused and ran his gaze over her from head to toe letting it linger along the way. "I like this whole commando attire you've got going on."

She swatted a hand at him. "I really like that you can be playful after such a tense situation."

"I'm not sure playful is the word, but yeah, I've learned how to let go of stress pretty fast or I'd be a basket case."

"Not me. I wish I did, but it usually stays with me for hours."

"Then maybe I'm a good influence on you."

"Maybe," she said, but it was followed by a frown of monstrous proportions, and he knew she was distancing herself again.

Two hours had passed since the interview, and Eryn was still riled up as she walked toward the back exit with Trey, Bekah, and the team. She managed to control outward signs of her distress, but not inside. All the while she wrote her report for Blake and started on the background checks, she stewed about how she might have better handled the interview with Coker until she felt anxious and overwrought. Thankfully, this trip to the playground with Bekah should ease some of her anxiety.

"Wanna take Trey's hand," Bekah said.

"Sorry, Kiddo," Trey said. "I need to talk to your mommy. Can you hold Gage's hand, and I'll make it up to you at the playground?"

She pouted but skipped ahead and slipped her hand into Gage's. Eryn smiled her thanks to her boss. He, Bekah, and Alex stepped outside. Trey slowed to scan the parking lot, and Eryn followed suit. Several officers were departing for the day and others were heading out to play golf. A perfectly normal day at the resort, and yet it wasn't. At least not for Eryn.

Trey caught her gaze. "I want to go on record as saying I don't think this trip to the playground is a good idea."

"If everyone on the team agreed with you, I would have

cancelled. But they didn't. Plus I promised Bekah, and I don't break my promises." Eryn pushed through the door.

Trey followed. "I respect that about you, but I don't like taking chances."

She gestured at Gage and Alex marching across the lot. "Pretty sure my safety is covered right now."

"Maybe from a close-up attack but what about a long shot?"

She inhaled a deep breath of the coastal air and let it out before speaking. He was just concerned for her well-being, and she didn't want to snap at him. "We have no reason to believe that will happen."

Trey sighed.

She stopped to rest her hand on his forearm. "We'll be watchful. And the team has already cleared the area, and Riley's on his scope on the rooftop. We'll be fine."

"Coker heading your way," Riley said into their earpieces.

"Gage, will you take Bekah ahead of us?" Eryn needed to make sure her daughter wasn't anywhere near a potential altercation with Coker. Not that Eryn thought he would try to harm her in the light of day. He was more of a hide-in-the-dark kind of guy. But as Trey kept saying, you could never be too careful.

Gage swung her up into his arms and started off at a fast clip.

"Hurry up, Mommy," Bekah called out. "Don't want to play without you."

"I'm coming baby girl," Eryn replied. "But I need to talk to Trey a minute."

The others headed down the path, and Trey looked at her. "Coker's pretty unstable, so humor me and stay behind me until he passes."

"Sure," she responded as it wasn't worth arguing about.

Coker soon crested the hill. His gaze was wild-eyed, his breathing hard. He barely gave them a glance, but she still stepped behind Trey like he requested. He slipped his shirt back and planted his hand on his sidearm. She heard Coker's thumping steps coming closer. Trey turned, bringing her with him. She took that to mean Coker had passed.

"You're clear," Riley said.

She moved around Trey, and they headed down the winding path to the playground area. "Coker must have someone else in his sights already."

"He's still a suspect."

"I know." But she couldn't think about that now. She needed to make sure Bekah had fun while Eryn still kept her eyes open for any danger. She doubted there would be any, but she would still be cautious.

They reached the play area with a huge jungle gym in bright orange and yellow. It also had three swings and two slides—one with a winding tunnel.

Bekah came sliding out of the tunnel. "Did you see me, Mommy? Did you?"

"I sure did, pumpkin."

She ran to a swing. "Push, Trey."

"Please," Eryn said.

"Please, Trey." Bekah peered up at him, her lower lip poking out.

"Looks exactly like you when you don't want to haul equipment," Alex said as he came up beside her.

She wanted to punch him, but he was right, so she simply shrugged.

"You sure you're okay?" His eyes narrowed.

She nodded, but felt tears prick her eyes at her teammate's concern. They'd all been so kind and ready and willing to come to her aid so she could fulfill her promise to Bekah.

"Good." His lips split in one of his famous grins. "We can't let our feisty know-it-all get hurt. Who would nag us all the time?"

She couldn't resist punching his arm this time, but laughed, and her tears evaporated. "You're a good friend, Alex. Even if you are a smart aleck. Wait, a smart Alex. Why have I never put that together before now?"

"Don't know, but I sure hope you forget it."

"Mommy, look." Bekah was swinging high thanks to Trey.

Eryn joined them and sat in the swing next to Bekah. She kicked it off swinging.

"I'm flying higher." Bekah's grin of pure joy erased the last of Eryn's anxiety, and she put all her effort into having fun.

After Bekah rode the swings and played on the slide a few more times, plus a stint on monkey bars that Trey held her up to navigate, she settled in the sandbox with him. Eryn stepped off to the side to watch them and still have a good view at the path leading down the hill.

At the edge of the play area, she noticed something fuzzy poking out of shrubbery. It looked like a large animal tail. Concerned, she eased over to the shrub, and her mouth dropped open.

Laying unmoving was a woman dressed in a fox costume that was so real, if Eryn hadn't seen her face, she would think it was a giant fox. Eryn ducked into the shrubs, and that's when she saw the bullet hole in the woman's forehead. The wound was circled in soot from a close-range shot and fresh blood had seeped into the ground. The woman's eyes were open and lifeless, making it clear that Eryn didn't need to check for a pulse.

For a moment, Eryn stood in shock. A woman had been murdered not less than twenty feet from where Bekah was playing.

Bekah. Eryn couldn't let her see this woman. Eryn shot out of the shrubs. "Gage will you take Bekah up to the room right now."

Gage cast her a questioning look.

"I'll tell you later. Hurry!"

Trey must have caught the panicked edge to her voice as he was already out of the sandbox and quickly at her side.

Gage stepped over to Bekah, no questions asked.

"But, Mommy. I'm having fun," Bekah complained.

"I know, pumpkin, but something has come up, and I need you to go with Gage. I'll make it up to you."

He scooped her up into his arms and took off despite her continued to protest.

"Riley," she said into her comm unit. "You see anyone in this area?"

"Negative. You're clear."

"What is it?" Trey asked sounding breathless.

Alex joined them.

"A woman in the shrubs," Eryn said. "She's dead. Bullet hole in her forehead. Close-up shot."

"Then we need to get you out of here." Trey reached for her arm.

"I'm fine." She stepped back. "Riley said we're clear. The danger has passed. Besides, the close-range shot says she likely knew her killer, and he's long gone."

"I don't like this, Eryn," Trey said. "Does she look like you? Like maybe a mistake was made."

"No chance of a mistake. Wait until you see what she's wearing." She led them back to the body.

"What in the world?" Trey said.

"Crazy, right?" Eryn asked.

"What's that in her hand?" Alex took a step toward the body.

"Stop! You might contaminate the scene," Trey commanded and took out his phone. "I'll zoom in with my camera, and we should be able to read the card she's holding."

He tapped the screen on his phone, and Eryn was impressed at his quick thinking. He used his fingers to zoom in. He suddenly looked up, his face pale. "Man. Just man."

"What is it?" Eryn asked, her stomach tightening

"She's holding your card, Eryn. Your business card."

11

The medical examiner loaded the victim onto his gurney, and Eryn stood in shock as she tried to come to grips with the murder. Alex had gone back to the room, but Trey stood next to her and Riley remained on overwatch until Blake was ready to release her.

Blake had arrived to take her statement, and then the medical examiner joined them. He confirmed Eryn's assessment of the powder burns from a close-range gunshot. Likely from the small caliber of a handgun, and they all agreed that the shooter used a silencer or the gun's report would've brought officers running. A silencer only masked the sound, didn't completely eliminate it, but with the playground located more than a football field away from the main buildings where officers attended classes, it would've sounded only like a pop to them.

She stepped back to let the ME and his assistant pass with the gurney. They started up the hill, one of the wheels squeaking with each turn.

"I wish we knew the woman's name so we could place her connection to you," Trey said.

Eryn was certain she'd never seen the victim before, much less given her a business card. But then, Eryn handed out cards in her classes and someone could have passed one along to this woman. "Hopefully when the ME removes the fox costume he'll find ID in a clothing pocket or her prints will return a name."

Blake finished a phone call and crossed over to them. "My forensics team is on the way. There's really nothing more we can do here."

"So Eryn's free to go, then?" Trey asked.

Blake eyed Trey for a moment before nodding. No doubt he was picking up on Trey's obvious concern for her safety.

"You planning to talk to Coker now?" Trey asked.

"I want to hash this over with the team before I interview him," Blake replied.

"I know Coker was in the area, but it's hard to believe he'd commit murder," she said. "I mean, don't get me wrong. He's a pain and underhanded, and honestly, I think he's mentally unstable, but that doesn't make him a killer."

"He was carrying, though." Trey's steely eyes narrowed as he glanced around. "And I could easily see him snapping and shooting someone in the heat of the moment."

Blake nodded. "He's been on law enforcement's radar for some time, and he's growing more and more desperate to bring his cause to the forefront."

"Desperate thinking isn't stable thinking," Trey added.

"Exactly," Blake nodded. "But we can't jump the gun here. Coker may have a solid alibi. I'll work on that once the ME pinpoints the woman's time of death." He lifted the fluttering crime scene tape and gestured at William Newton standing near the yellow tape. "Detective Newton will ensure the scene is protected. I'll walk up to your room with you."

"Heading back to the suite," she told Riley over her comm unit.

"Roger that," he replied. "Let me know when you're secure."

"Will do." She was suddenly struck by everything Riley did for the team. Of all the team members, he often had the most thankless, yet one of the most important jobs. She didn't know how he could hunker over a rifle scope for hours on end, but he could and did. Often. Serving as the frontline of defense for the team's safety. She made a mental note to thank him.

In the suite, she found her teammates seated in the living area, and her mother's bedroom door closed. When they were all inside, Trey let out a long sigh of relief, sounding like he might deflate. She'd never had anyone worry about her this much before, and despite being an independent person, she had to admit that she liked how much he cared. Maybe liked it too much.

She pointed at her mother's room. "I need to check in with my mom, and I'll be right out."

She knocked on the door and entered to find Bekah sound asleep next to her mother, which was unusual for this time of day.

"Is she feeling okay?" Eryn stepped over to touch her daughter's forehead.

"She's fine. She told me you cut the playtime short, started crying, and cried herself to sleep." Her mother sighed. "I'll be glad when we get back home, and she returns to her normal routine."

"She always does get out of sorts when her schedule is altered."

"She's definitely not like you in that regard. Except for being leery of water after that time our canoe tipped, I've never seen a child who could go with the flow like you did." Her mother chuckled.

Eryn smiled, but the memory of being trapped still made her breath catch. When the team's op involved water, she powered through her fear and did her job. And in her personal life, she did her best to make sure Bekah didn't pick up on the fear and had a carefree childhood.

Eryn shook off her thoughts. "Did Gage tell you about the woman I found?"

She frowned. "Yes. It's terrible. Was she really wearing a fox costume?"

Eryn nodded. "But why, I don't know and can't begin to figure out until she's identified. Still, I'll spend some time tonight looking for any connection to the hack."

"So you think this is related to you?"

"She was holding my business card."

"Oh, honey, I'm so sorry." Her mother shot to her feet and came over to hug her. She was a few inches shorter than Eryn and had to reach up to pull Eryn tight.

The minute her mom's arms went around Eryn, tears pricked her eyes, and she felt a crying jag coming on. That wouldn't do. She couldn't go out to meet with Blake and the team with blotchy red eyes. She stepped back and blinked hard. "Thanks, Mom, but if I let you hug me, I'm going to cry and the team is waiting for me."

"My tough baby girl." She smiled softly.

Eryn sighed. "I'm not a baby."

"You'll always be my baby. Like Bekah will be yours."

Eryn knew her mother was right, but she was an only child. What if Eryn had other children some day? Would she think of Bekah as her baby or would the youngest child fill that role? What was with thinking about having more

130

children anyway? Especially at this moment when she needed to join the others and help find a murderer.

"I'll come back when the meeting ends, and then we can grab dinner," Eryn said.

Her mother patted her arm. "I think we're all too emotionally worn out to manage Bekah in a restaurant. Let's do room service."

"Agreed." Eryn turned and swallowed hard before stepping into the room where all eyes focused on her. She gave herself a mental pep talk to keep out of the emotional danger zone.

The door opened, and Riley stepped in. He was carrying his rifle and set the bag on the hall table.

She met him in the middle of the room. "Thanks for having my back out there."

"No biggie." He had the softest blue eyes ringed in black that fit so well with his calm and levelheaded nature. She rarely saw him riled. Probably came from the patience he needed to learn to be a top-notch sniper.

"Actually, it is," she said. "You're always there for us, and we're never appreciative enough."

"She's right," Gage added. "After the threat made to Eryn, I couldn't help but think how valuable each of you are to the team."

A bright red flush crept up Riley's neck and over his face. The color highlighted the red undertint in his hair color. "Like I said. No biggie."

She wasn't surprised at the blush or humility. He was exactly like the other guys on the team. They were so tough, but the minute you complimented them, they were likely to get embarrassed—or in Alex's case, make a joke. They all thought the same way she did. They saw themselves as regular people doing a job and became uncomfortable when others tried to put them on a pedestal for their skills.

"Does that mean raises will be forthcoming?" Alex joked.

Riley cast him a thank you look for diverting the attention, and he crossed the room. Eryn followed him. He took a seat on the sofa with Alex and Gage. Blake sat in one side chair flanking the sofa, Trey in the other.

Trey got up and gestured at the chair. "Take my seat."

She smiled her thanks, and for some reason she couldn't possibly fathom, their gazes locked and held while sparks arced between them. Here. Now. Right in front of the team. She was helpless to look away even with everyone in the room.

Time seemed to stop, and she couldn't think of anything but how amazing Trey was and what it would be like to be held in his arms. To let go of the need to be so strong. For herself. For Bekah. To have someone to share her burdens with again.

Gage cleared his throat. "We should get started."

Trey jerked his gaze free.

Great Eryn. Let it all out in front of everyone.

She dropped into the chair. Trey perched nearby on the arm, and that further inflamed her nerves. The knowing looks she expected on her teammate's faces were clear and present. *Fine.* They could easily see she was equally attracted to Trey as he was to her. It was time to admit it. Not aloud, but to herself. That was the only way she would figure out how to deal with it.

"Let's discuss where we go from here." Gage met her gaze, and his look said his mind was fully on the business at hand.

She was so thankful for his ability to always bring them

back to task, but she knew this wasn't over. She would hear about her open display from her teammates. "I'll do some searching tonight for any reference to a fox in the hack. But honestly, I don't expect to find anything."

"What about another case you're working on or have worked in the past?" Riley asked. "Anything fox related there?"

She shook her head.

"Let's brainstorm on why anyone would be wearing a fox costume," Gage said.

"You mean other than they're a bit nutso?" Alex asked.

Eryn knew he was joking, but he could have a point. "Actually, I don't think we can rule out a mental condition."

"Maybe the costume itself can tell us something," Trey said. "It's not likely an off-the-shelf costume. The coloring is so intricate. Gray in the back and the head, blending into a bright orange chest and legs. Plus, the ears seemed extralarge. Seems custom made to me."

Blake sat forward. "I agree with that assessment."

"So maybe we should look for pictures of foxes with large ears that match the costume's coloring," Eryn suggested.

"I'll do it." Riley pulled out his phone. "Starting with the big ears."

"Okay, so say it's a custom costume." Blake tapped his pen on his small notepad. "It had to be expensive, right? Who would want something like that?"

"What about a person who does seminars about animals at schools," Gage suggested. "Or maybe a performer of some sort?"

"This looks right, doesn't it?" Riley held out his phone to Eryn.

She studied the picture of a small fox with coloring that matched the costume. "A kit fox. Never heard of it."

"Maybe you should check to see if kit foxes live in Oregon," Alex suggested.

"On it." Riley tapped the screen, and they all waited for him to update them on his search. "They live in the desert and semiarid regions of the state. Not many of them though. They're a Strategy Species and are part of the Oregon Conservation Strategy. Means they have a small or declining population or are otherwise at risk and in need of conservation."

"Sort of endangered, then." An idea struck Eryn. "The victim could be an animal activist." Eryn grabbed her phone to search for any activist organizations championing the kit fox.

"Found an article from last week about a kit fox being captured in the wild." She quickly scanned the story. "Someone posted pictures in an animal forum of a kit fox and claimed they captured it."

Blake's eyes narrowed. "You can say anything in a forum. Doesn't mean it really happened."

Eryn looked up from her phone. "Apparently, there's proof. Due to the kit foxes' rarity in Oregon, the state is monitoring them with trackers and cameras in the eastern part of the state. Their camera captured the fox being taken. Also, one of their trackers was cut off and left near the camera. The article says an animal rights group is up in arms. They want the fox found and returned to the wild. The writer doesn't name the group."

"I can see an activist dressing up in a suit to raise awareness for that," Gage said. "But why here? Why now, and why was this woman killed?"

"And how could it be related to Eryn?" Trey stared down at her as if he expected her to have the answer.

"The pictures," she said, thinking she was on to something. "The ones the guy posted in the forum. Maybe this woman wanted me to try to link them to a particular cell phone."

"That's a possibility, I suppose." Trey pursed his lips in thought. "But how would she even know about you?"

"Activists like to keep up on what's going on with other activists." Blake drummed his fingers on his knees. "Maybe she saw Coker was here. Since he has such a high public profile, she might have believed he'd be able to help her cause."

"Possible, I suppose." Trey's skeptical tone said he didn't think it was a strong possibility.

Riley stowed his phone. "So what's our next step here?"

Eryn pondered the question for a moment. "More Internet research on the kit fox, and we wait for the ME to provide an ID."

"And if we strike out there?" Riley asked.

"Then," Eryn said. "It looks like we'll be taking a chopper ride to eastern Oregon where the kit fox lives."

12

The next morning, the sound of protestors chanted in the distance, the heavy drapes not doing anything to mute their boisterous voices. Trey wished they'd go away. Bekah had already asked her Gammy about them a few times, and he didn't want her to have to learn about guys like Coker at such a young age. Shoot, he didn't want her to ever learn about guys like that. He wanted to protect her as much as he wanted to protect Eryn. Protect her in every way possible.

He almost sighed before he caught himself. He didn't want to draw Sandra's attention. She sat on the sofa across from him, overseeing Bekah's project of writing numbers on a lined paper. Bekah knelt on the floor by the coffee table. She bent over the paper, her face scrunched up in concentration, her tongue peeking out the corner of her mouth.

He changed his focus to Eryn who was at the desk doing background checks. Her concentration mimicked Bekah's, minus the poking-out tongue. With the way Eryn and her mother were raising Bekah, he could easily see she would grow into a special woman. She didn't seem to need or want for anything in her life, but he imagined how even more terrific it would be for her to have a father, too. And maybe a sibling or two. Or three. Just the way Trey would like it.

Eryn's phone rang. She snatched it from the desk. "Good morning, Blake. Anything new on the victim?" She sat back, listening intently for several minutes, tapping her fingers on the desk. "Yeah. I can make it. See you then." Without looking around, she started rapidly typing on the computer.

Her phone dinged, and after swiping the screen and reading the message, she stood. "Blake has the interview set up with Rodrick in two hours. Martha says Rudd's out of class right now so we should have time to interview her before talking to Rodrick."

Trey got to his feet.

Bekah popped up and hugged his leg. "Don't go."

Trey didn't know what to do or say, so he looked to Eryn for help. She joined them and knelt by her daughter to gently remove her hands from Trey's leg. "You know how mommy has to work at home every day."

Bekah nodded.

"Just because we're staying here at the resort, doesn't mean I don't have to work here, too. And I need Trey's help."

Bekah's lower lip poked out.

"But I brought you and Gammy along because I wanted you to be able to do fun things. Like go swimming and play at the playground. Are you having fun doing those things?"

Bekah nodded. "And I like the little jelly jars I get with breakfast. They're cute. And I like the syrup bottles. I can use them for my tea parties at home. Trey can come to my parties, too, okay? We'll have lotsa fun." She looked up at him and drew in a long breath. "Can we go to the big dining room for lunch?"

Trey almost laughed at her sudden change of topic but knew it wouldn't be well received.

"Sure, why not." Eryn gave Bekah a hug.

"See you later, squirt." Trey smiled at her and went to the door to make a quick check of the hallway, Eryn's voice floating back to him.

"Mom, can you look up the menu and make sure Bekah chooses something now? We won't have a lot of time at the restaurant."

With all they had to do today, he was honestly surprised Eryn committed to having lunch with Bekah. Maybe Eryn was hoping Coker was her guy, and Blake would have arrested him by lunchtime. Or she could be hoping one of the guys they planned to interview this morning would confess. He knew it didn't usually work that easily, but they could hope.

He looked over the ledge to the lobby. Classes were in session at the moment, leaving the area deserted and making it easier to spot a threat if one existed. But also, if Eryn's hacker wanted to harm her, now would be the time to do so with most of the officers in class.

She stepped out of the room, her gaze going down the hallway and back. She acted as if she was unaffected by finding the woman yesterday, but in unguarded moments, her expression revealed how deep her concern went.

He faced her. "Blake have anything new on the woman's ID?"

"No, but he doesn't think she was a resort guest. He's going to run all the license plates in the parking lot and cross-reference it to the guest list in hopes of locating her car. But she could've parked elsewhere and walked here."

"It's hard to miss a giant fox, so if that's the case, then someone probably saw her." The thought of seeing an enormous fox walking down the road brought a smile to his face but knowing what happened to the woman took it away in a flash.

"Blake also has his deputies canvassing the area. He said he might also put out a local news alert for witnesses."

Trey nodded his approval of Blake's thoroughness. "What about time of death and Blake's interview with Coker?"

"ME places time of death near the time we went to the playground." Eryn sighed. "If we'd gone a bit sooner, maybe she would still be alive."

"Or maybe you or Bekah would've been hurt."

"Yeah, I suppose. Anyway, Blake's waiting for the ME to remove the slug, and then he'll talk to Coker and hope he offers his weapon for comparison. If not, it could mean Coker's trying to hide something."

"Or he could be putting Blake through his paces and forcing him to get a warrant," Trey said. "At least that's my take on the guy."

"Agreed." She nodded down the hall. "Rudd's room is on this floor."

He gestured ahead. "Lead the way."

She moved down the hallway and knocked on a door. A woman wearing tactical pants and knit shirt much like Eryn's soon answered. She was around five ten, had a dark complexion, and big brown eyes that held the same wariness most officer's eyes would hold when a stranger showed up out of nowhere.

"Help you," she said, her voice low and throaty.

"Detective Gail Rudd?" Eryn asked.

She gave a clipped nod.

"I'm Eryn Calloway. I'll be teaching your computer class tomorrow." Eryn handed her business card to Rudd.

"The one about cell phone pictures." She smiled,

revealing even white teeth, and her gaze lightened. "I'm really looking forward to that."

"I was wondering if I could ask you a few questions."

"Sure, you want to come in?"

Eryn shook her head. "This shouldn't take long."

Rudd stared over Eryn's shoulder at Trey and smoothed her hand over her hair.

"This is my associate Trey Sawyer," Eryn said.

She nodded at Trey then focused on Eryn.

"Your partner, Ivan Petrov took my class already," Eryn said. "Did he mention it to you?"

She shook her head. "Not surprising. We're not what you would call real friendly. I've only been a detective for a few weeks, and Petrov made it clear he'd rather work with a male."

"I totally get that," Eryn said.

Trey knew women still had a hard time in law enforcement in certain places, but overall, things were better than they once were.

"Would you mind telling me why you're looking forward to this class?" Eryn asked.

"Petrov has this child porn case that's going nowhere fast, so our LT recently assigned me to work the investigation with him. When I saw your flyer about the photos, I knew I had to attend. He already signed up to attend and told me there was no point in both of us going. No offense to him, but he's not real capable on the computer, and I was worried he wouldn't understand it, so I registered, too."

"Sounds like you have some computer skills."

"Me? I have enough knowledge to at least ask the right questions."

"Then I look forward to having you in the class." Eryn

smiled, but it quickly evaporated. "Tell me about your porn case."

Rudd's relaxed postured vanished, and she stood at attention. "It involves a child who was in the care and custody of their paternal uncle while her mother worked. He sexually assaulted her and took pictures that ended up being posted on Facebook by a third party. Problem is, we can't prove the connection to the uncle. Being able to trace those photos back to his phone would resolve that."

Trey didn't like hearing this. Crimes were one thing, but crimes against children? Those were unfathomable to him.

Eryn fisted her hands. "I'd be glad to help you make that connection so he can put the creep behind bars where he belongs."

"Thank you." Rudd sighed out her relief. "I'll need to get my LT's permission to bring you onboard, but I know he'll approve."

"Once you do, call me, and I'll meet with you right away so we can get this child out of that environment."

"Thanks again. Your help is most welcome."

Anger built in Trey's gut. He hated that Rudd or any investigator had to deal with such things, but he was thankful that there were people who were willing to do so. And now that would include Eryn, which made Trey's heart ache even more.

"So back to my class," Eryn said, and Trey was thankful she moved on. "After that initial conversation, did Petrov ever ask you not to take the class again?"

Rudd scrunched her eyes together. "He do something wrong?"

"We're just asking questions of several people who have or are attending Eryn's classes," Trey said. It was technically the truth, but evasive, and he hoped Rudd bought it.

Her gaze cleared. "He did harp on it on the way over here. I figured he was mad I signed up when he didn't want me to."

"How long has he been on the force?" Eryn asked.

She shrugged. "Since I was in grade school—that much I know. He's retiring in a few months, and I'm training to take his job. I was one of the youngest officers to make detective. Figure that's another strike against me."

Eryn nodded. "Is he a good detective?"

"Yeah, I guess so. He has a good closure rate anyway, but he's too old school for me." She glanced between them. "I want to help, but these questions are out of the scope of the class and seem like you're fishing for information on him. I'm not comfortable with that."

A tight smile crossed Eryn's face. "I respect your position, and I'll see you in class."

"See you there."

Eryn headed for the elevator, and Trey kept up with her. "You thinking Petrov might be trying to keep her out of the class?"

"That's exactly what I'm thinking. Now proving it is another thing all together."

Petrov wasn't in his room so Eryn looked over the half wall to search for his telltale silvery hair. She spotted a possible guy standing in line for coffee. "I think that's Petrov at the coffee cart."

She didn't wait for Trey to weigh in but rushed to the elevator and stabbed the down button.

"Don't be in such a hurry to talk to him that you forget to take care," Trey warned.

She nodded, but her mind had already gone to the questions she would ask Petrov. When the doors opened, she quickly picked her way through the crowd of officers. Petrov had made his way to the front of the line and was paying for his coffee. She reached him as he turned to depart.

"Detective Petrov?" she asked, though now up close, she was certain of his identity.

"Yes," he said warily before he recognized her. "Ms. Calloway."

"Eryn," she said. "Would you have a few minutes to answer some questions for me?"

"About?" He blew on the top of his cup and stared down at her.

"The class."

"I suppose, but you have to make it quick."

He and Trey eyeballed each other like two evenly matched boxers in a ring, so she introduced Trey as her friend.

"Why don't we take a seat where it's less crowded." She didn't wait for them to agree but started toward a deserted area.

She found an empty seating group with windows overlooking the ocean and took a seat. Petrov sat across from her, and Trey stood next her, his hand on his sidearm. She gave him a pointed look, telling him to relax or she would never get Petrov to talk. Trey shifted and let his hand fall to his side. Petrov turned his attention to her.

"Did you enjoy the class?" she asked, hoping it would break the ice.

"Yeah, sure. I'm not big on computers, but I like to stay on the cutting edge." He was a master at veiling what he was thinking—not surprising for a seasoned detective—but his rigid posture said he was being cautious. But more important than posture or expression, according to Rudd, this guy didn't value technology in investigations at all... so he was lying, and it was up to Eryn to find out why.

"Do you have any cases that you can use it for?" she asked to see if he would tell the truth.

"Not right now." He angled his body away from her.

Okay, so he continued to lie, and his body language added to that. "I was surprised to see another detective from PPB attending the class, too, when you could share information with her."

He didn't flinch as her mention of Rudd. Not even a blink of his eye. "Yeah, Rudd seems to like computer stuff so I encouraged her to take the class even though I was already signed up. Figured since I'm not great at using electronics, we could compare notes."

"I don't have any other questions for you, detective." She stood and held out her hand.

He blinked a few times, and she knew she'd caught him off guard. "Oh, okay. That was quick."

They shook hands, and she noted his were moist, proving he was more uncomfortable than he let on.

"Thank you for your time," she said and watched him go.

Trey frowned. "The guy is obviously lying through his teeth. Why didn't you press him?"

"If he feels a need to lie about the innocuous questions I posed, he'll lie about the big questions, too, and I don't want him to know I'm on to him."

"But you think he's hiding something."

"Oh yeah, he's hiding something." She felt that old investigative spark that once consumed her when she zeroed in on criminals during her FBI days. "My only question is... what?"

Rodrick Newton was younger than Trey expected, maybe twenty-seven or so. He had dark scraggly hair and a mustache that he was either starting to grow or there was no hope of it developing into more than a few whiskers. He wore a blue hoodie over a green knit shirt.

"I musta done something really bad if it takes three of you." Rodrick laughed nervously and wiped his palms over his jeans.

Eryn sat across the metal table from him. "We have a few questions for you regarding your former rental home."

"Oh, okay." He scrunched thick eyebrows together into one large unibrow. "But I paid the rent and left it clean. Even got my security deposit back so don't know what the problem might be."

"It's regarding your cable." Blake joined Eryn at the table, and Trey leaned against the wall where he could see all faces and observe the conversation.

"Cable?" Rodrick asked. "I cancelled that the day after we moved out, so I'm not sure how that can be a problem either."

Blake slid a cable bill across the table. "As you can see, it hasn't been cancelled."

He scanned it, brow furrowed, then looked back up. "But I have the email confirmation."

"The company says you cancelled the service then chatted with them online and told them you changed your mind."

"No. No. I never did that."

Blake took another page from a file and slapped it on the table. "The chat transcript says otherwise."

Rodrick grabbed the page and stared at it. "I didn't chat with them. Someone else musta done it."

"The chat connection was tracked back to the house," Blake added.

Rodrick's mouth dropped open. Either the guy was surprised that he got caught, or he was surprised that someone impersonated him with the Internet provider.

"Then someone musta broke into the house and connected to the Internet."

"Why would someone do that?" Eryn asked.

"I don't know, but they did." He tapped his finger on the tabletop then suddenly his eyes brightened. "I took my modem with me so have them check the modem and serial number used to connect to chat."

Blake looked at Eryn. "Can they do that?"

She nodded. "Should be able to."

"Why's this a problem anyway?" Rodrick picked up the bill. "I would've gotten a bill for it, so it's not like someone is stealing the Internet."

Eryn leaned closer to draw his attention again. "It's a problem because a ransomware attack was launched from your former rental house. I confirmed it was deployed through the router we found in the home."

"Man," he said and his gaze shot around the room. "That's crazy." He dropped his hand. "Wait. Do you think I'm behind the attack, because I swear I'm not. No way. I didn't leave a router there, and I didn't launch any ransomware."

"But you have the skills to deploy a basic ransomware program," Eryn stated.

Trey knew if he admitted he had the ability to do so that he was more likely innocent.

"Yeah, I do. Maybe more than basic. But I didn't do it.

Not possible." He shoved a hand into his hair messing it up even more. "I got kids, you know. I wouldn't do something that stupid. My wife doesn't work, and they need me. I wouldn't hurt them like that."

He seemed so earnest that Trey believed the guy.

"So tell us who knew about your move," Blake said.

"Family. Close friends. People at work." He sat back and crossed his arms. "Guys on my gaming forum, too."

"Did you tell any of these people your rental address?" Eryn asked.

"Well work already knew it and so did my family and friends."

Eryn laid her hands on the table. "What about the forum?"

"Yeah, a guy asked about renting it so I gave him the address." Rodrick's eyes widened. "You think he did this?"

"Could be." Eryn passed her notepad and pen to him. "I'll need the forum URL and your login information."

"But I—" He shook his head. "I don't really want to share that with you."

Erin eyed him. "Would you rather be locked up for hacking a company network and deploying ransomware?"

He crossed his arms. "I have credit card information saved there, and I don't like others having that information."

"Look." Eryn leaned closer, her expression one that would make Trey take notice if he were Rodrick. "I can get that and more information on you if I tried hard enough. But I'd never use it, so relax and give me the login."

He grabbed the pen. "Fine, but when you get done I'm changing the login credentials."

"Not until I tell you you're clear to do so."

He scribbled on the notepad and pushed it back to Eryn, scowling the entire time.

Blake stood and handed the guy a business card. "You're free to go now, but I'd advise you against leaving the area without informing me first."

Rodrick charged for the door, and Blake escorted him out.

Eryn rose and faced Trey. "Let's get out of here, too. I have enough time to check out this forum and still make lunch with Bekah."

They exited the room, and by the time they reached Blake at the main lobby door, Rodrick was long gone.

"I'll contact the cable company and let you know what they say about the modem," Blake said.

She smiled at him. "And I'll get right on the forum."

He nodded and opened the door for them.

"Have you found the fox woman's car?" Trey asked before Blake could shoo them out the door.

He turned back and blew out a long breath. "My deputy just started on it. He has to gather all the plates, look up the registrations, and then compare them to the list. That takes time."

"We're eager to get her identified," Eryn said, likely in an attempt to appease Blake.

"As am I." Blake scrubbed a hand over his face.

His frustration didn't deter Trey. "I assume if you strike out with cars in the lot that you'll have deputies canvass the area and also watch for abandoned vehicles."

"Exactly. But let's not get ahead of ourselves here. The car could very well be in the lot, and we'll have the woman's ID soon."

13

Eryn sat back in the desk chair and pondered her recent discovery. On the popular computer forum, she located the private message where Rodrick shared the rental address with a guy who went by the screen name ShadowPrince. She'd gathered as much information as she could on the guy, short of having Blake get a warrant to request Shadow-Prince's login credentials. Something she would ask him to do if needed.

But first she had to give it some thought. Did the name mean anything? Was he a hacker who worked in the shadows? One who believed he was royalty? Maybe exceptional at what he did?

She quickly opened a search engine and typed in Shad-owPrince. A book series came up in the search results, but so did several forums where ShadowPrince was active. In those forums, he referred to the dark web, an area of the Internet that most people didn't know about and where criminals prospered. The perfect place to buy ransomware. She needed to dig deeper to find his true identity, but if he was familiar with the dark web, he also knew how to hide his identity from others.

Bekah cried out with joy, grabbing Eryn's attention. She was bouncing on Trey's lap and singing "This Little Light of Mine," her favorite Bible song. He watched her intently, a soft smile on his face, and if Eryn was right, a hint of longing for his own child.

One thing she knew for certain after these last few days with him. He really was a good guy. A great guy, even, and would make a wonderful dad. If she ever considered dating again, it would be with a man like him.

He looked up and caught her watching him. His smile widened, and her heart started thumping.

Man, he got to her in a way she hadn't experienced with anyone but Rich. And maybe not even this intensely with him. It had been too long to remember. And maybe that was all this was. She was longing for something she'd once had. But if she kept her mind focused on what had happened with Rich, surely she could resist Trey.

Bekah spun. "I'm hungry, Mommy."

"Then let's get that lunch." Eryn closed her laptop and tucked it under her arm so she could go straight to her class after their meal. "Go get Gammy."

Bekah ran to the bedroom as fast as her chubby legs could carry her, and Eryn had to smile over her daughter's enthusiasm for everything.

"She' s something else." Trey laughed as he got up.

Eryn stepped over to him. "If she ever gets to be too much for you, please tell me. You didn't sign up to be a babysitter. Well, at least not for anyone but me."

"No worries. It's been fun."

She kept her focus on him, searching for any hint that he was just being polite.

"What?"

"Does anything ever bother you?"

His eyes twinkled. "Sure, *you* do."

"What?" Her mouth dropped open.

He chuckled and with the tip of his finger, he lifted her chin. "In a good way, Eryn. A very good way."

"Mommy, how come Trey is holding your head up?" Bekah skipped up to them. "Is it too heavy?"

Trey burst out laughing and lowered his hand. Bekah immediately slipped hers into his and towed him toward the exit.

He paused by the door and released her hand. "Wait here a minute, sweetheart."

He stepped out.

Bekah pouted. "Where'd he go? I want him to come to lunch with us."

"Don't worry. He's waiting outside the door for us."

"But why? I want to hold his hand."

"Remember how I told you I have to work? Well, Trey does, too, and part of his job is to step outside before we leave to make sure the hallway is clear."

Her face screwed up like she planned to ask one of her famous questions, but Eryn's mother joined them, taking Bekah's attention. Eryn wasn't often thankful for a four-year-old's short attention span, but she was at the moment.

Eryn opened the door. Bekah bolted for Trey and took his hand. They made their way down to the restaurant and into a big booth, and once again it felt like they were a little family. She tried to ignore the feelings that warmed her heart, but they lingered through the entire meal.

Bekah pushed her empty ice cream bowl away. "Can we go to the playground again? Or swimming? Or for a walk? Or to the beach? Or—"

"It's time for your nap," Eryn interrupted before her daughter could mention another outing.

Bekah crossed her arms. "Don't want a nap. Not sleepy."

"Then you can take a rest," Eryn's mother said.

"No! Don't want to rest." Bekah's face screwed up, and she burst into tears, drawing the attention of the other diners.

Eryn scooped her sleepy daughter up into her arms, she snuck a quick peek at Trey but he seemed unaffected by the boisterous tantrum.

"Shh, pumpkin." Eryn rocked Bekah and rubbed her back until her tears wound down. "Gammy will take you up to the room, and when I get done teaching my class I'll come up, too. Then maybe we can do something fun."

"Promise we'll have fun?"

"Promise."

"K." She wiped her eyes and slid off Eryn's lap.

Eryn offered her mother an apologetic look for sending her off with a cranky child, but her mom simply smiled, patted Eryn's shoulder, and took Bekah's hand to leave.

Eryn watched them depart and sighed. "Now I'll bet you've had enough."

"Actually, no," Trey said, seeming as pleasant as usual. "She's bound to have cranky times. We all do."

"Who *are* you?" Eryn laughed, and their gazes locked.

His heated up, and she forgot all about the meltdown. About the people around them. The potential danger. She simply reveled in the way he was looking at her as if he never wanted to stop. And at the moment she didn't want him to.

His phone dinged, and he jerked his gaze away to look at the text. "It's from Riley. You're cleared, and we should get going."

She nodded, jumping up and reclaiming her work composure. What was she thinking? She had an important class to teach and needed to be vigilant of her surroundings at all times.

She followed him out of the restaurant and the security guard arrived to lead them into the staff catacombs. After a very roundabout trip, they reached the classroom and the guard departed. She connected her computer to the projector then brought up her PowerPoint presentation and made sure it displayed properly on the large screen.

She turned to Trey. "I'm all set, and I'm going to head to the main door. I usually greet the participants as they arrive."

He ran a hand over his hair. "Not today, okay?"

She loved how even with his apparent angst, he *asked* her, and it made her want to cooperate. Meeting the class members wasn't urgent, and she could let it go. "Okay."

She was rewarded with a wide smile that made her suck in a breath.

"Riley will remain at the front, and I'll take the back door," he said. "I've already notified the staff that they won't be allowed to come in during the class."

"This sounds like overkill to me, but I appreciate you arranging it."

He came closer and held her gaze. "I'll do anything I have to do when it comes to keeping you safe. Don't you know that by now?"

She nodded. "But I wish you weren't so invested. I feel like I'm taking advantage of that when there can never be anything between us."

"There's already something between us."

"Right, but I mean a relationship."

"Don't worry about that," he said, his good mood still in

place. "I've been thinking about it, too, and actually, it's not a good time for me to get involved either."

Just what she wanted to hear, so why did it bother her? Maybe she wanted an explanation. "Why's that?"

His smile faltered. "With the injury, my life is really unsettled. I can't support a family if I don't have a job."

"There's Gage's offer," she reminded him.

"Yeah, and I hope if I really can't return to patrol, I'll be able to accept it. But..." He shrugged.

"But you're still worried these feelings between us complicate it."

"Aren't you?" he asked, his tone quieter now.

"Maybe."

"Besides, I don't even know what Gage pays. And I have to make a good living to afford the five kids I plan to have." He smiled then, that wide luminous grin that sent her head spinning.

She let out a breath of relief at his ability to lighten the mood so she didn't have this on her mind during the class.

Riley opened the door. "We good to let participants in?"

"We're a go," Trey called out. "Be sure to scan everyone carefully."

"Roger that." Riley propped the door open and positioned himself so everyone had to file past him.

Eryn stood to the side and watched participants enter the room. Usually, she tried to predict the officers who would be strong interactors, but today she was watching for shady or evasive behavior. The hard part to accept was that most—if not all—of the officers would be carrying, so she couldn't use that as a reason to keep an eye on anyone in particular. She, on the other hand, never carried during her trainings. She'd learned that for some reason, many men were enamored by women who carried, and it changed the tone of her class. So she'd stopped long ago.

William Newton lumbered down the aisle toward her. She believed his story and wasn't concerned about him approaching. Obviously, Trey didn't feel the same way. He stepped closer, until barely an inch separated them.

"Afternoon, Ms. Calloway." William smiled at Eryn and gave Trey a cautious nod. William put his notepad on the table and dropped into the chair. "I'm looking forward to learning something today."

"You'll have to let me know what you think when the class is over," Eryn said.

"You can count on it." His phone chimed. He looked at the screen and lost interest in her.

"You need to chill a bit," she whispered to Trey. "Or the whole class is going to focus on you instead of the topic."

"Sorry." He pinched the bridge of his nose. "I don't like you in a room full of people who are likely carrying."

"I get that, but the odds of anyone pulling out a weapon in a room filled with officers has to be close to zero."

"Yeah."

"So relax." She took his hands and shook his arms to loosen his tension.

He laughed, giving her the reaction she hoped for, but then his awareness of her filled his eyes as it had at lunch, and she quickly released his hands before she acted like a lovesick teen in front of a room of professionals.

She moved to the podium, and when the clock hit two, she motioned for Riley to close the door.

"Break a leg, Calloway." Trey winked then turned toward the back exit.

She understood the wink but was confused by the use of her last name. Not unusual in her field, but he'd never

155

called her Calloway. Maybe it was a new tact to keep things professional, but then why add a wink? She abruptly remembered she had twenty or so officers looking at her and zeroed in on them.

She waited for Trey to reach the door before starting class. She tried to relax and keep the class' attention as she taught, but the officers kept casting glances at Riley and Trey. They were intuitive enough to know something was up, and like all good officers would react, they were on edge. So when she reached the halfway mark of the class she was more than ready to call a break.

"Be back in fifteen minutes when the door will close," she announced.

She heard a bit of grumbling from the back of the room, but the group filed out.

She joined Trey. "I need to use the restroom."

"I'll text Riley, and we'll go the back way." He took out his phone and thumbed the message.

She was impressed with his thorough care. He would make a welcome addition to Blackwell Tactical if he joined the team. She could easily see him fitting in. In fact, it would be great to have another guy on the team who wasn't so intense. She told him they could work together, but could she really see him every day and resist this attraction? If he continued to serve as a deputy or even join the team, he would be putting himself in danger all the time. She would worry that she might lose him.

"Ready?" he asked.

She nodded, and he led the way out of the maze to the main lobby. The hallway emptied out right by the restroom, and Trey stopped to stare at the door.

She tilted her head to look up at him. "You're not

thinking of coming in with me, are you? Because that's *so* not happening."

"I have to admit I was considering it."

She shook her head and pushed open the door. She waited for it to close to be sure Trey didn't ignore her request and follow.

He didn't, and she headed for a stall. She noticed a small sitting area ahead. Black and white penny tiles covered the floor, and the space held a small couch and large makeup mirror with vanity counter and stool. A big window filled the end wall, floral curtains framing the edges. So cute and quaint. She loved everything about this resort. Except the hacker, of course.

She reached for the stall door and heard movement behind her. Was another woman already in one of the stalls?

Eryn turned.

A tall beefy male wearing a black jacket and a nylon stocking over his head turned the lock on the main door.

She stood stunned for a moment.

He rushed toward her. His face was smashed and grotesque-looking in the stocking, so she couldn't identify him.

She let out a blood curdling scream and backed away, scrambling to find something to use as a weapon.

He charged like an angry bull and grabbed for her.

She instinctively used her training to shove him away.

He recovered quickly and managed to spin her around.

She tried to right herself but lost her balance.

He shot an arm around her chest, gripping her like a vice against his solid body.

"Trey," she screamed before the attacker clamped his other hand over her mouth.

She squirmed. Hard. Pushing. Prodding.

He jerked her harder, forcing her to lean back. He was trying to bring her down to the floor so he could subdue her. She tucked her chin to her chest to resist the pull.

"Eryn!" Trey's raised voice came from the other side of the door that rattled hard.

She tried to respond, but her attacker kept his hand clamped over her mouth. He slowly pushed her toward the window, and that's when she noticed the curtain fluttering in the breeze.

The window was open. Wide open.

"Eryn!" Trey pounded harder on the door.

She brought her arms up and dropped down into a squat.

Her attacker clamped his arm tighter and continued dragging her toward the window that faced over a parking area in the rear of the building.

He was trying to get her out the window. Maybe into a car or van. To drive away. Take her captive.

No. No.

She couldn't let that happen. Couldn't. Or she wouldn't live to see another day.

14

———

"Eryn," Trey shouted, his heart galloping. "I'm coming in."

He rammed his shoulder into the door. It didn't budge. He tried again.

"Need help?" William Newton's voice came from behind.

"Eryn. Being attacked." Trey didn't wait for help but slammed his shoulder into the door another time.

He felt it give some. He reared back for another attempt. Eryn's scream came from the other side, stopping his heart.

"Let me." William pushed past him and gave the door a linebacker slam.

The wood splintered.

Trey took another run and hit the wood hard. The lock gave way. The door sprung open. Hit the wall and bounced back.

Trey blocked it and raced into the room.

Eryn was staggering his way. Her face red. Her eyes glazed with fear.

"He's gone," she rasped. "Out the window. Go after him."

Trey shook his head. "I'm not leaving you alone."

"I'll go after him," William offered.

"He's six feet. Muscular. Maybe two twenty or so. Wore jeans and black jacket." She drew in a long breath. "He had a nylon stocking over his head so that's the best I can do."

"Got it." William bolted for the window.

Surprisingly, he was agile and managed to fit through the opening.

Trey ran his gaze over Eryn. She was shaking, and large red blotches covered her mouth. Rage boiled in his gut, but he tamped down the anger and focused. "What happened?"

"Guy was waiting in a stall. Came out and got his arm around my chest. Hand over my mouth. He tried to drag me to the window. Abduct me."

Explained the redness. "How did you get free?"

"I panicked at first. Foolish. But then I remembered my self-defense moves. Dropped. Jabbed him. Twisted and got free. You broke through, and he bailed before I could take him down."

Trey shook his head. "You're something else. You're what? Five seven or so and you intended to take down a two hundred plus pound man a good five inches taller than you."

"Guess so. Training helps. If you can remember it." She shook her body as if shaking off the incident.

Trey clenched his jaw. "Unless the hacker hired someone to try to abduct you, this guy's build fits Coker and Petrov, but rules out the other suspects."

She blinked. "Petrov and Coker would've had to hide their hair color, but they're both crafty enough to do that." She frowned. "But we won't get anywhere by speculating. We'll need to investigate. Now get out of here so I can use the restroom and get back to class."

"You want to finish the class?" He gaped at her.

"These officers or their department paid good money to

attend this training. I'm not going to let them down." She made shooing motions toward the door. "Try to keep the door closed please."

He shook his head and stepped outside, pulling the fractured door behind him. He didn't know what he thought would happen when he tore into the room and found her attacker gone. But if he really considered it, he realized he expected Eryn to throw herself into his arms where he would protect her. But she was still a fierce lioness—even after being attacked—shooing him away.

He didn't like that. Didn't like it at all.

He shoved the thoughts away and became aware of officers staring at him. "There's nothing to see here. Go back to your classes."

He used his patrol voice, but they didn't seem impressed enough to take action. He couldn't force them to move, but he wished he could so when Eryn stepped out she wouldn't have to face a curious crowd.

The resort security guard who let them into the back hallway pushed his way through the crowd. "What happened?"

Trey filled him in. "I'll call Sheriff Jenkins so Ms. Calloway can file a report, but I need you to stand guard at this door and not let anyone in. Understood?"

"Yes, of course." He wrung his hands together.

"Hold the door so I can make that call." Trey released the door to the guard and dialed Blake.

"Sheriff Jenkins," he answered on the second ring.

"It's Trey Sawyer. Eryn's been attacked at the resort. The guy tried to abduct her."

"Seriously?" Blake's tone went unusually high.

Trey stepped away from the security guard and lowered his voice. "We have to assume at this point the hacker was behind the attack. One of your detectives is in pursuit on foot."

"Only detective I have at the conference is William Newton, and he hasn't been engaged in a foot pursuit in years."

Trey had already guessed that based on the man's size.

"I have a patrol deputy attending the conference, too," Blake continued. "Give me your location, and I'll have him secure the scene, then I'll head over to take Eryn's statement."

Trey gave him directions to find the bathroom. "Eryn will be teaching for the next two hours in room 10a."

"Say what? She's seriously going to teach after that?" Blake let out a low whistle. "I always knew she was one tough cookie, but this is going above and beyond."

"I couldn't agree more. I'd like to get a bulletin out on the suspect if he's not apprehended by your detective."

"You might as well give me the details now," Blake said, indicating he didn't have a lot of confidence in William's ability to chase down the suspect.

Trey relayed the description Eryn had provided. "Coker and Detective Petrov have similar builds."

"I'll be the one to interview them and find out where there were at the time of the attack. Make sure Eryn knows that."

"I will." Trey hung up and went back to the door. Eryn tugged it open and stepped out.

She glanced around and stopped dead in her tracks. "I see I've got an audience."

Trey rushed to her side. "I tried to disburse them, but they're having nothing of it."

"Let's get going." She started off.

"Ms. Calloway," a heavy panting voice called out.

Trey's pulse skyrocketed. He spun and grabbed Eryn's hand to move her behind him.

William, sweaty and panting for air, came barreling through the crowd. Trey let out his breath and released Eryn. She stepped around him, and he noticed that she was breathing hard. It had freaked her out, too.

"Got away," William managed to get out. "Not as fast as I used to be."

"That's okay," Eryn said. "I am so grateful for your help."

Trey wished *he'd* taken off after the suspect and then maybe the jerk would be in custody, but if anything happened to Eryn, he would've never forgiven himself. "I called Sheriff Jenkins and put out an alert on the suspect."

Eryn cast Trey a questioning look.

"I talked to him while you were using the facilities. He's sending a patrol deputy to secure the scene, and then he'll take your statement when he gets here."

"The sheriff is coming." William's brow knotted. "I'm perfectly capable of taking the statement."

"It has nothing to do with your abilities," Eryn explained. "Blake's a friend, and we always call him directly."

William didn't respond, his eyes now tight with worry. He clearly didn't believe Eryn, but she spoke the truth.

She smiled at him. "You ready to sit down for the rest of that training?"

His eyes widened. "You're going ahead with it?"

"Sure."

"I better wait here for the sheriff." He sounded uneasy.

Eryn pressed her hand on his arm. "I can't thank you enough for going after the suspect. I'll make sure Blake knows how thankful I am for your help."

William gave a clipped nod, but his gaze remained wary.

Trey didn't want to keep Eryn out in the lobby any longer than necessary and easing William's worry wasn't necessary. Trey gestured for Eryn to depart first, and they made their way back to the classroom. Participants were up and milling about, murmuring, but when she entered the room they took their seats expectantly.

She stepped up to the podium. "Sorry I'm late. I ran into an unexpected guest."

She chuckled, and after a beat, some of the officers laughed with her.

Trey's respect for this strong, capable woman grew tenfold. Not that he didn't respect her before, but he now put her in the top one percent of people he'd ever encountered, and with his background in spec ops, that was saying a lot.

Eryn stepped from the shower and patted the towel gently over her upper body that was already covered in deep aching bruises. Simply breathing hurt, and she wanted to stay in her room and crawl under her covers. Typically she could tough out pretty much anything, but not this time. The attack terrified her.

Sure, she'd played it down for Trey. For Blake. The team. Everyone. Because maybe if she admitted her fear, she would fall apart as she had in the shower, letting her tears fall under the rush of water so hot she thought her skin might melt from her body. But she'd needed the searing heat. Needed to erase her attacker's touch.

She ignored the pain and got dressed. She'd promised to have dinner with Bekah and promised they would have fun. She couldn't let her daughter down.

She towel-dried her hair and put a little cover up around her mouth where smaller bruises were starting to appear. Satisfied that her eyes were no longer red and her bruises were disguised, she stepped into the living area.

Blake stood in the kitchenette talking to Trey and her mother, leaving Bekah in her mother's room. Both men turned to look at her. Trey's expression was unreadable, but he shoved his hands in his pockets. He seemed even more shaken than she was. And if she knew him like she thought she did, he was blaming himself for not clearing the bathroom before she used it. Her fault though. She rushed inside before he could do anything.

"How are you doing?" Blake asked.

"I'm fine." She waved off his concern, but the pain in her chest was so excruciating that she stopped. "Any news on my attacker?"

Blake shook his head. "I have an alert out for him, but even after canvassing all the officers, no one but you saw him."

"I kind of figured that. He must've come in through the window."

Blake nodded. "Coker claims he was with his group and they agreed, but then they'd lie for him so that means nothing."

"And Petrov?" Trey asked.

"Was in his room alone. So no alibi."

"I did hear back from the cable company though. The modem used for the chat was a different one than Rodrick had registered on his account."

"Then he was telling the truth," Trey said.

"Doesn't really mean anything," Eryn said. "He could've changed out the modem hoping we would think it exonerated him."

"Maybe," Blake said. "But he seemed pretty straightforward, and I'm not really liking him for this."

"Me neither," she admitted.

"So where does that leave us?" Trey asked.

"Coker's still a viable lead."

Blake nodded. "The ME has recovered an intact slug from the woman, and I plan to head over there now to see if it's in good enough shape to get a match and then talk to Coker. I'll ask for his alibi for woman's time of death. And if we figure out the murdered woman's ID, that could give us a lead, too. My deputy is almost finished with running plates, so we may get lucky there."

"If you don't, I'm still planning to head to Eastern Oregon to have a look around."

"I don't like that idea," Trey said. "Not one bit."

Blake narrowed his eyes. "I have to say, I agree with him."

Eryn understood their unease, but before they could progress in the investigation, they needed to know if this woman's murder related to her. It was looking like a quick flight in the helo was the best way to solve that mystery.

15

The suite was quiet and dark. A fun dinner was long over, and Trey was sitting without the lights on, brooding about the day while Eryn worked on her computer. Her head was bent forward, her glossy black hair shining in the light from her screen. Her fingers flew over the keyboard, and she was in her own world. A world he wanted to be part of.

Not that he deserved to be after he let a maniac nearly abduct her. A vision of a man with his paws on her wouldn't Trey him go, and his dinner churned in his gut. He had to do better tomorrow. Correction, tomorrow morning. Only the morning. The conference ended at noon, and then everyone would be heading home. The team in their SUVs and him in his car alone.

Eryn would be walking out of his life. Not for good. He could see to that by signing up for more classes at the compound, but he didn't like thinking that she might walk out tomorrow with her attacker still on the loose. Maybe the jerk would give up once the conference was over, but Trey didn't think he would. He'd gone to great extremes to stop her classes from being taught, or he wouldn't have risked trying to abduct her in a building filled with cops.

But if he was that adamant about stopping her, he could pop up again when she least expected him. Sure, with the compound's state-of-the-art security she would likely be safe, but what about when she stepped out of the gate? Maybe went into town for groceries? Or out for ice cream with Bekah? Or even on an op?

Trey wouldn't be there to protect her. Protect Bekah. They would be alone. Vulnerable.

The thought brought him to his feet, and he went to the window to look over the ocean rolling in under a full moon. They *had* to find this guy by noon tomorrow. Just had to.

Eryn's phone rang, splitting the quiet.

"Blake," she answered and listened intently.

He must have information on the woman or Eryn's attacker or he wouldn't call this late.

She slumped back in her chair. "Well, that's unfortunate."

Obviously not good news.

"No, nothing here either. But I'll keep up the search." She listened for some time. "I'm surprised Coker denied being involved in the murder. I figured even if he didn't do it, he'd want to somehow connect himself to get the publicity."

She ran a hand through her hair. "Okay. I'll check in with you in the morning."

She set her phone on the desk and rose to stretch her arms overhead. Trey was mesmerized by how the light silhouetted her frame, and he couldn't look away.

"That was Blake," she said, lowering her arms and coming toward him.

He swallowed hard to bring his mind back to work. "Oh."

"Coker claims he doesn't know the woman, and he refused to turn over his weapon without a court order, but Blake said he'd have no problem getting that warrant. He also said he reiterated that he was outside with his team when I was attacked. Blake will check with them, but you know they'll likely lie for him."

Trey wanted to go pound the truth out of Coker, but as a deputy he couldn't do that. "What about an ID on the woman?"

"The ME said she didn't have any ID nor did her finger-prints return a match. They also struck out on locating her car in the lot. Blake will have a deputy run plates on the nearby streets tomorrow."

"So we have a Jane Doe," Trey said, his mind still on Eryn, not the topic. How could he go from thinking they needed to do everything they could do to find her attacker, to not being able to focus? Maybe it was the dark sultry atmosphere of the room. Or maybe he was so tired of ignoring his interest in her that he couldn't keep up the pretense any longer.

She stopped next to him to look out the window. She smelled like a warm apple pie, and the scent wrapped around him. He wanted to reach out to touch her hair to see if it felt as sleek as it looked.

"I'll make some calls in the morning," she said. "To the people who are monitoring the foxes and to the reporter for the story I found. But unless they give me any leads, it looks like I'll be asking Riley to take me to eastern Oregon."

Trey didn't even hesitate. "I'm going with you."

"That's not necessary. Riley will be with me."

"I don't care. I'm going."

She turned to look up at him, likely wondering where

the agreeable guy he usually was had gone. He had his limits, and he'd reached them.

"Trey," she said, as if she planned to argue.

He didn't want to hear her pushing him away again. He let the curtains fall and rested his hands lightly on her shoulders. "Don't say it. Let me think for once that you don't mind my company."

"It's not that at all. I like being with you. You're a great guy."

"No buts. Not tonight. Not after today. I could have lost you." He gently drew her closer and wrapped his arms around her. He held his breath and waited for her to argue. To push away. But she didn't.

She snuggled closer and rested her head against his chest. He lifted a hand and ran it over her hair, not surprised to discover it indeed felt like silk under his hand. He relished the feel of her. The way she fit against him. Her warmth. Even her breathing that was speeding up.

She suddenly leaned back and looked up at him. Her eyes were glistening with tears.

"What is it?" he asked, hating to think she was crying because of him.

"Today. All of this. I don't know. I just feel like crying."

"Then let it go. Cry."

She bit her lip. "You wouldn't. Most guys wouldn't. Especially my teammates."

"But you're not me or them. You're a woman, and I don't care if that sounds sexist. It's not. God made us to be different." He cupped the side of her face and smiled. "And I'm so glad he did because as much as I admire your strength and toughness, I like you being vulnerable, too. A girl who might need someone. Maybe me."

"I do need people. My mom. Bekah."

"But not a guy."

She sighed. "I don't know anymore. These past few days with you have made me think about it."

"But you're still holding back."

She nodded.

"Maybe this will help change your mind." He slid his fingers into her hair and leaned down to kiss her. Her eyes widened when she realized what he planned to do. She didn't step away but raised up on her tiptoes.

His heart constricted, and he settled his lips on hers. Shock of awareness traveled through him. Kissing her was like an explosion of dynamite, warming him clean through. He forgot all about tomorrow. About the danger. About everything except their connection...and let his lips speak for him.

Eryn knew she should push back. Stop this kiss, but she was powerless to do so. She'd come alive again. Discovered emotions that she believed had died with Rich. She wanted the kiss to go on and on. Forever. To be connected to a man again. This man. This wonderful, wonderful, man.

The thought shocked her into pulling back. Trey opened his eyes and watched her under his hooded lids. His gaze started to turn wary. She reached up and pressed out a wrinkle by his mouth. "That was—"

"Amazing," he finished for her.

"Yes. And overwhelming, too."

He frowned. "I should have taken that into consideration. After the day you've had, I shouldn't have kissed you and added more stress."

She put her hand on his chest. "I'm not more stressed. Trust me. It's the best thing that's happened all day."

"I'm glad." His lips relaxed in a wide smile.

She wanted to reach up. To kiss that smile. Kiss him. But she wouldn't. Not now that she'd come to her senses. "That's as far as it goes, okay? I've got some serious thinking to do."

"About?" he asked and seemed to hold his breath.

"About what I want. Nothing has changed. Other than I liked kissing you and wouldn't mind doing it again sometime."

"But not now."

"No, not now."

"And what about tomorrow? Can I come with you?"

"If it's that important to you, then yes."

He nodded. "You're important to me."

She didn't like hearing him say that aloud, as it sounded so official. So much like a commitment of some sort that she wasn't ready for. She frowned.

"What did I say?"

She stepped out of his arms and instantly felt alone, the way she'd been for years, but now it felt lonely, and she almost moved back into his arms. But she couldn't. It was bad enough that she'd kissed him. She couldn't encourage him more.

She wrapped her arms around herself, wishing it was his arms instead. "I don't want to lead you on, Trey. I don't know what I want or what I'm capable of feeling for a man."

"And if you were capable and wanted a future with a guy? Would I be in the running?"

"Oh, yeah," she answered without hesitation. "First place."

"Then that's all I need to know for now. I won't think you're leading me on, and if I fall helplessly in love with you, it will be my own fault." He grinned again as if trying to tell her he wasn't serious, but his eyes told her a different story.

She agreed to let him accompany her tomorrow, but she was starting to regret making a decision when she was letting her emotions rule her, and she wasn't sure it was a good idea. Not a good idea at all.

16

Even eight hours later, Eryn couldn't quit thinking about the kiss. She should never have let Trey kiss her, much less encourage it to continue. She'd had a momentary lapse in judgement, but nothing had changed, and that meant her guard was up again this morning. She couldn't let it happen again. So why couldn't she quit staring at him across the breakfast table in their suite?

They'd just finished eating, and Bekah climbed up on his lap, looking like it was the most natural thing in the world. Perhaps Eryn was being shortsighted on thinking about a relationship when it prevented Bekah from having a father. But if Eryn constantly lived in fear of losing a future spouse, wouldn't it be better for Bekah not to have a father than to have one under those conditions?

Bekah swiveled on his lap and rested her hands on his shoulders. "I like you."

Trey grinned his soft, sweet, adorable heart-melting grin. "I like you, too."

"We're going home today. We get to drive by the ocean. It's pretty. And scary. I can't wait to get home. Mia and David got a puppy. A black one. It's cute. Sometimes it falls down when it runs. It's so funny. I want a puppy, too, but Mommy said I'm not 'sponsible enough. I'm only four. Maybe I'll be 'sponsible when I'm five." She drew in a deep breath and looked like she might start up again.

Eryn wanted to spare Trey from her daughter's early morning chatter. "I'm sure Trey isn't interested in the puppy."

"I love dogs."

"Me, too," Bekah said. "They named him Barkley. That's the dog's name on Sesame Street. He's only four months old. Do you want to come home with me and meet Barkley?"

"Maybe."

"Why maybe?"

"It depends on some things this morning."

Eryn assumed he meant that if they found the hacker then Trey wouldn't have a reason to come home with them. She had to admit saying goodbye to him in a few hours wasn't something she wanted to do.

Bekah moved her hands to his face. "I want you to come with us."

"And I want to as well."

She twisted her head to look at Eryn. "How soon can we go, Mommy?"

"I have a bit of work and a class to teach. Then we can go."

Her eyes narrowed as if confused.

"We'll leave after lunch." Eryn smiled at her daughter. "Now go with Gammy to get cleaned up so you can help pack your suitcase and be ready to leave when I am."

She pushed off Trey's lap and ran around the table to grab her Gammy's hand. "Hurry, Gammy. We have to pack."

Eryn's mother laughed, and as she passed behind Eryn, she bent down to kiss her head. "Be careful today."

"I will."

She looked at Trey. "I hope you *do* come with us. I like what's going on between the two of you."

"Mom!" Eryn turned to stare after her mother who was chuckling all the way to her door.

Trey grinned. "You have the best mom."

"I do," Eryn said, though right now she wanted to strangle her. "I located a contact with the Oregon Conservation Strategy and the reporter's information, too. You want to call one of them while I talk to the other?"

"Sure. I'll take the reporter."

She got up to retrieve the contact's information from the desk and handed the notepad to Trey. The moment he grabbed the paper she released it and swiveled because she could swear that a jolt of awareness traveled through that paper to her hand, and she wasn't about to let it take over and color her judgment again. This was the light of day not the dark of the night. She could ignore him. Easily.

Right. Like you did at breakfast.

She dialed Neil Moon, a biologist at the Oregon Department of Fish and Wildlife. When he answered, she introduced herself. "I'm interested in information on the kit fox."

"Then you've found the right person. I'm in charge of their monitoring."

"Where exactly have they been seen?" she asked as she heard Trey start his conversation with the reporter.

"We have cameras in the area between Sheepshead Mountains and Trout Creek Mountains. And if you're not familiar with that area, it's near the Idaho and Nevada borders."

She was very familiar with that area in Harney County.

It was just north of there that the FBI recently engaged in a nearly month-long standoff when militants illegally occupied the Malheur National Wildlife Refuge.

She'd followed the standoff with interest and learned a great deal about that section of her state that she hadn't known before. "I read that the camera recorded a kit fox being caught in a live trap."

"A sad thing. A sad thing indeed." He sighed. "Why would anyone take an animal out of its natural habitat like that?"

"I was wondering the same thing. Do you have any theories?"

"There's always a market for unique and interesting animals for private collectors."

"And the kit fox is unique?" she asked.

"Unique, yeah, maybe. In our state at least. It's more widely seen elsewhere. So, sure, I could see it being a valuable animal here and one that a collector might want."

She hated to ask the next question, but she had to understand. "When you say 'collector' are you talking about someone who collects live animals or taxidermy ones?"

"Live is more prevalent, but we can't rule out the later." He blew out a long breath. "Which is why we're so eager to find this little fella."

"What can you tell me about the pictures of the captured fox that were posted in the online forum?"

"All I know is the person who claimed to steal the fox published pictures and was bragging about his escapades. You could get more information by talking to someone in the enforcement division at the Burn's office."

She would make that call next. "Do you know of any animal rights groups championing the fox's return?"

"Not that I know of, but I don't pay attention to that stuff.

I'm a scientist, and I avoid everything political." He chuckled.

"Do you know of any animal rights groups in that general area?"

"Like I said, I don't pay attention, and I don't live in this area so I don't read the local news."

"Okay, thank you for the information. If I were to come over there, could you show me the area where the fox was taken?"

There was dead silence for a long moment. "I'm sorry, but no. We've only recently discovered the animals, and we don't want to disturb their habitat. But I'd be glad to answer any additional questions you might have."

"Thank you. I'll be in touch if I need more." Disappointed, she hung up. Instead of sulking over her strikeout, she located the correct contact at the Oregon State Police Division of Wildlife.

Trey was still on his call so she dialed the OSP number and asked to be put through to the sergeant in charge.

Surprisingly, her call was directed to his office without having to explain what she needed.

"Sergeant Corrigan," he answered.

"I'm Eryn Calloway. I work for Blackwell Tactical out of Cold Harbor." She paused and gave him a chance to respond to that so she knew how to proceed.

"I've seen your team's training flyers," he said. "How can I help you, Ms. Calloway?"

"We're looking into the murder of an unknown female in our county and think she might have something to do with the kit fox trapping. Is this something you're involved in?"

"We are."

"This woman was found at The Dunes Resort yesterday. She was dressed in an elaborate—and what looks like very expensive—kit fox costume. Cause of death was a gunshot to the forehead at a close range."

"Any idea why she was at the resort dressed like that?"

"No but let me share about another situation I'm involved in, and we're wondering if it's related." She explained about the hacker, the attack, and added the protest. "We suspect the deceased might be an animal rights advocate who came here to ask me to help with the pictures. Of course, this is a working theory, and we hoped you might have information about groups in your area so we can iden-tify this woman."

He didn't answer right away, and she was tempted to prompt him, but waited him out.

"I've never heard of an animal rights group around here," he finally said. "But that doesn't mean there isn't one. I can ask my troopers for more information."

"That would be great." She took a moment to gather her thoughts and come up with her next question so she didn't have to call him back. "Can you also explain exactly how OSP works with the Department of Fish and Wildlife so I can understand the investigation better?"

"Sure. We partner with ODFW to facilitate enforcement of resource management goals," he said as if spouting off an official position statement. "Basically, each year local biolo-gists set enforcement priorities by species, and we meet with them to discuss concerns regarding social issues, seasons, areas, and local issues so our troopers can enforce them. The foxes are part of those species concerns so when one was trapped, my investigator got involved."

"And have you had any success?"

"I'm not really free to discuss the investigation."

"I understand that, Sergeant, but I might be able to help you with those pictures."

"I'd appreciate your help, I really would. But right now, I think it best that I contact whoever's officially in charge of this murder investigation, and we go from there."

She didn't like his answer, but she understood it. And if he wouldn't talk to her, then putting him in touch with Blake was the next best option. "Sheriff Blake Jensen is in charge. I can have him call you."

"That would be perfect."

"Can I give you my phone number in case your deputies know of an animal rights group?"

"Go ahead," he said, but she could tell he really didn't plan to work outside official channels. Not unusual, but she didn't like it.

She gave him her number and hung up. Trey was still on the phone with the reporter so she called Blake.

"Anything new in the investigation since we talked?" she asked.

"Unfortunately, no."

She told him about her phone calls. "Would you give this sergeant a call?"

"I can do that."

She gave him the phone number. "Trey is talking to the reporter whose story I read. If he doesn't come up with a lead, I'm going to head over to Harney County to start asking around about this woman."

"I'd tell you that's a bit premature, but I know anything I say isn't going to stop you. Not once you have your mind set on it." He was so right.

"When we get home, I'll ask Hannah make a sketch of the woman for me to show around town. I'll let you know if I discover anything."

"Be careful, Eryn." He paused, maybe to let his warning sink in. "Many people who live in that remote part of the state don't appreciate people asking questions. They're out in the boonies for a reason."

His point was valid, but she wouldn't back down. "Trey and Riley will be with me."

"Then you're bound to draw a good bit of attention. Even more reason to be careful."

"I'll take that into account." She disconnected, found Trey had finished his call and was watching her. "That was mostly a waste of time. You learn anything?"

"The reporter couldn't give me any specific information on the animal rights group he mentioned in the story." Trey stood and shoved his phone into his pocket. "In fact, the longer I talked to him, the more his article seemed sketchy. I don't think he did much research. Maybe didn't even talk to an activist."

"That's odd, right?"

He came over to the desk and rested on the corner. "I don't know much about reporting, but the guy freelances—sells his stories to smaller papers. Maybe they don't fact check."

"Could be," she replied as she pondered the implications and did her very best not to notice that he was close enough for her to catch a hint of minty soap from his morning shower.

He crossed his legs at the ankle and leaned back, stretching out his long frame even more. "I'm starting to wonder if he was sensationalizing the rights group part of the story when there aren't any groups interested in this at all."

"Then how do you explain this woman's costume?"

"I can't."

"It's official, then. The only way we're going to figure this out is to take a trip."

He cocked his head in question. "Where exactly are we going?"

"Burns is our first stop."

"Why Burns?"

"The OSP office in charge of investigating the trapping is located there. Here, I'll show you." She opened a map of Oregon on her computer, located the mountains that Neil mentioned, and tapped the screen. "This is where the fox was taken."

He leaned closer to peer at the computer. "I've never been there but heard it's a pretty desolate part of the state."

"Definitely desert type landscape." She looked up at him and scooted back when she realized how close he was. "I only hope that Riley or Coop can find a spot to land, or we'll have a long drive ahead of us."

Her phone rang, and she saw Denise Frazier's name pop up on the screen.

"The resort's IT person," she told Trey in case he'd forgotten her name. Eryn tapped the phone to answer on speaker.

"We have a problem," Denise's voice shot into the room. "A big problem."

"What's going on?"

"We've had an intrusion, and before I even looked at the logs, it was clear we've been hacked again."

"I don't understand," Eryn said. "How can you know you've been hacked if you haven't looked at the logs?"

"Get to the lobby and look at a monitor. I promise, it'll be clear enough for you."

Trey found the lobby filled with officers. Not unusual.

Classes weren't in session. But they weren't engaged in conversation as usual. They were clustered around the various monitors. Trey pushed through so he and Eryn could see one of the screens. Filled with a firehouse red background, the message read, "When you can't get into your room, blame Eryn Calloway."

Trey fisted his hands. He was a fool to think they might make it through the morning without another threat. But he shouldn't be surprised. After all, Eryn was attacked and a woman was murdered. If their hacker was responsible for these actions, then the hacker meant business and wasn't going to give up.

Denise found her way through the crowd, her expression downcast. Trey was sorry she'd gotten caught up in this mess, and he wished he could fix things for her. At least, he knew Eryn would be kind again, and that would make it easier for the other woman.

Eryn turned to look at Denise. "Your look says this is worse than these monitors indicate."

Denise stepped closer and lowered her voice. "It's not only the keycards, which is a total nightmare in itself, but he has control of all of the resort computers including reservations and room management." She sighed, and it sounded to Trey like she felt like the world rested on her shoulders. "And all of these officers are going to be checking out soon."

"We'll figure this out." Eryn smiled, but Trey could see it was forced. "When was your last total system backup?"

"We do a daily back-up at four a.m., but honestly that could be compromised, too, right?"

Eryn nodded. "But hopefully he didn't touch it."

"So how do we fix this?"

"There's no ransom request so the resort can't pay to have the system released," Eryn said, sounding like she was thinking through the solution as she spoke. "If the backup is good, we can restore the system from that."

"But what about reservations, check outs, and registrations since that?"

"We won't be able to capture those. But it's early in the day so I doubt you'll be out a lot of information. You need to speak to your manager to get permission to restore from backup. Then I'll take the necessary forensic snapshots that the sheriff will need to prosecute once this guy is found, and we'll restore the system."

"I'll go talk to them." Denise looked skeptical.

Trey thought she had a right to be. Eryn was good at her job, but could she really do what she said here, or was she just trying to reduce Denise's stress?

Eryn laid a hand on Denise's arm. "Remember to breathe. We'll get through this together."

Denise's gaze remained skeptical. "Where will I find you after I talk to my manager?"

"Text me, and I'll come to your office."

Denise nodded and scuttled away.

Trey moved closer to Eryn. "Is it really not as big of a deal as you're making out?"

"No, it's a big deal. Huge." She frowned. "The resort has an online reservation system so hopefully we're only locked out of it, but the data will be intact. I won't know until I dig into the system."

"Sounds like that could take some time. Can you do this and teach the class at ten?" he asked, honestly hoping the answer was no.

Her frown deepened. "Not likely. "

"Which is probably what the hacker was hoping for."

She crossed her arms and widened her stance. "Well he's

not going to win. I'll talk to Martha and see if we can postpone the class a few hours."

Not the answer Trey had hoped for. She spun and stormed down the hall toward Martha's room. He hurried to keep up with her and wished he could convince her to let the last class slide. Not that even with his plea, she would. She'd find a way to notify each participant of the change, and he wouldn't be surprised if she even offered to buy them all lunch. She really was quite a woman.

It took Martha little time to get the classes rescheduled, and then he escorted Eryn to Denise's office where she sat down behind a computer proclaiming the same message. The screen suddenly cleared.

"Say what?" Denise gaped at the screen. "Just like that, we have the system back?"

Eryn rubbed her forehead and stared ahead. "I don't know what this guy's up to. If all he wanted to do was display a message on the hotel's monitors, he could have easily done so without locking up your entire network only to release it. Makes no sense."

"Maybe he's trying to prove his skills to get your attention," Trey suggested.

"He got my attention all right," Eryn muttered.

"So what do we do?" Denise circled her arms around her waist, and her face took on a blank stare.

"He may have infected the network with additional malware so I'll take it offline. And then, I'll dig for his code for later review."

Denise's gaze flitted around the room as if she was searching for a solution. "This is awful. Just awful."

"Hey, look on the bright side." Eryn smiled. "With the system unlocked, we can locate any new reservations since the last backup and print those out for later entry. I'll then restore from backup, clearing out his code, and you'll be back in business soon."

Denise released her arms. "You sure that will work?"

"I can only hope so." Eryn swiveled back to the computer. "I'll know more once I take the network down."

17

Eryn had so looked forward to her time at the resort, but she was now glad that the place was in the SUV's rearview mirror, and she could get home and let her guard down a bit. Trey left his car at the hotel and would pick it up after they returned from their trip to Eastern Oregon, so Gage drove, Trey rode shotgun, and she sat in the back with her mother and Bekah. Riley and Alex followed in the other SUV with everyone's luggage and equipment.

Eryn glanced at her daughter, sleeping peacefully. Her head was tilted to the side, her thumb in her mouth, and her blanket scrunched up next to her face. She'd dropped off to sleep almost the moment they'd left the resort. Not surprising. They didn't depart until two, which was Bekah's naptime. But at least Eryn got the resort's systems restored and was able to teach her class, too.

Now they were finally heading south on Highway 101, which had some of the most amazing views out over the ocean. Beauty this majestic couldn't be randomly created, and Eryn often felt closer to God on this road. It also helped keep her mind off Trey. She still wasn't sure why she agreed to let him come along, but she obviously let her emotions from last night sway her common sense.

She had to forget all about that. With everything she had on her plate, that shouldn't be hard. First, she would meet with Hannah who was a sketch artist to complete a drawing of the victim. Then Eryn would spend the night at her computer reviewing the logs and code from the resort hack in hopes of finding a signature to lead her to the actor. For some reason, it appeared that he wanted her to see his code. Maybe he left her a message in it. Maybe he wanted her to know who he was. But why? That was what she couldn't figure out.

Her phone rang, and seeing Blake's name, she quickly answered.

"I talked to Sergeant Corrigan," he said. "His deputies didn't have any insight on local animal rights groups. He said the only group that was mentioned at all is located in Bend."

She brought up a mental map and plotted the city in relationship to Burns. "That's two hours away, right?"

"About that," Blake replied. "Why are you looking in Burns? I don't get it."

She wasn't sure of anything, but she wouldn't admit that aloud. "It's the closest town of any size to the kit fox abduction area."

"About the fox. Corrigan said they don't have much to go on in their investigation. The video taken at the crime scene didn't capture any faces. And the forum was a dead-end for them."

Might be a dead-end for them, but that didn't mean it would be for her. "Did you get the forum name?"

"Yeah. ACT—Animals Count Too. You gonna dig into it?"

"Yes. It would help when we head to Burns if I had more to go on." She asked Blake to keep her updated and disconnected.

Trey swiveled to look at her, and before he could ask about the call, she shared Blake's information.

"So you'll be looking into ACT then," he said.

She held up her phone. "I'll start right now."

He tilted his head and looked at her like Barkley often did when confused. "Could you ever go anywhere without an electronic device?"

"I could, I suppose, but why would I?" She chuckled.

"Honestly," her mother said. "I don't think you could."

"I agree," Gage said. "Never seen you without your phone."

"I don't sleep with it."

"But you do keep it on your nightstand."

"That's for safety reasons."

"Um-hm," her mother said.

"Well, computers *are* my job." Eryn fired her a mother a testy look.

"But you don't have to work 24/7," her mother said, ignoring the look.

Eryn wasn't going to get started on that subject with the guys around so she turned away and opened the Internet to enter Animals Count Too into the search engine. She found the forum and kit fox listing right away. She opened the pictures to look for any leads but saw only desert-like surroundings and a cage holding a small terrified fox. She also saw the transmitter laying on the ground.

She imagined it wouldn't be easy to remove the device from a scared fox, but it didn't look like the animal had been tranquilized. So the person who cut it off was either not very bright or had experience in working with wild animals. A vet maybe.

She moved on to the comments but felt the SUV slow and turn so she'd have to wait to read all one hundred of them. Tonight she would have to try to track down each person who'd weighed in. She was in for a long night.

She stowed her phone as Gage pulled up to the compound's heavy iron gate and lowered his window to press his finger on the print reader. The gate swung open, and he drove into the compound. Because they kept a large weapon arsenal and owned very expensive equipment, the property was surrounded with a tall fence and state-of-the-art security. She was safer here than anywhere else, and as the gate clanked closed behind them, she could feel the stress pouring from her body.

Gage glanced at Trey. "You can bunk in a cabin, or you're welcome to stay with my family if you want."

"Actually, I'm staying with Eryn."

"What?" Eryn and her mother asked at the same time.

He looked back at them, his gaze going between them both before settling on Eryn. "In case you forgot, I'm in charge of your safety. I'll be taking the couch so no worries about propriety."

"But the compound is secure," Eryn replied. "You don't need to stay with us."

"Is it? Didn't someone breach the perimeter a while back?"

"Yes, but..."

"But he was bent on hurting Hannah," Trey interrupted. "And a guy who wanted to hurt you could do the same thing. Especially someone who has the skills to take the security cameras and system offline."

"Good point." Gage pulled up outside his single-story

house. "I'm sure Eryn will be glad to let you bunk on her couch."

Glad? "Sure. Whatever. That will be fine."

The front door of Gage's house burst open, and his children, Mia and David, came racing out. A jumping black puppy followed, nipping at their heels.

"Looks like my welcoming committee has spotted me." Grinning from ear to ear, Gage hopped out, and the kids rushed him. Barkley danced on his hind legs, and then bumped into Gage and tumbled to the ground.

Hannah stepped out, too, wiping her hands on a kitchen towel. She was about Eryn's height with bright red hair and freckles that matched her son David's. This past month Gage had officially adopted David, Hannah adopted Mia, and both kids were over-the-moon happy.

Hannah reached over the children and kissed Gage. Not a quick peck, but a lingering kiss that reminded Eryn of last night, and she felt herself color. Hoping no one noticed, she turned to Bekah and gently woke her. She stretched her arms overhead and rubbed her eyes.

"We're home, pumpkin."

She frowned and buried her head in her blanket, telling Eryn her daughter could use more sleep, and they might be in for another cranky fit.

"Mia and David are outside," Eryn said hoping to help her daughter come fully awake.

Bekah didn't respond.

"Barkley's with them."

Her eyes popped open, and she squirmed to free herself from the straps. "I want down."

Trey got out and opened the back door. Bekah hopped down from her seat and scrambled past Trey without even a glance.

"Replaced by a puppy." He laughed.

Eryn was honestly glad to see that her daughter could let go of Trey that easily. Question was, could she do so long-term? An even bigger question was—as Trey held out his hand to help Eryn down— could she let go of him at all?

~

Trey closed the SUV door and heard a vehicle pulling into the compound. He spun to make sure it was Alex and Riley. When he confirmed their identity, he sighed out a breath of relief, drawing Hannah's scrutiny. He'd saved Gage's life a while back, and she'd made it her mission to ensure he was happy. And to her, that included a wife and family.

Alex and Riley joined the others, and Trey started in their direction, but Hannah left the group behind to approach Trey.

"I didn't expect to see you with the team," she said.

He worked hard to eliminate all worry from his tone. "I'm on security detail for Eryn."

Hannah's eyes narrowed in an assessing gaze. "From your look it seems like something more than hacking has occurred."

So much for evading Hannah's sharp intuition. He looked around to make sure the kids had moved out of earshot before speaking. "She was attacked by a man trying to abduct her."

Hannah spun on Gage. "Why didn't you tell me?"

Trey thought he would feel sheepish being called out in front of the team, but his gaze didn't waver. "You couldn't do anything about it, and I knew you'd worry yourself sick until we got home."

"Then let me worry. I need to know when one of my

family members gets hurt." She rushed over to Eryn and swept her into her arms. "Trey told me about the attack. Are you okay?"

"My chest hurts a bit from where he held me," Eryn said. "But otherwise I'm fine."

Sandra scoffed. "A bit? You're in serious pain and have been since it happened."

"And I'm probably hurting you more." Hannah set Eryn away. "And how are you doing emotionally?"

"I'm a wreck," Eryn readily admitted.

Trey gaped at the three of them. Eryn had been stoic about her injuries with the team and here she was sharing that she *had* been hurt. Pretty seriously if her mother was to be believed. Eryn should probably have been checked out by a medic. In fact, if Trey had known about her pain, he would've insisted.

Gage clapped him on the back. "If you and Eryn get together you'll have to get used to this. The sisterhood is strong, man. Very strong."

"We won't get—"

Gage held up a hand. "Save your breath. You will. We all know it, and you know it."

"It's just Eryn who has to come around," Riley said.

Trey couldn't believe they were discussing her when she was standing so close. "Yeah, well, she's pretty stubborn."

"And you're a former operator," Gage said. "Surely, you can figure out how to get past a little stubbornness."

"Um, boss," Alex said. "Wasn't too long ago that you were in the same place."

"Oh, no." Gage shook his head, but grinned. "A single guy without prospects can't weigh in here. Find the love of your life first, and then you can comment."

"Guess I won't say anything then." Riley laughed.

Hannah turned to face them. "What's so funny?"

Gage looked like he didn't want to answer, so Trey decided he would take the bullet for his friend. "Just life in general."

She was smart enough to see right through his comment, but she was also polite enough not to question them.

"I should get going," Sandra said.

Trey once thought Sandra lived with Eryn, but she only stayed at the compound when Eryn needed babysitting.

Eryn took a deep satisfied breath as if glad to be home—maybe in a place where she felt safer. "Let me get Bekah, and we can head home."

"I'll get Bekah for you," Trey offered to save her a few steps when she was in pain.

He expected her to argue, but she nodded.

He jogged across the yard to where the kids were playing with Barkley. They were all laying on their backs, and Barkley was running over the them, stopping to lick faces along the way. Mia and Bekah's giggles filled the air, and Trey's heart lifted. He wanted a family. Always had, but not when he was a Beret. Which is why he'd left the army. And yet, he hadn't found a woman he wanted to be the mother of his children.

Until Eryn. That day they met. He fell hard. Right there and hadn't been able to come up for air since. Now he wanted it all, including the little munchkin rolling in the grass and staining her clothes green.

"Bekah," he said. "It's time to go home."

She looked like she might pout. "Are you coming home with me?"

"Yes."

"Yippee." She jumped up and took his hand. "This is my new friend Trey. He's the bestest."

"He's our friend, too," David announced. "He comes to see dad sometimes."

That pout that had threatened before, materialized on Bekah's mouth as if she didn't want to share him with the others. His heart melted on the spot.

"How about I give you a ride on my shoulders?" He suggested to stave off tears.

Her eyes brightened. "Yes, please."

He swung her up on his shoulders, and she clutched her fingers in his hair to hold on. "Say goodbye to your friends now."

"Bye," she called out.

"Bye, David and Mia," he added. "Maybe I can come over in the morning, and we can play outside for a while."

"Yes, please," Mia answered, struggling to get to her feet. She'd suffered a brain injury in the car accident that had killed her mother, and she had some physical difficulties as a result. But she was a sweet little thing, and since Hannah had come into Mia's life, the child opened up more and wasn't quite as shy.

Trey rejoined the group, and Eryn frowned at him as if she didn't like him carrying Bekah. Maybe he should've asked.

"Look, Mommy, I'm *really* tall." Bekah giggled.

"I need to put you down now," Trey said. "So I can carry the luggage."

"I have my own suitcase," she said as he swung her down. She ran for the bags that the guys had unloaded and grabbed a small Dora the Explorer suitcase on wheels. She didn't wait for anyone but started down the drive.

So like her mother. Focused with single-minded

purpose and rushing headlong to accomplish it. He grabbed as many bags as he could, but before he could take Eryn's, she slung the strap for her computer case over her shoulder and took hold of her suitcase. He released it and grabbed Sandra's instead.

"I'm not about to be stubborn and say no." Sandra laughed, earning a look from Eryn.

Sandra held up her hands. "Message received."

"I'm sorry," Eryn said. "It's just..." She shrugged.

"The attack," her mother said. "Trey. Being back home. I'll choose one so you don't have to."

Eryn smiled as her mother had obviously intended. Trey liked Sandra from the start, and he liked her even more now. Eryn hurried to catch up to Bekah, and Sandra fell into step by him.

"So tell me your story," she said.

"Story?"

"You know. Your life story—in as much time as we have before reaching the cabin." She grinned.

"I grew up in Portland. Great parents. Two brothers. Two sisters. I'm the second child. I always loved military things and felt a calling to join up. My parents didn't have the same desire, so I compromised. Went to college first. They believed it would give me time to get over my military fascination. But it only grew. So I joined up the day I graduated. Worked my way into the Green Berets."

"I thought so," she said quietly.

"Pardon?"

"Special ops. I figured as much. I can tell one a mile away."

"How's that?"

"It's in the way you carry yourself. Such supreme confidence. Nothing phases you."

"You sound pretty well versed in spec op guys."

"My husband was a Ranger."

"So that's where Eryn gets it."

"If you mean her tenacity and unwillingness to give up —yes. And her desire to be in a career where she can carry a gun." Sandra laughed. "I had better luck than your parents in keeping her out of the military, but then she goes and works for the FBI. And when that ends, she hooks up with Blackwell." Sandra shook her head. "At least that's not as dangerous as going to war."

"That it's not." The guys he served with who lost their lives in duty to their country came to mind, and he was supremely thankful for their sacrifice. "Is that how your husband died?"

"No. Cancer. One year after he retired." She shook her head again. "Here I worried about him on duty all those years, and I should have been prepared for cancer instead."

"Sounds a bit like me. I served for so many years with not more than a scratch and then get shot as a deputy."

"Eryn mentioned that you might not be able to go back to patrol."

"Might not."

"Maybe Gage has a position for you here."

"He's already offered."

She mocked rubbing her hands together. "Well, doesn't that make things interesting."

"Why's that?"

"You. Eryn. Working together when there's this attraction between you." She stepped past him toward the cabin door but glanced back. "I almost wish I was on the team to see that."

Glad this discussion had ended, Trey followed everyone inside the small building. From the log exterior, he expected a rustic feel inside, but the walls were drywalled and painted a pale gray. The main living area was one big room with furniture that was overstuffed and looked comfy. He could easily imagine sitting on the sofa and watching a football game on the large-screen TV mounted over a fireplace. Her kitchen had white cabinets and gray countertops, and he could also imagine sitting at the island having a meal with her and Bekah. All thoughts he needed to stow.

"Gammy has to go home," Sandra said to Bekah.

"Aw," Bekah replied.

Trey waited for a meltdown since she didn't get a long nap, but she gave her Gammy a big hug and stepped back. Sandra hugged Eryn, too, and Trey was suddenly homesick for his own family.

He didn't visit them as often as he should. Maybe that was why he was so attracted to Eryn. He simply wanted family around. *Yeah, right.*

He carried Sandra's bag to her small Honda. She stared at him for a long uncomfortable moment. "Don't hurt my daughter. You hear?"

"I won't," he said, but then he really didn't have any control over if Eryn got hurt or not. All he could do was control his actions. And he needed to be cognizant of that until he resolved his employment issues. After that kiss, it was very clear that there was no way he could spend each day working with her while longing to be a part of her personal life. Once she was safe, he would look for other employment in the event that he wasn't cleared by the doctor and she didn't want a relationship with him.

He went back inside and found Bekah at the island eating a snack of cheese and crackers. Eryn stood on the other side. She gestured at the food. "Dinner's going to be a few hours so you might want to join us."

She didn't have to ask twice.

"Thanks." He took a seat next to Bekah. "I like your cabin."

Eryn looked around. "I still can't believe I had a big part in building it. Gage hired workers to frame the place, do the big things, but I did all of the finishing work with the team's help. We all worked together on each other's places. It was a lot of fun."

"I helped, too," Bekah said around a mouthful of crackers.

"Not with food in your mouth," Eryn said.

Bekah finished chewing and swallowed hard. "I painted. Mommy said I was a big help."

"That you were." Eryn's fond expression landed on her daughter. "I could never have finished without you."

Trey knew Eryn was exaggerating, but little Bekah's chest puffed up under the compliment. How wonderful it must be to have the chance to raise a child and know you were doing one of the most important jobs God entrusted to people.

"Full." Bekah hopped down from her place and took her plate and glass to the sink. "Going to play with Dora."

She scampered through a doorway on the far wall.

"You're doing an amazing job raising her." Trey took a slice of cheese and placed it on a cracker.

"Thank you. That's nice to hear. Sometimes I think I'm failing miserably." She sighed. "Rich and I planned for me to not to work and stay home with her, but then he died and everything changed. Still, I have the best situation possible. Gage made sure of that. I can spend many of my days with her and work while she naps and at night after she goes to bed."

"Do you want more children?"

She tilted her head as if she hadn't really considered that option before. "Sure. I mean if I ever marry again. Which as I told you, I can't imagine right now."

"Mind if I throw something out there about your fear of losing someone again?"

Wariness darkened her eyes. "I suppose."

He took a long drink of water as he organized his thoughts. The last thing he wanted to do was offend her. "First, I need to say I have to apply this to my own life, so there's no judgement on my part, okay?"

She nodded but still looked wary.

"When I was first shot and put on desk duty, I was in a pretty foul mood. So my pastor took me aside and reminded me that I wasn't trusting God. I told him I was asking for direction, but not hearing anything back. It was a one-way street."

She nodded vigorously. "That's me for sure. Since Rich died, I'm not hearing God at all."

"He mentioned a verse in Jeremiah that talks about seeking God. I'd read it like a hundred times before and couldn't see why my pastor was pointing it out. I mean doesn't every Christian know we're supposed to seek God?"

She nodded again, this time less forcefully.

"But then my pastor highlighted the part of the verse that said we only find God when we seek Him with our whole heart. I realized I wasn't seeking with all my heart because part of me wanted what I wanted to happen, not what God wanted to happen. Even now, I want to go back on patrol, but maybe that's not what God wants for me. I'm not ready to accept that, I guess, so I ask half-heartedly."

She stood quietly, staring down at her hands that were resting on the counter.

"So maybe you're hanging on to the past, too, when God

wants you to let it go. It seems like you're using the pain as a way to avoid falling for someone again so you don't get hurt."

She paused for a long moment. "You could be right. Probably are. But...I'm powerless to do anything about it right now." She looked up at him, her eyes glistening with tears.

His heart tore at her sadness. He couldn't sit there and do nothing, so he got up and circled the island to take her into his arms, being careful not to aggravate her injuries. She didn't fight him but let him hold her as she softly cried. Not big sobs, only little puffs.

"It'll be okay." He stroked her hair.

Gradually, her tears subsided, and she leaned back to look at him. "I don't know what's come over me. I'm not a big crier, but I guess the stress of the last few days have finally hit home."

"No need to apologize. I totally get it."

She reached up then and gently touched the side of his face. "You're an amazing man, Trey, and if I could find a way over my issues to be with anyone, it would be you."

He appreciated her comment, but he knew that the only way she would get over her fear was if she wanted it for herself. Not for him or any other man. And as much as he wanted to help her, he couldn't. It was all up to her.

18

The morning came too soon, and Eryn wasn't ready for the bright sunlight that filtered through her bedroom blinds. She stayed up way too late last night reviewing the logs and code and tracking down comments on the forum. And thinking about Trey's words of wisdom.

It was funny how a person often couldn't see their own problem, but someone else could succinctly nail it. Trey had done that for her. She was choosing not to let go of her fear of getting hurt. She got that now. But get it or not, she still wasn't ready to let it go. Only someone who'd lost a close loved one could truly understand her reasoning.

Maybe Trey understood. She didn't know, but he likely lost close friends in the army—soldiers who were like family to him. And he was smart enough to see his own problem, which she had to give him big kudos for. He really was an exceptional man, and she meant what she said last night. He was worth getting over her issues for, but she didn't know how to do that. At least not on her own.

"Please help me," she said and lay there, trying to come

up with additional words, but that was all she could think to say. Her heart really wasn't in it, as Trey pointed out.

She got out of bed and took a quick shower then dressed in her usual work attire. First, she would meet with Hannah to do the sketch of the deceased woman. Then later in the afternoon after Riley finished teaching his urban sniper course, he would fly her and Trey to Eastern Oregon, and she wanted to be wearing her Blackwell uniform when she questioned people.

She stepped into the family room and found Trey in the kitchen, a delicious smell drifting across the space. He'd folded the sheets and blanket from the couch and was now cooking breakfast? He was a keeper for sure.

He looked up and smiled. "I hope you don't mind that I made myself at home in your kitchen."

"Are you kidding? You're making breakfast. How could I mind?" She laughed and joined him at the island.

"Just sausage and waffles. I was hungry and figured I could keep everything hot until you and Bekah were ready."

Eryn went to the cupboard and grabbed a mug then poured a cup of rich black coffee. She took a sip and had to admit he made good coffee. And his waffles looked equally as appetizing.

"I usually drink a cup of coffee to wake up and then get Bekah, but let me wake her now so we can all eat together."

"That would be nice," he said, not looking up from the stovetop.

Would eating together seem too personal with them behaving like a little family? Likely, she supposed, and she should watch that. But then she was watching so much with him already—could she add another thing?

She sighed, drawing his attention, and their gazes locked. She could easily get lost in those soft morning eyes, but she exerted iron will and set down her mug to go wake her daughter. She found Bekah sleepy-eyed but lying awake in her bed.

"Is Trey still here, Mommy?" she asked. "He promised he would be."

"Yes, he's in the kitchen making waffles so we need to get you dressed and ready."

She dropped her blanket and jumped out of bed. "I'll pick my clothes."

She went to her closet and grabbed a purple and pink striped T-shirt, and then from her dresser she took out red plaid shorts. They didn't go together in the least, but Bekah wouldn't be leaving the compound today so there was no reason to mention it.

Chattering about how she was going to take Trey to play with Mia, David, and Barkley, Bekah quickly shed her pajamas and got dressed.

"Remember, when I finish my work with Hannah, Trey and I will be going for a short trip. I might not be home tonight so Gammy will come to stay with you."

"I like it when Gammy stays, but I wish Trey could, too."

Eryn didn't take it personally that her daughter left her out in this discussion as Bekah took having her mother around for granted. After Bekah fastened the Velcro tabs on her tennis shoes, they went into the family room.

"Trey!" Bekah ran across the room to him, and he scooped her up in his arms.

There was something about those powerful arms gently holding her child that got to Eryn in a way nothing else had before, and a vision of them as a true family saturated her heart.

Is that you God? Trying to tell me I really am ready for something?

She squashed those thoughts immediately. In her experience, prayer wasn't usually answered that quickly, and she hadn't even been living her faith much of late.

"Are you ready for a waffle?" Trey asked.

"I am!" Bekah clapped. "With lotsa syrup. And you havta cut it for me." She wiggled, and he put her down.

He gestured at place settings. "Sit, and I'll serve you both."

Eryn helped Bekah onto her stool, and then took a seat across from her. Eryn also steeled her heart against letting this little episode get to her. She cut Bekah's waffle but let her pour the syrup herself—stopping her before she drowned the waffle. Then Eryn turned to her own plate and ate silently, half-listening to Trey and Bekah chat while she focused on the tasks ahead.

When they left the cabin, they stepped into a glorious day of sunshine and a cool ocean breeze whisking over the area. Cooper Ashcroft and Jackson Lockhart, her other two teammates, were passing by. Both men were tall and powerful, and they stopped defensively near Eryn. Coop's and Jackson's eyes were filled with suspicion as they focused on Trey. She appreciated that her teammates were protective of her, but this was overkill.

"You guys both know Trey, don't you?" she said pointedly. "I'm assuming Gage filled you in on what's going on and why Trey is staying with me."

"It's because he's my friend," Bekah announced.

Jackson laughed, but Coop didn't crack a smile. He was more reserved than Jackson, and his intense gaze said he was still unsure about Trey's intentions.

"I'm on protective detail for Eryn." Trey shook hands with Jackson then Coop. "What class are you teaching today?"

"Close quarter combat," Jackson said. "You've taken that one, right? You've taken almost all of our classes."

Trey nodded. "Yep, I've learned many excellent skills."

Bekah grabbed his hand. "Want to play."

He smiled down at her.

"Catch you guys later," she said to her teammates and let Bekah draw them away.

As they walked, Trey started whistling, and Bekah skipped to the beat of his tune. Eryn felt the warmth of the sun. Caught the scent of the salty sea breeze.

How much more perfect could the morning get?

For some reason that thought made her cranky. By the time she bid Trey and Bekah goodbye and was seated at Hannah's island, she wanted to snap at Hannah's good mood.

"Someone got out of the wrong side of the bed this morning," Hannah said as she laid her drawing supplies on the island. "Did you fight with Trey?"

"No. The opposite. Everything was wonderful. He made breakfast. Treats Bekah like a princess." Eryn shook her head.

"That sounds totally awful." Hannah chuckled.

"Well it was. You know I'm not ready for something like that."

"I know no such thing."

"I've told you often enough."

"Yeah, but that doesn't mean you're right."

Eryn held up her hands. "It's way too early in the day for that discussion. Let's just do the sketch."

"You know the drill. Start describing the woman." Hannah's tone was terse and to the point. She was never terse. Ever.

Eryn had obviously hurt her feelings. "I'm sorry. It's not you. It's me."

"I get it. I was there not too long ago with Gage."

Eryn blew wayward strands of hair from her face. "And I know you want to help, but I have to work through this myself."

"Okay." Hannah smiled. "As long as you know I'm always available to talk."

She snorted. "Yeah, but you're rooting for Trey, too, and I need an impartial opinion."

Hannah sputtered. "Like you're impartial on this matter?"

Eryn slapped the countertop. "Ohhhh—that's not fair!"

Hannah sighed before sitting on a stool. "Look, sweetie. I'm sorry. I'll stick to the drawing and let you bring up Trey again when you're ready." She picked up her pencil.

Eryn took a deep breath and exhaled as she shifted to relax her body. Using the skills she learned in the FBI, she cleared her mind of everything but the woman's facial details. "She had an oval face with a fairly pronounced chin. It's wide. Kind of masculine. She also had big brown eyes with bushy eyebrows that looked like she never plucked them."

Hannah looked up. "You're sure it was a woman? Because you're describing a man."

"Positively a woman, but now that you mention it, she was kind of manly."

Eryn paused to let Hannah get started on the image. Her pencil scratched across the surface, and Eryn sought out other details from her memory. She avoided thinking about the gunshot wound and tried to remember if she saw any hair sticking out from the fox costume.

She remembered an auburn lock by her ear, so she

relayed that to Hannah. "But I have no idea of her hairstyle. Except for one lock, her hair was tucked up in the fox hood."

"Bangs make a world of difference in a woman's appearance. I'll start without bangs since you didn't see them. Then once we have everything else right, I'll do one with bangs, too, in case it will help ID her."

That was Hannah. A woman who went above and beyond and could always be counted on. She'd opened her arms to all of the team members, including Coop's fiancé Kiera and Jackson's fiancé Maggie. In fact, Hannah was serving as Kiera's maid of honor for the wedding next month and Eryn would be a bridesmaid.

"How are preparations going for the wedding?" Eryn asked, trying to lighten the mood.

"Good." Hannah didn't look up. "But when this is all over, I know Kiera wants your help with a few things."

Eryn thought of her friends getting married, and her crankiness evaporated. "They're going to be so happy."

Hannah looked up and opened her mouth as if to say something, then snapped it shut and looked back at her pad. Eryn wasn't about to ask what she was going to say.

"What was the woman's nose like?" Hannah asked.

"Narrow, but big. Kind of hawkish."

"Okay, let me get that added, and you can have a look."

"While you do that, I'll take a quick peek outside to see how Trey's doing with watching Bekah."

"He often plays with Mia and David when he visit's Gage, so he should be fine."

"He really likes kids, doesn't he?" Eryn asked.

"He said he has several nieces and nephews."

"And he wants like four or five of his own kids!"

Hannah's head popped up. "And how do you feel about that?"

"Not that it matters, but I'd never thought about having more than three kids."

"Best work that out before the ring goes on your finger, then."

Eryn sighed. "There's not going to be a ring on my finger anytime soon."

"If you say so." Hannah went back to drawing.

Shaking her head, Eryn headed to the patio door to look out over the large yard with a sandbox, huge play structure, and garden beds all built by Gage and the team.

Trey was walking over to the play structure from the sandbox, and she noticed a pronounced limp today. Or maybe it was always there, but he hid it when he was around her. Men were like that. Never wanting anyone to see they were hurt or in pain. She was the same way, but only with the team, and then never to cover up an injury so she could go on an op that she wasn't fit for.

Trey stepped up to Bekah who was seated on a swing and started pushing her. He stared off into the distance and absently pushed like his mind was filled with something he was working out. Maybe he was spending as much time thinking about his issue with his leg as she was about getting hurt again. Neither of which would find her hacker. She spun and marched back to the kitchen with purpose.

Hannah turned her sketchpad to face Eryn. "Am I close?"

"Close, but no. Her eyes are bigger. Nose narrower and chin broader."

"So I got the eyebrows right then?" She chuckled and exaggeratedly wiggled her own eyebrows.

Eryn laughed with her and grabbed some coffee as Hannah made the changes. They went around and around like this for the rest of the morning, but finally Hannah produced a sketch that Eryn felt realistically portrayed the deceased woman.

"That's perfect." Eryn gave Hannah a hug. "I owe you one."

"Then I aim to collect right now." Hannah pushed back.

Eryn rolled her eyes. "What do you want?"

"Don't close yourself off from Trey. Why not let things develop, and then see how you feel?"

She crossed her arms. "Then I'm bound to be hurt because he's a great guy, and I know exactly where it could lead."

"I'm pretty sure if you open your heart, you'll forget all about being afraid."

"Maybe," Eryn replied, but she still wasn't willing to find out.

19

Trey sat next to Eryn in the company helicopter. He'd been in more helos than he could count in his military career, but that had been a while ago. And none of them were as nice as Gage's aircraft. Trey knew his buddy would buy top-of-the-line equipment, but this baby must have set him back a pretty penny.

Trey glanced at Eryn. She was still busy reading information she'd printed out for the trip. She told him it was part of the code from the hack, but it all looked like gibberish to him. Every now and then she scribbled something on a page and then sat and stared at it.

"Finding anything?" he asked using the mic on his headset so she could hear.

"I'm seeing something familiar, but I don't know what yet. I still have a lot of code to go through." She turned her attention back to the pages.

He wanted her to be able to find the hacker so he let the conversation drop. Or maybe he didn't want to have a conversation with her. Not when she wasn't open to him in the way he wanted. Besides, Riley had a headset on, too, and he would hear anything they said.

Trey shifted to look out the window on the far side of the helo. Since leaving Cold Harbor, they'd gone from the ocean to heavy lush forests to mountains, then the populated Willamette Valley. Over another mountain range, they hovered over the high desert portion of the state covered in big sagebrush and rabbit brush along with hardy grasses. Yellow and purple spring wildflowers dotted the area, making it pretty in a stark kind of way, but it was totally opposite of the western side of the state that was lush and green most of the year from abundant rainfall.

"ETA two minutes," Riley announced over the headset.

Trey strained his neck to see the private airstrip where they would put down about fifteen miles out of Burns. Ahead he spotted what amounted to a flat piece of land serving as a dirt strip. Not much of a runway, but then Trey had landed in far more difficult terrain in the past and a helicopter didn't need a runway at all.

Near the end sat an older model Jeep. "Looks like the car's there waiting for us."

"Did you doubt it would be?" Eryn asked.

"You never know," he said, but he really did know. The airstrip belonged to one of Gage's many military contacts, and when a military brother said he would do something, you could count on him to follow through.

Riley set the helo down smoothly, and Trey took off his headset. Eryn packed her papers into her computer case. Trey didn't wait for her but slid the door open and hopped down. The temperature was about the same as Cold Harbor, but without the coastal wind it felt warmer than sixty-five degrees. The rotors slowed above, and Riley joined Trey as did Eryn.

"I'll keep you updated on our progress," Eryn told Riley.

Trey wasn't surprised he was staying with the pricey helicopter. It was on private property, but the airstrip was next to a main road, and they would never risk leaving such an expensive machine where it could be vandalized.

"I'll try to stay awake to hear your calls." Riley laughed.

She rolled her eyes good-naturedly and set off for the Jeep. They were supposed to find the keys under the floor mat, and that's exactly where Trey located them. He needed something to keep his mind busy so he didn't even ask if Eryn wanted to drive.

He got the Jeep on the road, and they headed east toward Burns. Trey had looked up the city last night and discovered it was less than three thousand people. It was also the county seat and made up nearly fifty percent of the entire county population. Told him how sparsely populated the large county was.

Eryn rummaged through her bag, and he expected her to grab her code pages again, but she took out a folder and removed the victim's sketches.

"Hannah does good work," he said.

"She's very talented."

"And you did a good job describing the woman. She looks like I remember her."

Eryn turned to face him. "Is this entire trip going to be this tense between us?"

"Tense?"

"You know, small talk. Avoiding anything of importance."

"I figured that's what you would want."

"What I want is not to be stressed out over this when we have such important work to do."

"Then I'll just be myself and won't filter what I say."

"Good. I'll do the same thing."

He smiled at her. "You look really nice today."

"What?" she asked, her eyes widening.

"You look nice."

She lifted her chin. "I look like I look all the time."

He smiled at her. "Yeah, you always look nice."

She groaned. "Oh, brother."

"Hey, you were the one who wanted my unfiltered thoughts."

"Maybe put a little filter on them." She grinned, which was his intent, and the tension evaporated. Maybe he was going to enjoy this trip after all.

Eryn pushed her empty plate away in the vintage drug store with an old-fashioned lunch counter and refused to get disappointed over striking out. They'd spent three hours showing the woman's photo around town and asking about an animal rights group to no avail. Giving up for the day, they'd stopped in to have a late dinner in one of the few places still open.

Trey set his iced tea down on the scarred Formica countertop. "I thought at least one person would be willing to hear us out today, didn't you?"

"Blake warned me that people in this part of the state were cautious. But yeah, I hoped someone would look at the woman's drawing before saying they didn't know her." She sighed. "I was almost tempted to mention that the woman was murdered, and we needed to locate her next of kin."

"But you wouldn't want that information to get back to the woman's family via the grapevine, right?"

"Exactly. I'll never forget when I heard about Rich. It was

hard enough to take coming from official police officers. But if I'd heard it via the grapevine?" She shook her head and didn't elaborate about that dark rainy night when her husband lost his life on a mountain road.

Trey swiveled on the chrome barstool. "We're running out of daylight."

"Looks like we'll need to spend the night here and should make a reservation somewhere."

He nodded. "What about Riley?"

"He'll have to bunk in the chopper. Won't be the first time."

Their waitress carried the coffee pot over to them. Her stick-straight brown hair was in disarray, and she pushed up her wire rim glasses. "Refill?"

Eryn nodded. "Can you recommend a hotel here?"

She leaned a hip against the counter, bunching up her red and white striped apron with *Bee* engraved near the top. "Are you looking for modern conveniences or a quaint bed and breakfast?"

"Modern," Eryn answered quickly. She didn't need to spend the night under the roof of a homey place with Trey.

"Then I recommend the East Side Motel. Local mom-and-pop business with clean and updated rooms." She poured the coffee. "I hear you folks are looking for a woman."

Encouraged by Bee bringing up the subject, Eryn pulled out both sketches and turned them to face Bee. She bent over the sketches for a long while.

She looked up, and pushed up her glasses, her expression wary. "Are you the law?"

"No," Eryn said, though technically Trey was, but this had nothing to do with his job.

"Bill collectors."

"Absolutely not."

Bee settled her free hand on her hip. "You both have honest faces, but I have to ask if you mean her any harm."

"Harm?" Eryn shook her head. "No, definitely not."

Bee shifted to look at Trey.

"Me neither."

She gave a curt nod. "In that case, I know her."

"You do?" Eryn couldn't contain her enthusiasm.

"Well, I don't really *know her*, but I know her name." Bee frowned. "Unfortunately, I know her because she gets her prescriptions filled here, so that means I can't break confidentiality and share her name or address."

Eryn's enthusiasm evaporated. "There must be some way you can help us find her."

"I suppose I could give general directions to her house. Then you could knock on a few doors until you find the right place."

Eryn grabbed her notepad and pen. "Okay, go ahead."

Bee rested the pot on the counter. "Before I do, I want to make sure my name won't be mentioned."

"We're glad to leave you out of it," Trey said.

She provided directions that would take them out of town and into a remote area. "Now I don't recommend you go out there in the dark. You might find a shotgun or two in your face."

"Do you know if she might be involved with an animal rights group?" Eryn asked.

Bee shifted and looked up at the ceiling. "I don't really know. She's a sweet lady with a kind and generous heart, so I could see her championing animals who are abused."

Eryn took a business card and slid it over to Bee. "If you think of anything else that might help, would you please call me?"

"Doubt that will happen, but I hear a lot of gossip in here so anything's possible." Bee scooped up the card.

Eryn nodded. "Thank you for your help."

"Be careful," Bee said. "People around here like their privacy."

She turned and walked away, and Eryn swiveled her stool to face Trey. "You willing to risk going out there tonight?"

He shook his head. "Are you?"

"No. Too bad we couldn't have gotten an earlier start today." She wouldn't let that ruin her good mood over the lead. "But we can check into the motel, and then I can keep reviewing the code."

"About the motel."

"Yes."

"I'm not going to leave you alone in a room." His tone was soft, but his intense gaze was locked on hers.

"But I can't stay with you."

"Then if they don't have a room with an adjoining door, we'll have to check out other hotels." He sat up straight, his neck stiff, his expression unyielding.

She nodded but didn't like the fact that his room would be attached to hers. Sure, at the suite they were in the same general area, but his room had been on one side, hers on the other. Not that she thought he would try anything, nor would she. It was just that with him being so close, she would think about him more, and that wasn't good on any level.

He took money from his wallet and grabbed the check. Before she could protest, he was up and on his way to the register. A young woman at the end of the counter followed his progress, admiration and interest burning in her eyes.

Eryn had to wonder if she was looking at him the same

way, so she snapped her gaze back to the counter and gathered her things together. They were soon pulling into the quaint motel with a cactus theme that was a bit corny. But Eryn's room was clean and remodeled like Bee had said. It held a queen-sized bed, small dining table with two chairs, and a plush chair in the corner.

Trey went to clear the bathroom. She knew there couldn't be anyone lying in wait for her, but she appreciated his thoroughness.

He turned the lock on the adjoining door. "I'll head to my room and open my side."

She nodded and set her computer bag on the dining table. "I'm going to get started on the code again, so if you want to watch TV in your room or something, feel free."

"I'd rather be in here with you."

"But why?"

"Because being with you beats being alone."

"But I'll have my nose in my computer."

"That's okay," he said and went out the door.

She didn't get him. He wanted to be with her. Was totally into her, and yet, he was giving her space. Well, except for the kiss. Something she was going to make sure they didn't repeat.

His room door opened and closed, then the adjoining lock clicked open, and he stepped into the room. She didn't look up and continued booting up her computer, but she heard him settle in the plush chair. She brought up the files and glanced at him. His gaze was locked on her.

"You're not going to watch me all night, are you?" she asked.

"I wouldn't mind it, but I won't." He held up his phone. "I have email to check and a few calls to make."

"Wouldn't you rather have privacy for those calls?"

"I will."

"What?"

"By the time I finish my email, you'll be so lost in your work you won't hear a word I say." He grinned at her.

She wanted to be mad at him but couldn't resist the crooked grin and smiled back. "You're infuriating, you know that?"

"Yeah. You look really mad." His grin widened.

"Grr," she muttered. "We need to go back to you *not* saying whatever pops into your head."

"Oh, but I like this so much more."

"I wish I could say the same thing," she said, but she had to admit she enjoyed the good-natured bantering with him. She wouldn't let it distract her, though. She turned her attention back to her computer.

"Exactly what are you looking for there?" he asked. "In layman's terms."

"Without any physical evidence to find our attacker, I'm trying to find any digital attribution."

"Attribution?"

"Sophisticated actors can cover their digital tracks, but looking closely at files or data left behind as part of the incursion can help me attribute the hack to someone. One of the most common ways to do that is look for comments in the software code, as programmers often leave notes in the code. Notes to others or for future developers."

She paused and took a long breath before continuing. "I can also look at metadata, to see if the text has been translated from one language to another. Plus, code customization can reveal clues, such as programming style or even choice of programming language, and if I combine that with other things I find, it can suggest the responsible party."

"I don't get it. How does that point you to a particular hacker?"

She sat back. "So think of this like you would a police investigation. When a detective doesn't have a strong lead, they often compare a crime to past crimes in the area or with the same MO. It's the same with a hack. I can compare what I find in this hack to previous ones and maybe it will reveal links that add pieces to my puzzle."

"But how do you know about other attacks?"

"Hackers usually work alone. Sometimes in small groups. Always in secret. But ethical hackers are different. They partner together all across the world. When a clue is found in an investigation, hackers share that information."

"Where?"

"You can find it publicly on blogs or in scholarly papers. And over the years, I've developed a wide list of trusted investigators. I've solved many investigations at the FBI by comparing the leads I find with other information."

"You're amazing, you know that?" He sat without moving, his focus attentive. "I can't imagine how long it took you learn all of this stuff."

"When you love your work, it's not difficult to become proficient. You know that from being a Beret. Maybe your current job."

His expression turned pensive.

"What is it?" she asked.

"I'm not sure I love my job. I mean, I like it and enjoy going to work every day. And I most definitely don't like desk duty, but love it?" He shook his head. "Not like I loved being a Beret."

She suddenly realized she had no idea why he left the army. "Why did you leave?"

"I wanted to settle down and have a family. Being a Beret

doesn't lend itself to being the kind of family man I want to be."

"That's quite a sacrifice to make."

He shrugged. "From what you've said, you'd give up your job for a family, too."

"Yeah, I guess I would," she said, turning around, but she couldn't think about that now. She had her work cut out for her in this investigation and that was where her focus needed to be tonight. Only there.

20

After breakfast at a local diner, Trey pulled into the first driveway on the road where Bee said they'd find the woman's house. It had taken them fifteen minutes to reach this location, and he hoped for a little conversation along the way, but when he met with Eryn first thing that morning, she said she was on to something in the electronic files, and she continued to work on her computer even through breakfast.

"Oh my gosh." She sat back and gaped at the screen.

"Did you find something?"

"Yes. The hacker is Russian."

"How can you tell that?"

She looked at him, fire burning in her eyes. "The metadata contains text converted from the Cyrillic characters of the Russian alphabet to the Latin characters of English."

He pulled up to the house and parked. "So you're looking for someone in Russia?"

"Not necessarily. Just someone whose native language is Russian, and he feels more comfortable using it."

"Petrov," Trey said as he shifted into gear. "He's American-born, but of Russian descent."

"Right. And he fits my attacker's build. We'll need to look into him more. Maybe stop in Portland on the way back to Cold Harbor to talk to him again." She closed her computer. "But now we have a woman to find."

They exited the vehicle and stepped toward the single-story adobe home built in a common desert style. Trey scanned the area but didn't see anything that raised red flags. They approached the door, and a dog started barking from inside. Eryn knocked loudly, and they both stepped to the side out of habit to protect themselves.

A young woman, maybe thirty, with wavy blond hair and a friendly face answered the door. She was holding a Rottweiler back by the collar. "Don't mind Rascal here. He's a real sweetie and is likely to lick you to death before biting you."

Eryn introduced herself and held out her hand.

The woman took it. "Lacey Kramer."

"Nice to meet you, Lacey." Eryn smiled and Trey could see she was putting Lacey at ease. "We're working on an investigation and are looking for this woman." Eryn held out one of the sketches. "We were told she lives on this road."

"That's Veronika 'spelled with a K,' as she says." Lacey frowned. "Did something bad happen to her?"

"Why would you think that?" Trey asked.

"She went out of town but was supposed to be back yesterday. I'm watching her pets. Three dogs and three cats. She hasn't come home and isn't answering her cell." Lacey patted Rascal's head, and he settled to the floor. She released his leash.

Trey had to admit he wasn't comfortable with the dog

looking up at him, but this woman must know her dog and it was safe to release him. "Does Veronika live alone or did her family travel with her?"

"Lives alone." Lacey's eyes narrowed. "*Did* something happen to her?"

Trey didn't want to tell this woman that Veronika had been murdered. Not until they had a positive identification with her driver's license. "We're not at liberty to discuss the details of our investigation right now."

"What's Veronika's last name?" Eryn asked, quickly jumping in, likely to defect a follow-up question from Lacey.

"You know, I don't know." Lacey shook her head. "I didn't realize that until right now. She moved in about six months ago, and we've only talked a few times."

"But you're sure she's the woman in my sketch?" Eryn asked.

"Positive. I mean the one without the bangs."

"Is she Russian?" Trey asked, as using a "k" in a name was common in Russian spelling.

"Not that I know of."

"How about part of an animal rights group?" Eryn asked.

Lacey shrugged. "She loves animals but that's all I can tell you."

"Did she ever mention a kit fox?"

Lacey cocked an eyebrow. "Did she have something to do with that stolen fox?"

"We have reason to believe she's fond of foxes."

"If she is, she never mentioned them to me. But like I said—I haven't known her all that long."

Trey tipped his head at the street. "Which house is hers?"

Lacey frowned. "I should probably have asked what you

want with Veronika before giving you all of this information."

"I wish we could explain," Eryn said sincerely. "But know we mean her no harm."

Lacey nodded, but her frown lingered. "It's the last house on the right before the intersection."

"Thank you." Trey smiled at her.

They departed, and Lacey stood—hand over her eyes to block the sun—watching them. Trey didn't want her to overhear anything he might say, so he held off speaking until they were settled in the Jeep. "I hated not telling her about Veronika."

"Me, too." Eryn sighed. "But we owe it to Veronika to look for her next of kin first."

"So what's your plan now? We can't very well break into her house and look for more information."

"No, but we can take a peek in the mailbox to get her last name then call Blake so he can move forward in the investigation."

"But you're not going to drop it, are you?" He eyed her.

"Are you kidding? No way."

"I didn't think so." Trey didn't like the answer, but he expected it.

He started the Jeep and took them down the road to the old farm-style house with peeling white paint. He pulled onto the shoulder short of the rusty blue mailbox.

"She didn't buy the nicest of places, did she?" Eryn asked.

He shook his head. "I assume you want to be the one to look at the mail."

She nodded and stepped out. She opened the mailbox and laid out five pieces of mail on the hood of the car. Phone in hand, she snapped a picture of the envelopes and put them back before sliding into the vehicle.

"Well?" he asked.

"Abram. Veronika Abram."

"Is that Russian?"

Eryn shrugged and settled her computer on her lap. "I'll check it and any connection to Petrov while you get us back to the helo."

He made a U-turn and drove straight to the airfield. She didn't look up until he pulled up near the aircraft.

She closed her computer. "I found a Veronika Abram in an animal rights forum. Looks like she's an activist as suspected, but I don't see any group affiliation."

"So maybe she does this on her own." He turned the key, stilling the engine, and the absolute quiet of the country settled around them.

"Could be," Eryn said. "The posts I see aren't related to wild animals like the kit fox, but abused dogs."

He removed the keys. "Still, if she loved animals she could've read about the fox and decided to do something about it. Or she could be part of an underground group that you haven't located yet."

"True. I don't have access to all the tools I need since leaving law enforcement. Hopefully, Blake will be able to find information that will help."

Trey tucked the keys under the mat. "Did you check social media?"

She nodded. "First thing I looked at. Nothing."

"What about the name Abram? Is it Russian?"

"Not according to my research, but there are Russian surnames like Abramov, so it could've been shortened over the years, I suppose."

"I really think we need to talk to Petrov," Trey said. "So I hope you're planning to stop in Portland."

"Absolutely." A grin lit up her face. "We not only need to interview him, but it's also time to call him out on lying to us."

Eryn had been to the Portland Police Bureau's downtown precinct many times when she worked at the Portland FBI office, but she was always impressed with the modern and clean lobby. Not that it compared to the new FBI building opened about six years ago, but it was still nice for a police department.

Detective Petrov met them in the lobby and escorted them up to the detective's division. Eryn spotted Detective Rudd sitting at her desk, but she didn't want Petrov to know that they'd talked, so she didn't acknowledge Rudd. He led them into a conference room. Based on the podium and posters on the wall, she suspected this was their roll call room where they disseminated needed information to patrol officers before their shifts.

Eryn wanted to see Petrov's face when she questioned him, so she took a seat across from him. Trey sat next to her. They'd decided on the drive over that since Petrov was a detective and would be difficult to interview, she would handle the questioning and Trey would sit back and observe.

Today, Petrov wore a long-sleeved white dress shirt with black slacks, and his gun was stowed in a shoulder holster. He sat forward and planted his hands on the table. "What can I do for you?"

Eryn sat up straight, ready for anything he might throw

at her. "As I said on the phone, we have a few follow up questions from the resort."

"And as I told you then, I know little about computers, so I doubt I can help you."

"Ah, but I'm sure if you were interviewing a person of interest in a crime who gave you such a reply, you'd point out that you could easily know someone who is a computer expert."

"A crime?" He met her gaze and held it. "And I'm a person of interest?"

"Honestly, yes," she said. "We have a working theory that you might have tried to stop my class."

His eyes widened in genuine surprise. "Why on earth would I want to do that?"

"That's what we'd like to know."

He ran a hand over his hair that was cut short but seemed to have a mind of its own, sticking out at odd angles even after he pressed it down. "Look. Let's cut to the chase here. What do you have on me?"

"For starters, you lied to me when I talked to you last."

He crossed his hands behind his head and leaned back. "Refresh my memory about what we discussed."

"I asked you if you were working on any cases you could use my specific class for, and you said no."

"And?"

"And you have quite a big investigation going on right now."

He eyed her. "How do you know about that?"

She was finally garnering a reaction from him. "I'll be helping Detective Rudd with the pictures in the child porn investigation to link them back to the suspect's phone."

He crossed his arms. "Rudd needs to learn to keep her mouth shut."

"Why, when I can potentially help you close this case?"

He shot forward in his chair, veins bulging in his neck. "Because we don't share investigation details with civilians, that's why. Not with anyone outside the department. And we especially don't do it without talking to our partner."

Eryn resisted leaning back from his aggressive posture as she was sure that was what he hoped she would do. Detectives were masters at intimidation, but so was she. "Rudd didn't tell me anything that isn't in an interview you did with the local newspaper. Plus, she's going to get your LT's permission before sharing the photos. So your reaction is overkill. Mind telling me why that is?"

He scowled. "She's a rookie detective who doesn't know her place. Always pushing. Overstepping." Eryn thought his attitude had more to do with Rudd being female than her pushiness.

Eryn leaned closer to rile him. "Point is, why didn't you mention that you had an investigation where the new techniques could be used? You wouldn't have had to share anything. Just say yes instead of no."

His jaw clenched. "Because it's none of your business."

"Sounds like you resent that I asked you about it. Do you have something to hide?"

He slapped his hands on the arms of his chair and gripped tightly. "What's this really about?"

"ShadowPrince," she said and watched to see if recognition flashed in his eyes.

"Excuse me," he said sounding and looking surprised. "Should I know something about this ShadowPrince?"

"ShadowPrince is the screen name for whoever deployed ransomware on my computer, warning me not to teach my next classes. I've confirmed the software was written by someone who prefers the Russian alphabet to American."

"And because my family came over from Russia you think it's me?" He swung his head side-to-side with exaggerated movements. "Of course, you would think all Russians are bad, so you figure this points to me. But you're forgetting I don't know diddly about computer programming."

"And you're forgetting that I know you could've hired ShadowPrince to write the code and deploy it. With your years as a detective, it wouldn't be farfetched to think you could find a criminal to do your bidding."

"But why? Why would I do that?"

"Because you didn't want Rudd to attend that class. You were worried she would learn something that you didn't want her to know. Is it related to your porn investigation or something else? I don't know, but now's your chance to tell me before I figure it out and you pay the price for not cooperating."

He growled. "I won't even bother justifying myself to you. Get out of here. *Now*."

He shot to his feet and started for Eryn, his chest rising and falling with each breath. Eryn could easily see him getting angry enough to murder someone.

Trey jumped up, standing there in full warrior mode, stance wide, his chest rising and falling, and Eryn couldn't take her eyes from the sight he made.

"I'd stand down if I were you," he said in a low, threatening tone.

"Right, like you're gonna do anything in a room full of my fellow detectives." He laughed mockingly. "Get moving, or I'll ask them to help me throw you out."

Detective Rudd pushed open the door and poked her head in. "Anything I can help with?"

"Yeah," Petrov snapped. "You can show your buddies out of the building."

"Glad to." She stepped back, and Eryn got up to join Rudd in the hallway. Trey backed out of the room, his gaze remaining on Petrov. Eryn didn't think the detective was foolish enough to try anything, but she was thankful for Trey's protection.

In the elevator, Rudd turned to her. "I'm glad you stopped by. I was going to call you."

"Did you get your LT's permission to bring me in?" Eryn asked.

"No. Not yet. This is about Petrov. I overheard him on the phone this morning when he didn't know I was nearby. I think he's blackmailing someone, and it might have to do with our porn investigation."

Really? "I'm surprised you're telling me this instead of reporting it to your LT."

Rudd scratched her neck, leaving long red marks. "I hate to go outside the brotherhood, but if I go to my LT, I'll be branded as a whistle-blower and my career will be over. I already have issues because of my age and sex. I can't add to that. And I can't lose my job. I'm a single mom and my kids depend on me."

Eryn nodded. "I totally get that. So did you hear who he was talking to?"

"He called the guy Olson. Petrov warned him that if he didn't pay up, he'd expose him."

"Is there anyone named Olson in this investigation?" Trey asked.

"Not that I'm aware of, but Petrov hasn't shared his old files with me. I've asked, but he keeps stonewalling me. This might be why." Rudd frowned.

Eryn hated that this guy was making Rudd's job difficult,

but it was looking like he was into something illegal, and he was going to pay for it if Eryn had anything to do about it. "Any way you can get a look at the files without him catching on?"

"Maybe. I'll try anyway and get back to you."

"And watch for any mention of the name ShadowPrince, too," Eryn added.

"Explain," Rudd demanded.

It was time Rudd knew about the ransomware, so Eryn told her about it. "I'm thinking Petrov hired someone to do the hack."

"But why?"

"To stop me from teaching the class where you'd learn how to prove pictures came from certain phones."

"Do you think some of the pictures in our investigation could lead back to this Olson guy? If so, Petrov wouldn't want me to be able to expose his blackmailing scheme."

Eryn nodded. "See what you can find out. In the meantime, we'll do some digging on our own."

The elevator doors opened, and Rudd escorted them through the locked door to the lobby. "I'll be in touch."

Eryn and Trey stepped onto the busy downtown Portland street, and Eryn caught a whiff of something savory cooking, making her stomach growl.

Trey faced her. "If Petrov is blackmailing the person who took the pictures, it makes sense that he wouldn't want Rudd to take your class so she could figure out who took them."

"Agreed, but I think he's telling the truth about not being computer literate. So he had to have hired someone to deploy the software to scare me off. Our best bet now is to try to figure out who he's blackmailing."

"Olson is a common name. How exactly do you plan to do some digging?"

"I'll start with public figures or influential businessmen. These are the guys who have the most to lose and would be very susceptible to blackmail."

"Then you best be careful," Trey warned. "Men who have something to lose can be dangerous. Very dangerous."

21
———

Eryn didn't want to leave town without at least doing a cursory investigation into potential blackmail subjects. "Mind if we find a coffee shop so I can do a little research on the name Olson? Maybe grab something to eat."

"Works for me. I saw a Starbucks south of here on the way in." He gestured for her to go ahead of him, but when she did, he gently guided her to the inside of the sidewalk.

He never forgot about her safety, and her heart was touched by his care and compassion. She didn't know how much longer she could ignore these feelings she was developing for him. Even more important, she didn't know if she wanted to anymore.

She sighed, drawing Trey's attention.

"Anything I can help you work out?"

"No." She picked up her pace, winding in and out of pedestrians and forcing her mind from Trey. She enjoyed strolling along the tree-lined streets. Enjoyed the warm breeze when it was often so chilly in Cold Harbor. Enjoyed the smell of coffee filling the air as they reached the Starbucks.

Trey held the door for her, and surprisingly there was no line. She ordered a chicken and quinoa protein bowl while he got a chicken wrap, and they both ordered black coffee.

As they waited for their food, she took out her phone and typed "elected officials Portland, Oregon" in a search engine. She opened the official City of Portland website and scanned the list of positions. Near the top of the page she saw a city commissioner named Avery Olson. She clicked on his link and brought up his bio. He'd held office for three successive terms, and he was very involved in education.

The barista called Trey's name, and he collected their order. They found a small table by the window and took a seat.

Trey distributed the food. "Anything?"

"I found Commissioner Avery Olson. One of his passions is education."

"Which might give him access to children, fitting the porn aspect of the investigation."

"Exactly." She grimaced. "I really hate the way we have to think sometimes. I'd much rather think he's a good guy passionate about education."

"I hear you on that." Trey opened his wrap and took a large bite.

She uncovered her bowl, scooped up a bite, and tapped the "In the News" link on her phone. A page of listings opened, and she read down them to the first post involving education. She continued to eat and read the articles until a photo opened, and she sat back stunned.

"What is it?" Trey asked.

"Olson knows Petrov." She held out the picture of Olson and Petrov shaking hands outside a downtown preschool where they'd worked on a fundraiser together.

Trey frowned when she expected excitement. "This isn't

enough to go barreling into a councilman's office and accuse him of child porn."

"I know. What we really need are phone records and bank account information. Or for Rudd to get those files on the investigation that she hasn't seen yet." Eryn took her phone back. "I'll call her and give her a heads up on Olson so she can watch for anything referencing him in the investigation. And maybe she can also get a look at Petrov's phone."

After the call, Eryn started eating in earnest as she pondered their next move.

"Are you still thinking Veronika Abram is involved in the ransomware?" Trey balled up his wrapper and took a sip of his coffee.

Eryn shook her head. "I'm convinced Petrov is behind this hack now, and we haven't found anything yet to connect him to Veronika. But if she's not involved in the ransomware, why did she have my business card?"

"Actually," he said. "I can't seem to let that go. I think you were right earlier. That she wanted your help with finding whoever took the pictures of the captured fox."

"If so, her death is totally unrelated to the ransomware. So who killed her and why?"

"Someone in direct opposition to her goal. Like the person who took the fox."

"Could be, I suppose. But if she came to the resort to talk to me, why dress up like a fox?"

"Maybe she thought you wouldn't talk to her, and she had to do something to get your attention." He paused for a minute. "I know Blake interviewed Coker, but I'm liking him for this murder."

She frowned, tapping her finger on the table. "What's his motive?"

Trey set down his cup and leaned closer. "Imagine Veronika arriving at the resort. She wants to get your attention. Maybe she's out front planning to upstage Coker, but he's not having anything of it. So he lures her away. She tells him she's here to get your help. He can't let that happen, right? I mean, if you helped save the cute fox, people would side in your favor, and he would strike out. He takes her aside because he doesn't want people to see her. When they're alone, he asks her to let it go. She refuses, and he shoots her."

"He's just unstable enough to do that." Eryn's eyes burned with intensity. "We need to track him down while we're in town and question him again."

"Sounds like a good idea to me." Trey started clearing the table. "But shouldn't we check in with Blake first? You know. Keep him informed."

"Yeah, probably." She got out her phone and dialed Blake, but the call went to voicemail.

"He's not answering," she said. "I'll try him again later, but first I'll get Coker's contact information."

"Can you find him?"

"Are you seriously asking *me*—the great computer master—that question?" She wrinkled her nose at him. "I'll be talking to him in a few minutes. Mark my words."

Trey loved that Eryn could find humor after all she'd been through. She really was resilient, and he was beginning to think she didn't need anyone's help. But the hacker and her attacker were most likely hoping he'd let his guard down, when in fact, the closer they got to the suspect, the more vigilant Trey needed to be.

"Got Coker's phone number. Let's see if he'll meet with us." She dialed and held out the phone for Trey to hear the conversation.

He leaned close to her, and her nearness sent his thoughts whirling in every direction they shouldn't go. He shoved them away and focused on the phone, willing Coker to answer. On the fourth ring, he muttered a grumpy hello.

Trey didn't like Coker's tone, and Trey prayed that the guy would be amenable to Eryn's request.

"Eryn Calloway, here," she said as pleasantly as if she were calling a friend.

"Didn't get enough of harassing me at the resort?" Coker replied. "Now you need to do it by phone?"

"Are you afraid of a little conversation?" she asked, taunting him, and Trey loved seeing her give back as good as she got.

"I'm not afraid of anything," he snarled.

Her lips tipped in a victorious smile. "Then you wouldn't mind if I stopped by your place to have a chat with you. I'm in Portland now."

"Bring it on."

"Your address?" she asked casually.

He rattled off a nearby location, and she said goodbye.

"To the Batmobile, Robin." She grinned widely and shot to her feet.

"If anyone in the relationship is Robin, it's you." Trey mocked tossing a cape over his shoulder as he stood. "I'm Batman all the way."

Laughing together, they disposed of their trash and headed outside. The minute they hit the street, Trey forgot all about joking to deliver her safely to the parking garage. The place was dark and dank after the sunshine in the busy downtown Portland street, raising Trey's vigilance even higher.

She settled in the car, and when he slammed the door, he felt a sense of relief. He didn't know how many times he could escort her somewhere before something bad happened. The odds had to be growing that the suspect was going to try something again soon.

Inside the car, he punched Coker's address into the GPS and started the vehicle. He was starting to have regrets over agreeing to take her to this lunatic's place. He looked at her. "You should try Blake again so someone knows where we're going."

"Good idea." She dialed his number, and Trey heard it ring until voicemail picked up. "Blake, it's Eryn. We're headed over to Coker's place to question him. Call me when you get a chance."

"Maybe we should reconsider this little visit."

"Are you kidding?" She gaped at him. "No way. Not when he agreed to see us."

"I don't know. I don't like it all of a sudden. He could be a killer, and I'm bringing you right into his lair."

She waved her hand. "We're both carrying. We'll be fine. Let's go before he changes his mind and doesn't let us in."

Hoping she was right, Trey backed out of the space and headed down the ramp.

She turned to him. "I appreciate you remembering Blake in all of this. I should do it more often, but I've been out of law enforcement long enough that I tend to act first then think of him later."

"I'm sure he wouldn't like to hear that." Trey stopped to pay their fee then drove into the bright sunshine.

The GPS voice told him to take a right, and he followed

the directions until they pulled up to a tall concrete-and-glass apartment building a few short miles away.

"He's on the fifth floor." Eryn slid out of the vehicle.

Trey jumped out and rushed around the front to the sidewalk. "Let's take a few seconds to case the place and not rush into danger."

She placed her hands on her hips and stared up at him.

"Humor me," he said. "If our theory is correct and Coker killed Veronika, then he's likely willing to kill you, too."

Her attitude vanished. "We'll proceed with caution then."

"Starting with a vest."

"It's in the chopper."

He shook his head. "I grabbed both of our 'Go Bags' while you were talking with Riley."

One side of her mouth tipped up. "You really are the best, aren't you?"

"I've been trying to tell you that for *days*." He grinned. "Shoot—every time I caught your attention for this past year."

"I'm kind of thickheaded."

"Kind of?"

Her mouth dropped open.

He laughed and considered tipping up her chin, but movement to his side snagged his attention. He instinctively shoved her behind him. It was only a squirrel, but it sobered him up, and he urged her away from the windows. She put on her vest and covered it with a large shirt.

Tucking her under his arm, he slowly moved them to the front door. She didn't question his actions, but actually eased even closer to him. He loved the feel of her body next to his as if she belonged there. He had to work doubly hard not to let that distract him. They reached the building without any incidents, and he pulled open the lobby door. They located the elevator and were standing outside Coker's apartment within minutes.

She slipped out from under Trey's arm and knocked. He immediately felt the loss, but stood aside, ready for action, his focus firmly fixed ahead.

Coker jerked open the door. He eyed Trey. "See you had to bring your bodyguard again. You must really be afraid of me."

"Right." Eryn rolled her eyes.

Coker stepped back, and they entered the studio apartment. A kitchenette filled one wall. The living room ahead and was only big enough for a sofa, a console table behind it, and a television mounted on the wall. Newspapers were piled on the sofa and stacked on the floor. Behind it sat an unmade queen-sized bed.

Trey took particular interest in the suitcase sitting by the door. Was Coker planning to run? But why, when Blake had nothing on the guy? If so, why let them come talk to him? Maybe he was taking a trip to stage another protest.

Trey wouldn't mention the suitcase now, let things play out, and bring it up when the timing seemed right.

Coker swept the papers to the floor, revealing a stained sofa. "Go ahead and sit."

"I'll stand," Eryn said.

"Suit yourself." He plopped down.

Trey stationed himself near Eryn.

"What did you want to talk about?" he asked casually, but his expression was anything but casual.

"ShadowPrince," she said.

"Say what?" Coker tilted his head.

"ShadowPrince. Your online screen name."

He snorted. "You pretend to be a talented computer person, but you're so wrong it's funny."

"I'm not wrong when I say you murdered Veronika Abram, though, am I?" Eryn kept her focus locked on Coker.

He didn't move. Didn't blink. Not even a twitch of his finger. A perfect tell for his guilt. He finally narrowed his eyes.

"Veronika who?" he asked, but the damage had been done. His body language told them he had indeed killed Veronika.

"The woman dressed in the fox costume," Eryn said, her voice steely. "I expected you'd at least have learned her name before you killed her."

He crossed his arms. "I didn't kill anyone."

"Why don't I believe you?" Eryn said, tapping her finger on her chin. "Let's see. You were seen near the playground at her time of death. You were carrying. The police have matched your gun to the bullet recovered from Veronika's body."

Trey was shocked that she added the last bit as they knew no such thing. Maybe she was hoping as a layperson he didn't understand the process of matching a bullet to a particular weapon.

Coker leapt up from the couch, his gaze spiteful and challenging. "Right, like I'd buy that. You must think I'm stupid. If the police had anything on me, they'd have arrested me."

Trey took a step in his direction.

"Down boy." Coker waved his arm dismissively. "I'm going to get a glass of water. Either of you want anything?"

"No," Eryn said. "Other than for you to admit you killed Veronika."

Coker snorted and went to the kitchenette. With his back to them, he grabbed a glass from a cupboard and filled it. "Maybe you could tell me the reason I would want to kill a woman I don't even know."

Trey gave Eryn a look trying to tell her that she should take things down a notch, but she shook her head and put a finger up.

Coker spun, sipped on his glass, and stared at Eryn over the rim. His eyes were unfocused and seemed to be glazing over with anger. He crossed back to the living room and set his glass on the console table. He was only a few feet from Eryn. Trey took a step to insert himself between them.

"Why the suitcase?" Trey asked thinking it was the right time as Coker seemed to be losing it and might not be able to focus later.

"Suitcase?"

Trey gestured at the packed bag. "You running from something?"

A knock sounded on the door, grabbing their attention.

"Police. Open up, Coker. We have a warrant for your arrest." Trey recognized Blake's voice.

Trey turned back to see Coker whipping out a large butcher knife from his sleeve, grabbing Eryn, and pressing the blade against Eryn's throat.

"No!" Trey yelled. He wouldn't let Coker hurt her. *Couldn't* let Coker hurt her.

Fierce pounding sounded at the door.

Coker glanced over, panicked, and his hold on Eryn loosened.

Trey seized the moment and karate chopped Coker's arm away from Eryn. She stumbled away.

Coker lunged at Trey with the knife.

Trey jerked back. Not fast enough.

The knife came down in a furious slash. Bit into Trey's left arm. Deep. Tearing. Ripping.

Coker yanked back, and the gash widened. Blood spurted out. He must have hit bone. Pain razored into Trey's arm and the room swam.

Eryn screamed. "Drop it, Coker! I'll shoot!"

Coker whipped around with the bloody knife, and Trey slammed him to the ground. He writhed and screeched like a banshee, trying to stab Trey.

Trey saw Eryn aiming her gun, but they were grappling too furiously for her to get a shot in. Blood was spurting everywhere.

The world was going black. Dark and welcoming. He swallowed and fought hard not to pass out when Eryn needed him.

～

Then door splintered and cracked as Blake and another officer burst in the room, yelling.

Trey seized the moment to slam Coker's arm down and dislodge the knife. Eryn sighed out her relief and kicked it away. Blake got Coker's arms behind his back and cuffed him. Officers rushed in and hauled the screaming man out of the apartment.

Trey dragged himself away to lean against the couch and gripped his arm. There was blood everywhere, and panic reared up in Eryn's body. An eight-inch gash ripped open Trey's forearm, deep and jagged.

Could she stop this much bleeding before the medics arrived? She had to. Trey depended on her.

She charged to the kitchen and grabbed towels. She swallowed down her queasiness and wrapped the gaping wound tightly then applied firm pressure. She hated that she must be hurting Trey. The color had drained from his face, but he remained conscious. His jaw twitched and sweat ran down his face as he breathed rapidly.

"I'm so sorry." Her voice wavered as she locked on to his gaze.

"For what?" He tried to smile but his lips trembled. "You didn't cut me."

"I should've listened to you. Known Coker would try something like this and leave it to Blake." She grabbed another towel to cover the first which was saturated with blood.

Blake, standing in the doorway, snorted. "If only I had a recording of that to play back to you." He looked down the hall. "Hang in there, Trey. Medics are a few minutes out."

"Coker?" Trey asked.

"On his way to booking." Blake responded. "FYI, we took possession of Coker's gun this morning. Likely why he needed to use a knife. The rifling on the bullet removed from Veronika's body matched Coker's gun. Which is why we're here."

"So he *was* planning to run," Trey muttered.

"Yeah, saw the suitcase," Blake replied.

"If only you would've answered your phone." Eryn protested.

He eyed her. "If only you would've waited until you'd spoken to me. I was strategizing with PPB."

"Point taken."

An ambulance siren screamed nearby, and she almost sighed with relief, but Trey wasn't out of danger yet.

Blake focused on Trey. "I'll be adding assault with a deadly weapon to Coker's murder charge."

Trey nodded.

Eryn's heart shredded from seeing him so pale and limp.

Father, please. Please watch over Trey and let him recover. I can't lose him. I just can't.

Blake looked at Eryn. "Are you any closer to proving he hacked your computer?"

She knew he wanted the answer, but even more, he was trying to keep Trey's mind from the injury. She kept an eye on Trey and shared their theory about Coker's motives.

"You could be right," Blake said. "Hopefully, when I question him, he'll explain."

"I don't think he had anything to do with the ransomware, though." She told Blake about their interview with Petrov.

Blake frowned. "You better be certain of what you're saying before you accuse a veteran detective of blackmail."

"I'm not ready to make any accusations. Just a working theory."

"Well, when you do have proof, don't confront Petrov like you did Coker. With Petrov's law enforcement training, he could be even more dangerous." Blake rushed in the hallway. "Medics—in here!"

She turned her gaze back to Trey. "Looks like the bleeding's slowed."

"Thanks for that." He tried to rise up on his elbow but fell back.

"Relax, tough guy. Let the medics do their job." She backed away as two medics rushed into the room and began working on him.

She looked down at her blood-saturated hands. Trey's blood. His lifeline. Poured out here. Because of her. He could've died.

A flood of anxiety crashed through her body, and she

panicked, remembering Rich's death. That terrible night when he'd died in a bloody crash. She put a wall up around her heart. She couldn't survive the pain of another loss. She'd see Trey all the way through recovery, and then they'd go their separate ways.

22

On the chopper heading to Cold Harbor, Eryn watched Trey like a hawk as the sun started its descent toward the horizon. Trey had suffered only a class II hemorrhage and didn't need a blood transfusion, only a Lactated Ringer's solution.

Thank you, God.

The ER doctor offered strong pain meds, but Trey adamantly refused. The only pain relief he'd gotten was a lidocaine injection before the doctor cleaned and closed the deep wound with thirty stitches. Thirty pain-filled agonizing stitches. And that didn't count the subcutaneous sutures. Eryn had held his other hand through it, even when he tried to refuse, and had felt him jerk with the deeper stitches.

When the doctor was done, Eryn continued to hold his hand, watching him breathe as the IV dripped into him. His color was better and he didn't look as weak, but she didn't like that he wasn't under a doctor's care. She'd told the doctor as much. He said the pain was most likely causing Trey's symptoms, and that the best thing she could do for him was to convince him to take his pain meds. She would try.

After the IV ran out, they released him and now they were back in the helo. He shifted in his seat and winced.

"I wish you'd take the pain meds," she said into her headset.

"Maybe when we get to the compound."

Translated, once she was behind secured fences and safer.

"No one's coming for me, Trey. Not up here in the chopper and not in the compound." She met his gaze and held it. "Please take the meds. For me, if not for yourself."

"You?"

"I don't like seeing you like this. Pale. Sweating. Obviously in pain from an injury you incurred while saving my life."

"I'm fine."

"You say that, but that's because you can't see yourself."

"I don't have to see me. I am me."

She sighed. "And you said *I* was stubborn."

He quirked a smile. "Never claimed I wasn't equally stubborn at times."

She took the hand of his uninjured arm. "I'll let this go for now, but expect me to bring it up again once we land. And know that Hannah will join me in my quest."

"She will, won't she." He shook his head. "I don't know which of you is a bigger mother hen."

"Eryn is," Riley chimed in. "No question. She tries to boss us around on ops all the time, and Hannah sticks to our private lives."

Trey chuckled then grimaced.

"Time for us to all be quiet so you can get some rest."

She released his hand and gently pulled his head toward her shoulder.

"See what I mean?" Riley said.

She ignored Riley while Trey shifted in his seat and settled his head in place. His soft hair caressed her cheek, and her heart nearly exploded with joy at having him so close. She didn't like that he was injured, but she loved that it gave her a reason to touch him and not have to worry he would take it the wrong way.

She rested her head against his, her heart swimming with emotions. She heard him breathe easier and could tell by the even rise and fall of his chest that he'd drifted off to sleep.

They remained that way until Riley set the chopper down. Trey came awake in a startle and sat up. He glanced around then met her gaze and smiled. A soft smile that said he couldn't think of anything better than waking to find her at his side. She couldn't resist the gentleness in his look and touched the side of his face. He pressed his hand over hers, and they lingered there. Looking at each other. Mesmerized. Unwilling to pull away.

"Um...guys. We're home." Riley's voice came through the headset. "You have a welcoming committee so maybe take this back to your place."

Eryn snapped her gaze free and felt her face flush with embarrassment at her lack of restraint. She removed her headset.

"Mind helping me with mine?" Trey asked.

She lifted it off and moved a lock of his hair back into place.

"For the record, I like it when you blush like that." He grinned again. "You're this incredibly tough woman who can handle herself with killers and other criminals, and then you blush over being caught looking at me. It's really sweet."

His comment made her face burn even more, and she hurried to climb past him to the door. She spotted Hannah and Gage standing near the utility vehicle, both gazes dark with concern, the sun a glowing ball behind them. Eryn turned to offer her hand to help Trey, but he ignored it and jumped down. She saw him cringe and his eyes go dark, but he quickly whisked the emotions away. They ducked under the slowing rotors and made their way to Gage and Hannah.

Gage eyed Trey. "How bad is it?"

"Just a scratch," Trey said.

"Hah!" Eryn said. "A scratch that took over thirty stitches to close and that doesn't count the subcutaneous sutures."

Gage frowned. "Sorry, man. You know I hate it when my people get hurt."

"No biggie," Trey replied, also not addressing the "my people" comment.

Hannah took a step closer. "Your face says something else."

"See?" Eryn looked up at him. "I told you your pain is obvious." She looked at Hannah. "He won't take his pain meds because he thinks he has to protect me."

"I get that," Gage said.

Trey gave a quick nod. "Knew you would."

"But she's safe here at the compound," Hannah said.

Gage looked at his wife. "Reasonably, yeah. But if her attacker is as determined as yours was—"

"He could try to breach security," Hannah finished for him.

"Right now, I don't even want to think about that," Eryn said. "I want to get Trey back to my place and settle him on the couch so he can rest."

Trey's eyes narrowed. "I rested on the helo."

"Doesn't mean you don't need more." Eryn almost clucked at him like the mother hen they'd accused her of being but refrained from doing so. "And food. I plan to feed you until you pop, then we'll all get a good night's sleep."

"Let me bring dinner over," Hannah offered. "I've got a big roast beef in the oven and there's plenty."

Trey shook his head. "You don't have to baby—"

"That would be wonderful," Eryn said.

Gage's mouth turned up in a wry smile. "Go with the pampering, man. Or you'll wear yourself out arguing."

Trey smiled, but it was half grimace.

"Let's get you home." It wasn't lost on Eryn that she'd said "home" when it wasn't his home, so she quickly gestured at the vehicle to cover up her comment, but the others didn't miss it. Of course, they didn't. They didn't miss anything.

"You two go ahead," Hannah said. "We'll walk with Riley."

Eryn knew Hannah hoped to give them privacy, something they totally didn't need, but Eryn wanted to get Trey off his feet so she didn't argue. He slipped behind the wheel before she could protest, so she let him drive. It wasn't far.

They drove down the road, and Eryn was happy to see familiar sights that included a big training facility about the size of a basketball court. Next came a small town made of cutout storefronts that they used for urban training, and then they drove past cabins where trainees stayed, until they finally reached the staff cabin area.

Eryn's mother met them at the door. She peered up at Trey. "Are you all right?"

"Fine, and let's not talk about it again," he said sounding a bit put out. "I don't want to worry Bekah."

Even now he was concerned about others. A character trait Eryn had to add to the long list of traits that was swaying her toward getting involved with him when she'd just resolved to walk away from him.

Is that you again, God?

Bekah was playing on the floor with Legos. She caught sight of Trey, and her face lit up. She hopped up and came barreling toward Trey. Eryn stepped between them and intercepted her daughter before she slammed into him.

Eryn knelt down next to Bekah. "Trey hurt his arm today, and you need to be extra careful not to bump him. Or even touch his arm. Okay, sweetie?"

Bekah looked up at Trey, a serious expression on her face. "I have Disney Band-Aids if you want one."

Trey's soft smile spread across his face. "I would be most honored to have one."

She spun and ran toward the bathroom.

"I need to get going," Eryn's mother said. "I have laundry waiting at home."

"Thanks, mom." Eryn turned to Trey and pointed at the couch. "Sit. Now. I'll get you some juice to start with."

He settled on the sofa and gave her a mischievous smile. "Can I have cookies, too?"

"Me, too, Mommy." Bekah raced back into the room. "Cookies and juice."

"Yes, to both of you, but you have to sit down and not bounce."

"I won't bounce," Trey promised and grinned.

Eryn heard her mother chuckling as she stepped out the door.

"She means me," Bekah said. "I like to bounce. It will hurt your arm. I don't want to hurt your arm." She stared at his bandaged arm. "Hey! No fair! You already have a biggest Band-Aid."

"Yes, but it's not special like yours." He tweaked Bekah's nose. "We can put one right at the end of this one."

Bekah ripped open the package and looked at Trey's arm in the same way she did when she mothered her dolls. Eryn knew he was in for a zealous Band-Aid application, and she needed to prevent that.

"Better let me help with that." Eryn knelt near Trey and held out her hand for the Band-Aid. She tore off the plastic strips and gently placed it as far to the end of his real bandage as possible, being extra careful not to hurt him.

He lifted his arm. "There. It's all better now."

Eryn stood. "Remember—no bouncing, Bekah."

She looked up at him, her eyes wide. "Can I sit on your lap if I'm very, very careful, and you can read me a book?"

Eryn shook her head. "Trey needs to rest."

"I don't need rest," he replied. "I'm happy to read a book, but you're going to have to hold it."

"Yippee." She started to launch herself at him, and Eryn took hold of her daughter's arm to slow her down.

Trey quickly lifted his injured arm to the back of the sofa, and Bekah settled in place.

"I'll get a book," Eryn said.

Eryn picked a short one so Trey could move quickly through the story and then rest. She handed it to Bekah who frowned. "Wanted a different one."

"Not me," Trey said and looked at the cover. "Now that I've seen this, I have to know everything about *Jesus and the Twelve Dudes Who Did*."

"K." Bekah slid back on his lap, stretched out her legs, and perched the book on her knees.

Trey started reading, and the picture of the two of them

filled Eryn's heart with such emotion and longing she had to take a breath. She'd become more than fond of Trey. Without a doubt, this was what she wanted in life. A man she loved and who loved Bekah.

Shocked, she stood staring as the familiar pain of loss came rushing in. The feel of Trey's blood on her hands not yet gone. She may know now what she wanted for her future, but her reaction said she wasn't ready for it.

Not yet.

Father, can you help? I feel like you put Trey in our life for a reason. But you also allowed him to be hurt by Coker for a reason. The blood. It was too much. Is Trey here to protect us, or is it more than that? I really want to know. Truly. With my whole heart this time. Please show me, and if I have the chance at a future with Trey, help me to get over this fear of losing him.

He looked up and caught her gaze. A slow smile slid across his face, and she wanted to stand and look at him forever.

"Keep reading, Trey," Bekah said, drawing his attention again.

Eryn felt lighter inside as she went into the kitchen for their snacks. She almost felt like humming. She'd forgotten how wonderful it was to cast her cares on God. To stop trying to do things on her own and be open for His leading. How blessed she was that despite her distance since Rich died, God was still there. His arms open. Waiting. Welcoming her back.

She poured two glasses of juice, one in a covered container for Bekah, and seeing them together on the tray brought back her newfound wishes. Could they really have a future? She suddenly hoped it was possible. Hoped more than she could imagine.

She grabbed a container of peanut butter cookies her

mother had baked and plated them, then carried the tray into the living room. Trey was just reaching the end of the book. She set the snack on the coffee table.

Bekah closed the book and spotted the cookies. "Gammy made the cookies. Peanut butter is my favorite."

"One of mine, too," Trey said.

She pushed off his lap and looked up at Eryn. "Can I eat in here, Mommy? Can I?"

Bekah was never allowed to eat anywhere but at the dining table or kitchen island, but today, Eryn would make an exception. "If you sit nice and quiet and hold your cookie over your plate."

"Yippee," she said and grabbed her cookie to start munching.

Trey leaned forward, and Eryn held up a hand. "Relax, I'll get yours for you."

He frowned.

"What's wrong?"

"I don't need to be babied. I'm fine."

"You're not fine, but you're right. You are more than capable of getting your own snack." She handed it to him and sat on the sofa. "This is my way of saying thank you."

"No thanks needed." He met her gaze. "You know that, right? I would move heaven and earth to keep you safe."

His tone was urgent and forceful, and she felt his commitment to her bones. What had she done to deserve this man wanting to protect her so fiercely?

Thank you, Father.

She peered at Trey's bandage where blood had seeped through. Panic assailed her. She swallowed it down and said another prayer. Forced the panic to subside. Could she really overcome this? She certainly had a reason to.

They ate their snacks in silence.

Bekah brushed the crumbs from her chin onto the plate. "Can I play in my room?"

"Sorry, pumpkin. It's way past your bedtime."

"Wanna play with Trey."

"He needs to go to bed, too," Eryn said. "Now scoot and get your jammies on and I'll be in to brush your teeth soon."

Bekah scampered away, her lip still protruding.

"Looks like I'm the world's worst mother today." Eryn's phone dinged with a text. She glanced to see a message from Gage. "That's odd. Gage says to turn on the Portland news right away."

She grabbed the remote and clicked on the TV. A reporter was standing outside PPB's central precinct, a picture of Petrov in the upper right corner. She turned up the volume.

"In a startling discovery today," the female reporter said. "Twenty-five-year veteran of the police force, Detective Ivan Petrov has been arrested and charged with ignoring evidence in a child pornography investigation and using that evidence to blackmail Councilman Avery Olson."

Eryn gawked at the screen. "Oh my gosh. We were right."

"And Rudd must've found a way to prove it," Trey said, looking equally stunned.

Eryn grabbed her phone and dialed Detective Rudd. The call went to voicemail. "Detective Rudd, it's Eryn Calloway. I saw that Petrov has been arrested for blackmail. How did that happen? And did you find anything in the files about ShadowPrince? Call me as soon as you can."

Eryn hung up and looked at Trey. "If Petrov is behind the hacking, then with him in jail, it could mean this is all over."

"Could," he said, but didn't sound enthusiastic.

"Why the gloomy face? We can get on with life again. Go

back to the way things were," she said before she remem-bered that wasn't actually what she wanted anymore.

His body stiffened. "Trust me, I'm all for you being safe again. But my old life without you? I'm not sure I can go back to that ever again."

23

Hours later, Trey shifted on the couch and finally sat up. The house was quiet. Way too quiet. Bekah had gone to bed three hours ago, and Eryn had taken her laptop to her room to work. He'd hoped she would stay in the living room with him, but she said she wanted him to rest. She was more than likely running from his declaration that he didn't want to go back to his old life without her.

He'd felt safe in saying it because she'd been so tender and caring. It felt like she crossed some line as if she might want to risk a future with him. Until he'd mentioned that future. Then she shut down. Now he didn't know how to get back to the easiness before he'd said that.

He sighed, and he wasn't a sighing kind of guy. He was a *take action* kind of guy. *A get to the point* kind of guy. He'd been so patient. Letting her come to grips with how she was feeling. But he was done tiptoeing around the subject. Time to talk it out once and for all.

He got up, his arm aching with the movement. Tylenol had dulled the pain a bit, but he still wished he was free to take the pain meds. He wouldn't. Even with Petrov in jail they didn't know for sure that he was behind the hacking and Eryn's attack. And as long as Trey was in charge of watching over Eryn, he wouldn't let drugs alter his mental state.

He strode to her room. She sat on her bed piled high with girly type pillows he never expected she would own. She was such a study in contrasts, and he loved everything he was learning about her. She was so wrapped up in staring at the same computer she'd had at the resort that she didn't even notice him standing there. Another reason he needed to keep an eye on her.

He tapped on the doorjamb.

She looked up and a soft smile spread across her face before she quickly erased it. Yeah, she was definitely giving off mixed signals, and he was going to find out why.

"How's the arm?" she asked. "Do you need something? Food. A drink. Tylenol."

"No."

"Then—" Something flashed on her computer screen lighting her face in a red tint. She moved her focus to the screen. She shot straight up, her mouth falling open.

Trey rushed over to her. "What is it?"

"More ransomware and another message."

He waited for her to show him the message, but when she didn't, he turned the computer so he could see the screen. He read the bold black letters on the red screen.

Did you think I wouldn't know how to find you? How to hack into your network?

He swallowed hard. "This means Petrov isn't behind the hack, and whoever is has gotten to your computer again."

She snatched up her phone and tapped the screen, then gasped. "Not only my computer. He's taken control of our entire network."

Trey didn't like the sound of that. "What does that mean exactly?"

She looked up at him, face white. "With our network down, we have no security system."

His gut twisted into a tight knot. "How long to fix it? A couple of hours like when you did the computers at the resort?"

"I wish," she said. "He got through security I worked months to develop. It'll take me all night—if not longer—to restore it and ensure he can't hack into it again."

"I can put on a pot of coffee."

"Thanks, but I can't do this here." She swung her legs over the edge of the bed. "I need to work in our server room at our training building."

"Then I'll make the coffee there."

She shook her head. "You stay here. Our weapons arsenal is in that building, and Gage will assign one of the guys to protect it. So I'll be fine."

Trey fisted his hands. "This isn't up for discussion. I'm coming with you."

She closed her computer and stood up, dark eyes flashing. "I need you to stay here with Bekah. She's my first priority, and I need to know she's safe so I can work without distraction."

"You're the one who's in danger. I'm sure someone else can watch her."

"She's in danger, too, by virtue of the fact that she's in my cabin. If this hacker comes for me, then she'll be in danger. Or maybe he'll try to hurt her to get to me. Either way, she shouldn't be with me, and I can't be worried about her."

"Then we'll move her to Gage's house and under his protection. I'm sure he'll agree."

Eryn locked eyes with him. "I still want you with her."

261

He didn't buy her argument. "Are you sure this isn't about my injury? That you don't trust me to be able to protect you?"

"It's not that at all." She yanked her hand through her hair. "Here's the thing, Trey. Over the last few days I've come to care for you more than I want to."

His heart soared, but the danger brought it back down to earth. "And that's a bad thing?"

"Yeah, because nothing else has changed for me." She pinched the bridge of her nose. "No, that's not true. What *has* changed is that you're constantly in my thoughts, and when you're nearby, my mind wanders to you and what might be, and I can't work."

"Which is why you came in here tonight."

"Exactly. And I've *got* to fix this—we are in serious danger. So can you take Bekah to Gage's place and stay with her?" She squeezed his uninjured arm. "Please?"

How could he say no to her pleading look? He nodded.

"Good. Thank you." She smiled but it quickly evaporated. "You should know how dangerous this is. Our business network is so secure only an extremely talented actor could bring it down. We don't use it for the Internet. We have a separate network for that, so there's no chance he deployed the ransomware by one of our people inadvertently opening an email or uploading a malware file from a flash drive."

"But you do think this is the same hacker from the resort."

"Yes, but he didn't show his true abilities with the earlier hacks. Gave me just enough to lead me on, but he limited my knowledge of his protocols and that kept me from seeing his expertise."

"So why reveal it now?"

"Because it appears he wanted to bring down our network." She met his gaze, and he didn't like the look in her eyes. "And that tells me he's far more dangerous than we ever imagined. If he's after me—or wants to destroy our systems—we may not be able to stop him. He could be breaking into the compound right now."

∼

Eryn notified the team who kicked into high gear with emergency protocols. Trey got Bekah safely to Gage's house, and Riley escorted Eryn to their main hub. Eryn settled behind the network computer, heart pounding. But the ransomware message vanished.

Not again. Seriously, what is this guy up to?

She quickly took the network down before he could do additional damage and went straight to work on locating and reviewing his code. It took almost two hours, but she finally let out a long breath and sat back.

This actor had skills. Mad skills. In her many year of working cyber crimes, she'd only run across one actor who displayed such complex abilities. Kirill Velichko. She assumed there were other actors with top-notch skills like his, but she had to wonder if Velichko was behind this code and the attack.

Memories of the day she'd arrested him came rushing back. He'd glared at her, acting all cocky and declaring he'd be released before the day was out. She'd lost it. Snapped at him to take him down a peg. And she had. He'd gone to prison and was still there.

The door opened behind her, and she turned.

Riley poked his head in. "Got a text from Trey. He said he hasn't heard from you in a while, and he didn't want to bother you, so asked me to poke my head in to be sure you were okay."

"Guess he figured I'd be too wrapped up in my work to notice the time." She stretched to get the kinks out of her tense muscles, inwardly smiling over Trey's ongoing attention and how much this simple gesture of kindness impacted her. "You can tell him I'm fine."

"I doubt he'll believe me, but yeah, I'll tell him." He pointed at her computer. "Any luck?"

"Not on getting the network up yet, but I'm getting a déjà vu feeling on this ransomware code."

He rested against the doorframe. "How's that?"

"When I was at the FBI, I arrested this really crafty actor named Kirill Velichko. He stands out in my mind because he was so talented and could've gotten rich from hacking, but in an odd way he hacked for the good of the Internet."

Riley leaned closer. "Okay, now you've got to explain that to me."

"He went by the online name of Gatekeeper and built a malicious botnet."

"Botnet?"

"The term comes from combining robot with network, i.e. a network of robot computers." He still looked confused so she continued, "When malware is deployed on a computer these days, it's usually used to take control of the computer, not harm it."

"What do you mean by take control?" Riley asked.

She loved that he was willing to hang in there to figure out how this worked. "If you open malware on your computer, it's like you've given the actor permission to sit down at your keyboard and use your machine. His script gives the computer directions, and it acts on his behalf. Once he has enough computers under his control, he mobi-

264

lizes them like a zombie army to launch cyberattacks that—in almost all cases—involve making money for him."

Riley pushed off the doorjamb. "So let me get this straight. You have this guy who deploys malware and the computer user falls for his tricks. Then he can remotely take control of the computer and make it do things without the user knowing."

She nodded. "There are millions of infected computers in botnets. One of the largest botnets out there is purported to control a half million machines alone."

He whistled under his breath. "But you said this guy is different, and he doesn't make money."

"Right. He claimed that a huge number of Internet of Things devices—like webcams, routers, smart TVs, etc.—are unsecured and vulnerable. Which is right. And he worried about Internet safety, so his solution was to take control of the unsecured devices before anyone else could and kill them before they were zombified. The code he wrote completely destroyed the IoT devices, or *bricked* them as we say in the IT world, rendering them completely useless. Totally useless, even after factory reset. Sure, he was doing something illegal, but he claimed it was for the user's own good to show the danger of hackers exploiting vulnerabilities."

"But you stopped him."

She nodded and felt the same pride today that she felt the day she cracked his code leading to his discovery.

"And you think he's the guy behind this ransomware?" Riley asked.

She shrugged. "He's of Russian descent, so that fits with the code I found, and his build fits my attackers build. Still, this guy's in prison. Or at least he should still be unless he was released early for good behavior."

"Any way you check on that?"

"My FBI contacts should be able to help. Still, if it's not him, the code is sophisticated enough that it has to be someone as talented as he is."

"Then you've got your work cut out for you, right?"

She nodded. "You can tell Trey that I'll be working on this for hours, maybe days, and he should go ahead and get some rest."

"Will do." He started to leave then turned back. "You want a cup of coffee?"

She pointed at her mug and held up a trembling hand. "I'm already way past my limit."

"Then I'll leave you to work and won't bother you again."

"Wait, before you go. Have there been any issues with security?"

He shook his head. "The others are all in position, implementing emergency security protocol."

She rubbed her forehead. "Good. I'll get back to work."

He closed the door. She knew he was headed back to guard their weapon storage room on the far side of the building.

She picked up her phone to call her friend Piper Nash at the FBI. They'd worked cyber crimes together for years, and she would be able to check on Velichko's whereabouts. Eryn started to press Piper's number but saw that it was three a.m. She didn't want to wake Piper over such a remote possibility, so she sent an email instead. She called Gage to update him, and he said he and Trey would search for current information on Velichko.

She worked for another hour and hit a line of code that caused her mouth to fall open before she snapped it shut. She blinked a few times and read it again. "The floodgates are open, Calloway, and your problems are just beginning."

Stunned, she sat back. This guy was quoting her. She remembered the moment she'd said this very thing, and she'd said it only once. To one person. Kirill Velichko.

Seriously. Velichko was behind this.

At least she didn't think Velichko would hire out his services to and especially not for a detective like Petrov. And besides, Petrov was in jail, and his arrest so recent he hadn't likely had contact with anyone on the outside except his lawyer. That meant this was unlikely related to Petrov, and Velichko was messing with her for some reason.

She sat forward to keep moving down the code. She heard the door open again. Likely Riley back for another update. But now that she suspected Velichko, she couldn't pull her eyes from the code until she found his signature.

"Tell Gage I'm getting close," she said.

"Would do," the voice from her past said. "But I don't think I'll see him."

She whirled her chair around, her heart racing as fast as the wheels on her chair.

Kirill Velichko stood there. No disguise. No pretense. Just a gun with a silencer pointed in her direction.

"Don't make a sound," he warned. "I have no qualms about dropping you right here."

24

Trey's arm ached, his head ached, and his worry over Eryn made him edgy. Ever since she called an hour ago, he and Gage had been searching for information on Velichko. It gave him something to do, but when he read about the man, it ratcheted up his anxiety. He had to check in with her. Just had to. A short text should be fine.

You still doing okay? he tapped into his phone.

He watched the screen for a reply, but none came.

You there? he typed.

No response, and a sliver of worry pierced his heart.

"Calm down," he told himself. "She could be using the restroom."

He would give her a few minutes to respond. He got up to pace the length of the family room. He'd kept his shoes on so he could bolt if needed, and they sounded like thunder in the quiet room. He hoped he didn't wake anyone.

Gage stepped into the living room. "I heard you in my office. What's up? Did you find anything?"

"Nothing current, but what I read so far about the guy was disturbing. I texted Eryn, and she's not responding."

"Did you call her?"

"No. I don't want to bother her but thought a quick text was okay. She might be in the restroom."

"Call her." Gage's worried tone upped Trey's anxiety.

He dialed her phone. It rang. Once. Twice. Three times. Four. Five. Voicemail.

"No answer. I'm calling Riley to check on her." He dialed Riley who picked up on the second ring. "Eryn's not answering her phone. When's the last time you saw her?"

"When I checked in on her." There was a pause. "About an hour ago."

"Go check on her. Hurry. Run." Trey heard Riley's boots pounding on the concrete floor, and he could easily visualize him running from the back of the building and around the outside of the conference room to the hallway for the server room.

"Door's open," he said. "She's not in there."

"Check the restroom," the words came out on a strangled breath.

Trey heard Riley's boots again and a door squeak open.

"Eryn," Riley called out. "You in there?"

No response and Trey almost crawled through the phone as he heard Riley banging open stall doors. "She's not here either."

"Maybe she went home for something."

"She would've gone out the front door, and I would've seen her leave."

"Search the building from top to bottom. I'm going to her place to check for her. Let me know what you find." Trey spun on Gage. "Keep an eye out for Bekah. I'll let you know what's happening."

Trey didn't wait for Gage to agree but bolted out the door and jumped into her car, which she insisted on bringing due to his injury. He was very thankful that she'd given him the keys in case he needed to get anything from the cabin for Bekah. He barreled down the road and slammed to a stop in front of her cabin. He hoped to see lights gleaming through the window, but all was dark. If she was in there, she wouldn't be sleeping because he knew the security system wasn't back up. His heart raced, imagining what he might find.

He quietly unlocked the door and flipped on the light, ducking out quickly in case Velichko or someone was there.

After no sound, he cautiously stepped inside and ran his gaze over the room. Everything was exactly the same as when they'd departed, except the answering machine on the countertop was blinking red. He thought it odd that a technophile like Eryn had a landline, but Gage insisted that each team member had one so a 9-1-1 dispatcher could easily trace their call.

Trey slipped into the bedroom and turned on the light. Her bed was empty. He checked the bathroom. Nothing. Then Bekah's room. The other bathroom. Still nothing. His panic grew with each step.

Where are you?

Maybe the message on her answering machine would tell him something. He pressed play.

"Eryn, it's Piper Nash," a woman's voice said. "I got your email about Kirill Velichko."

The hacker.

"He was released early last week. Turns out, on his way out, he told his cellmate that the first thing he was going to do was shut you up. Permanently. The cellmate didn't bother to share that information until he saw a chance to use it to his advantage. I've got one of the Bureau analysts trying to track Velichko down. Will let you know what I find."

Trey's heart clenched, and he grabbed his phone to call Gage. It rang in his hand, and he nearly jumped out of his own skin. "Whatcha got, Riley?"

"I found Eryn's phone. It was in the bushes outside the back door. She would never voluntarily ditch her phone. Her whole life is on that thing."

"I know, call Gage. Velichko has her." That was all he could get out before his heart stuttered like it might stop beating.

Eryn shifted in the car's truck and tried to undo the ropes cutting into her wrists. She had to get free before Velichko exacted whatever revenge he had planned for her. She wished she could get the ratty gag out of her mouth, too. Velichko had bound her wrists, then jerked the rag out of his trunk and tied it around her mouth. It smelled like old gym socks.

She tried to forget about the stench and gouged her fingers into the thick knot at her wrists. She soon felt something wet near her fingertips. Likely blood from clawing at the rope for so long, but so what? Her life was in her own hands right now, and she couldn't give up. She fought through the pain and kept working.

The car slowed and bumped off the road, then slowed even more, coming to crawl.

No. No. She was still bound. She had to hurry. She clawed at the rope. Dug hard. The pain was nearly unbearable. But if Trey could handle his arm being sliced open, she could handle raw and bloody fingertips.

The brakes squeaked and the vehicle stopped.

Faster. Faster. Hurry.

She dug harder.

A car door opened.

Harder. Dig harder.

The door slammed.

She got a finger in the knot. Tugged.

Footsteps sounded over gravel.

She pried hard. Gained movement.

Yes! She was almost there. Almost free. Just another minute. That was all she needed.

The trunk latch popped.

No. Not yet. No.

The trunk opened, revealing Velichko's big body blocking a sparkling starry night.

"I warned you." He scowled, making his narrow face even longer and emphasizing his nose resembling an eagle's beak. He had a cleft in his chin that she remembered him touching during the trial where her testimony put him behind bars. Above it, he had a soul patch that was as black as his bushy brows and thick hair.

She wanted so desperately for him to take off her gag so she could ask him why he abducted her, but he didn't seem the least inclined to. She feared this was payback for arresting and testifying against him. But maybe he was abducting her to help him with a computer issue. It was possible anyway, and she preferred that thought to him killing her.

He jerked her up and lifted her from the trunk to settle her on the ground, the infernal gun going back to her temple. "We're going for a walk."

She stared at his darkly shadowed face. He looked sinister and dangerous. She knew he was. Sure, he claimed to do be doing his hacking for the good of the Internet, but in reality, he did it to feel powerful after a childhood of abuse. And she'd ended his chosen method of relief from his pain. Now she was afraid he planned to inflict that terrible pain on her.

He kept hold of her arm and urged her forward. The first light of dawn illuminated an overgrown path, and she could hear the ocean waves pounding. So much for helping him with a computer issue. He was taking her down to the beach.

No. No. Don't let him take me into the water. Anything but water.

Her footsteps faltered. He shoved her ahead, and they wound down the sandy slope toward the waves pulsing in. Panic stole her breath. She wanted to beg him to stop but couldn't. And she hoped even if she *could* speak, she wouldn't let him see the fear seizing her insides.

At a large outcropping of rocks, he urged her to turn right and walk parallel to the shoreline.

Yes, good! Not the ocean. Thank you, God! Thank you.

They crested a hill and below she saw a small opening in the rocks likely leading to a cave.

A cave? He didn't plan to put her in there, did he?

He shoved her forward. She took slow steps. He yanked her to the opening. If he abandoned her inside until high tide, the place would become a stone grave.

She had to stop him. But how with a gun to her head?

She couldn't. Only God could. She stopped to lift her face in prayer and knew her life was totally in His hands now. Totally. Completely. She'd come to the end of herself and could do nothing.

Velichko flicked on a flashlight and pushed her ahead. A sudden dawning hit her. Her life had always been in God's hands. She knew that subconsciously, but did she really think about it? Realize what it practically meant? Not really. He was in supreme control. Absolute. No matter what she wanted...what she feared...as a believer, God's will would be done.

She sought His comfort now. His assurance. And she felt Him with her whole heart. Like Trey had said would happen when she truly sought God. She knew deep in her being that whatever the outcome, God had her in His hands.

25

Trey charged toward the training facility, the dawning light making the trip easier. He felt numb inside. And afraid. And worried. Terrified actually. All at once. But he had to swallow it all down and find Eryn.

Gage and Riley met him right inside the door, their tight expressions doing nothing to aid Trey in calming down.

"I found a Piper Nash in Eryn's contacts." Riley held out Eryn's phone.

Trey grabbed it and dialed this Piper woman.

"Special Agent Piper Nash," she answered, her cheerful voice grating on Trey's nerves.

"You called Eryn Calloway a few minutes ago. She's missing, and we're trying to find her." His words rushed out so fast he was surprised that they were clear.

"Who is this?" Her tone had turned wary.

"Deschutes County Deputy Trey Sawyer. I've been in charge of Eryn's security detail this week when a hacker took control of her computer with ransomware and threatened her life."

"Okay, I'm listening now. Tell me more."

He reviewed each hack and their subsequent actions. "She was working in the server room, and now she's missing."

"Can you send me a screenshot of what she was working on when she went missing?"

"Maybe. At least I can try. Hold on, and I'll check the computer."

Trey didn't wait to explain what was going on but ran to the server room. He sat down behind the computer. "Looks like gibberish to me."

He took a better look at the writing on the black background. "No, wait. Wait. There's a message here. I assume this is the ransomware code."

"What does it say?"

"The floodgates are open, Calloway, and your problems are just beginning." Trey had no idea what that meant other than it was directed at Eryn. "Does that make any sense to you?"

"Unfortunately, yes." The worry in her tone ratcheted up Trey's concern to near panic level. "Eryn said that to Velichko when we arrested him, and he went ballistic. Tried to attack her. He's out of prison and has threatened her."

"So in all likelihood he has her."

"Sounds like it, and he has a history of violence when things don't go his way."

"Do you have a last known address for Velichko?"

"I don't have the address he gave the prison when he was released, but before he went away, he owned a house near Rugged Point. He was forced to pay restitution for the equipment he bricked, so he had to sell it—it's not likely he'd be there." She paused for a moment. "My analyst is contacting the prison for a forwarding address for Velichko. I'll check with him and call you back."

"Use my cell, not Eryn's." He gave her the number and hung up.

He got up to find Gage and Riley at the door, and he could hardly think well enough to communicate. He took a long breath and let it out. "It's almost certain that Kirill Velichko has her."

Gage shoved a hand in his hair. "This is usually when we ask Eryn to do her thing on the computer and find information on the abductor."

Trey ran through the things Piper had told him, but all he could see in his mind's eye was this creep holding Eryn hostage. Maybe hurting her. Maybe killing her.

No! He wouldn't think that way.

"Piper's trying to get Velichko's forwarding address from the prison, but that could take hours. Even days." Trey slammed a fist into the wall. The pain radiated up his good arm, competing for a moment with the ache in his injured one.

Gage laid a hand on his shoulder. "Won't do any good if you do more damage to your body."

"You're right. I need to think straight. Velichko had to sell his house to pay restitution, but maybe he went back there. It's just up the coast. We should head there to check it out."

"Actually," Gage said. "We're better off taking the time to gather equipment we might need for a hostage rescue. Then if Piper hasn't called back, we'll head up the coast."

He was making sense in this crazy situation, and Trey was suddenly very thankful for his friend. "Okay, we prepare for as many rescue scenarios as we can think of. But if Piper hasn't contacted us by the time we're ready to roll, we're deploying." He met Gage's gaze and held it. "No excuses. No reasons not to go. We go."

"Get into the cave," Velichko said. "One false move and I shoot."

Why was he doing this? Bringing her here instead of killing her? What would he gain?

She stumbled forward through the damp sand. She'd come in via a side entrance and took a quick look at the main entrance. Rocks faced the beach, standing as sentries protecting the cave in high tide. Entering from that direction was virtually impossible, and the person would have to risk getting trapped in rocks to make it in. With high tide, they'd crash over the sharp rocks, ending their life.

Velichko pressed his hand on her back, shoving her toward the wall. "Sit."

As she lowered her body to the cold ground, she noticed thick metal eyebolts secured into the rock. Did he plan to tie her up here and leave her for the tide to come in? Had he somehow discovered her worst fear, or it was just a coincidence?

Either way, she was faced with water that could end her life. Panic assailed her, and she tried to breathe it away. Tried to remember God had her in His hands. She felt light-headed and made noises to let him know she couldn't get her breath.

"Tough," he said. "You'll need to work it out."

Work it out? Work it out? How?

The worst thing that would happen was she'd hyperventilate and pass out. Nothing worse.

She could do this. Just breathe. Even. Slow. Pray.

God, please help me! Please!

The sun was fully up by the time they got the SUV loaded with gear and Riley, Gage, and Trey were prepared to go after Eryn. Trey wished Coop and Jackson could join them, but with the security system down, they had to remain at the compound to protect Hannah and the kids plus the team assets.

Trey shook his hands, his injured arm aching, but he needed to get rid of his jitters. He always had them before an op in the Berets—most guys did—but not like this. Nothing like this.

Please keep Eryn safe. I know I should be trusting you. Funny how I told Eryn to seek you with her whole heart and she'd find you, but man, I'm seeking now, and I don't feel your presence. Are you there? Watching over her?

He had to be. Trey couldn't lose her. He couldn't imagine life without her.

Hah! Now he understood how she felt. She'd gone through the searing pain of losing a spouse, and it had to create an anguish a hundred times worse than tightened Trey's gut. No wonder she didn't want to get involved again.

His phone rang, and he startled, but recovered to grab it from his pocket.

"It's Piper," he told the others and put her on speaker.

"I've got the forwarding address Velichko left at the prison." She shared an apartment address in Rugged Point. By the time she finished, Gage was already looking it up on his phone. "It's a rental. We didn't find phone or utilities in his name, but he could be living with someone and not have a landline."

"Roger that," Trey said, his mind going to how they would breach this apartment and rescue Eryn.

"Let me know the minute you find her. Or if you need

more help." Trey disconnected and shoved the phone into his pocket.

"I've got the address up on my phone, and we'll make a plan on the way," Gage said.

They piled into the SUV. Riley drove, Alex rode shotgun, and Gage sat next to Trey in the second row of seats. Trey's arm and leg ached beyond description, but he shoved down the pain as Riley got them out of the compound and onto the highway. Alex swiveled to look over the seat.

Gage held out his phone. "This is the 3-D map."

"Eryn would be proud of you for loading the right map." Riley glanced in the mirror.

A wry smile crossed Gage's face. "She would, wouldn't she."

"So the map," Trey said, keeping them on task. "Building looks like an eight-plex with two entrances. Velichko is on the south side of the first floor which makes for an easier breach."

"Problem is, we don't even know if he's there or if there are civilians inside," Alex said.

Gage looked up. "Then we surveil the place until we do."

Trey shook his head. "We can't sit there for hours while he could kill Eryn."

Gage eyed Trey. "I'm not going to authorize a breach until I know my actions won't endanger her or a civilian."

He was right. Of course, he was, but Trey couldn't think straight right now, and he sure couldn't imagine sitting inside this vehicle for hours, not knowing what was going on in the apartment. He would get nowhere by arguing, though, so he would table it for now. "We'll play it by ear."

He turned his attention back to the map and jabbed his finger on a nearby apartment building. "Riley can take over-watch here. It'll give him a perfect view of the small window on the front of Velichko's unit. Hopefully the blinds are open. Patio door's on the south side. We can park in the front lot, and then one of us takes this door."

"I've got it," Alex volunteered.

Trey took out his phone. "I'll look online for floor plans for the complex."

He located the apartment website and found the layouts. He held out his phone. "They have one- and two-bed units. The entrance for all is through the living room. Bedroom one is to the right. Bedroom two is to the left in a two-bedroom unit. If it's a one-bed, we have a direct line of sight into the bedroom from the front window."

"Two-bed will pose a problem," Gage said.

Trey stabbed a finger at the plan. "It has a window facing the courtyard. It'll be a risk to expose our location to get that close for a good look, but it can't be helped."

"Once we're clear, we can make a simultaneous breach from the front and the patio door," Alex pointed out.

"Agreed." Gage glanced at his watch. "At this time of day, we need to be cognizant of neighbors. One look at us in our gear and our weapons, and they could derail our plan to surprise Velichko."

Trey nodded and stowed his phone. Plan in place, he settled back to close his eyes and calm his nerves enough to be able to follow the plan and not make a deadly mistake.

Eryn wanted to rest back against the wall, but her arms were wrenched behind her back and secured to an eyebolt mounted low in the thick cave wall, preventing that. Velichko had snugged handcuffs around her wrists and run a thick chain through them and the bolt, then secured it with a padlock. If that wasn't enough, he added a pair of zip ties, too. He wasn't taking any chances.

He stood and peered down on her, his narrow lips tipped in a snide smile. "I would be remiss if I left without telling you the plan."

She didn't want to know how he planned to kill her, but being gagged and bound, she couldn't do anything to stop him from tormenting her.

"As much fun as it was playing with you at the resort, watching you run around to try to figure out why someone wanted your classes cancelled when I was just messing with you, today is the real deal. First high tide of the day is in a couple of hours, but the water will begin filling the cave before then. You'll have plenty of time to sit here and watch the water roll in and think about your upcoming death. Just like the hours I had in prison to think about killing you." He sneered. "You messed with the wrong man."

He lifted his shoulders. "Maybe I would've cut you some slack, but you had to go all righteous that day you arrested me. Spouting some nonsense about floodgates opening. When high tide rolls in, you'll know all about an open flood-gate." He laughed, but kept his glazed eyes trained on her.

"And don't think your buddies are going to find you. I gave the prison a bogus address." He grinned widely. "They'll be setting up to bust some poor schmuck who happens to live in that apartment. No way they'll find you here."

She wished she could ask how he knew about this location.

"Spent hours here as a kid," he said as if reading her mind. "My old man was pretty free with his fists. He worked nights so I hid out here during the day. He never did figure out where I went and couldn't find me. Stupid old man. He tried following me so many times, but I lost him every time. Earned me a beating, but I never talked. Never cracked. I learned the hard way how to take a beating, so if your buddies somehow find me, they can pound me to within an inch of my life, and I won't tell them where you are."

He turned to leave then looked back. "You can count on that, Calloway. They'll never find you. Never!"

Panic flared up, and Eryn almost cried out. Almost pleaded through her gag for him to stay. But he wouldn't remain here because she asked, and he would only get a kick out of her begging. She wasn't about to let him have that satisfaction.

As he left, she closed her eyes to stop looking at the waves crashing on the shore and to think. Her only hope of getting out of here was to find something to cut the zip ties and also break the cuffs. But what might she find in the cave?

Sure, Velichko would have removed anything she could use to gain freedom, but maybe something washed in on the evening tide that he didn't notice.

She opened her eyes and searched the space. A small shell and piece of driftwood lay near the mouth of the cave. They seemed too far away, but she stretched her legs out as far as possible. The muscles in her arms cramped from the time in an unnatural position, and she had to sit back to release the tension and cramps. She remained still until the muscles released and then waited a bit longer for good measure. Only then did she stretch out again. Her foot was so close. Maybe if she took off her shoe, she could bend her foot at the needed angle to capture the items.

She pulled in her leg and used her other foot to remove her shoe, then reached out again. She felt the wood through her sock. If she could remove it, she should be able to grasp it with bare toes. She lifted her leg again. Pushed off her other shoe. Used her other foot to remove her sock. She was gasping for breath by the time she got the wet fabric off and took a moment to relax.

Breathing normally again, she reached out. Grasped the wood. Dragged it closer. Dropped it. Picked it up and moved it close. She braced it against her other leg and rolled it closer until it lay in her lap.

But now what?

She couldn't get her hands around front. Couldn't bend and use her teeth. She had to maneuver to the side and dump it near the wall. Then maybe she could reach it.

She shifted slowly, making sure not to lose the stick. She inched closer to the wall. Her arms screamed in agony, her wrists threatened to dislocate, the cold metal cuffs biting into her tender skin. But she continued.

When she could move no closer, she paused to catch her breath then heaved her body sideways. The stick launched into the air and hit the wall.

Yes! She'd done it.

She scrambled around, digging her toes into the cold sand and pushing until she faced as far in the other direction as possible. She reached out with her fingers. Felt the tip of the stick. Pressed on it to flip it her way. She felt it move. Waited for it to hit her hands. Nothing.

No. Oh no. Did she send it in the other direction?

She turned to look. It lay by the wall. Out of her reach.

No. No. She'd failed. Big time. And this failure could cost her life.

26

"We're a go," Gage said into their comm unit.

Trey took off from the vehicle, assault rifle out, marching straight to the front door. Alex was already in place in the rear of the building, and Gage trailed Trey while Riley had their backs on overwatch. Trey stepped to the side, and Gage inserted the breaching tool in the metal door's jamb. He lifted then put his shoulder under the tool and pressed up. The door swung free.

Trey shot inside. Alex had picked the patio door lock and he ripped it open to enter. They met in a small living area. The space was clear. Too clear. Not a scrap of furniture in sight.

Still, they continued on. Trey led. Alex fell in second, and Gage took up the rear. They cleared the kitchen. The bathroom. The single bedroom and closet.

Trey sighed out his adrenaline. "You guys thinking what I'm thinking?"

"Not Velichko's place," Alex said.

Gage frowned. "He must've given a false address at the prison."

"Early release means he's still technically serving his sentence, just outside the prison walls," Trey said. "So he has to know that if he gets caught lying, it's an immediate return to prison."

Gage met Trey's gaze. "Then I'd say he doesn't plan on getting caught."

Trey eyed Gage. "You mean he plans to disappear."

"Sounds like it."

"Then we need to alert the authorities to be on the lookout for him at transit points."

Gage got out his phone. "I'll call Blake. Get him on it, while you two figure out where we go from here."

"I'm calling Piper." Trey pulled out his phone and dialed. "Velichko played us." He explained. "I want to know everything you know about him."

"Starting where?"

"The beginning." Trey rested against the counter, but was too antsy to stay in one place, so he started pacing instead.

"Mom took off when he was in grade school," Piper said. "He lived with a dad who beat him. Spent some time in foster care but was ultimately returned to the dad."

"Where did he grow up?"

"Rugged Point. Dad was a commercial fisherman until he got hurt then he was a night watchman at one of the fisheries. Dad owned a small house on the beach, and that's where we located Velichko after he got cocky, made a mistake, and Eryn tracked him."

"So he lived his whole life in Rugged Point?"

"Yeah. In middle school, a computer teacher took an interest in him, and he got involved in computers. He worked a legit job as a repair tech at a local computer store until it closed. Then he dropped out of sight."

"Sounds like we need to visit his old house."

"But he sold it."

"Was forced to sell it," Trey clarified. "Doesn't mean he doesn't still think the place is his and took it back."

"You may have a point," she said and gave him the address on Beach Way in Rugged Point. "While you check the place out, I'll listen to our old interviews with him. Maybe he said something that'll help."

Trey hung up and filled Alex and Gage in on his conversation. "We need to check out the house."

Gage frowned. "Breaching this door is going to cost me. Maybe the complex will press charges, too, so we're not going in there guns blazing."

"Let's move," Trey said, without agreeing to Gage's terms.

If Trey had to breach that place, he would and wouldn't think twice about it. And when push came to shove, he knew Gage would do the same thing. He was just trying to warn them not to be stupid.

In the car, Gage called the apartment complex management and explained their breach. He held the phone away from his ear, and Trey could hear the man on the other end of the call shouting. When he calmed, Gage said, "I'll pay to repair the damage and make the trouble worth your while. Perhaps you can tell me who the apartment is registered to."

He answered but Trey couldn't make out his response.

"Thank you." Gage tapped his phone and sighed out a long breath. "That's gonna cost me."

"I'll pay for it," Trey said. "Was the place leased to Velichko?"

"No. Vacant."

"He *is* planning to disappear, then." Trey didn't like that thought. Didn't like it at all. "He could be taking Eryn with him, and we'll never find her."

"Hey, man," Gage said. "Don't talk like that. We'll find her. Besides she's resourceful. She may already be free."

It was obvious Gage was trying to make Trey feel better, but there was no validity to his claim. Because if Eryn was free, she'd have found a way to contact them.

So Trey didn't feel better. Not one bit.

Eryn may have bungled the driftwood, but she had to try for the seashell. It wouldn't help free her from the cuffs, but she might be able to slice through the zip ties and gain more flexibility to go for the stick again.

She twisted and stretched her body until she gripped the ragged shell between her toes. The sharp edge bit into her tender flesh, but she held tight. Instead of trying to move it up her leg, which she doubted she could succeed at, she lifted her foot and flicked the shell against the wall. It dropped down next to her.

Yes! Yes! Her first real break.

She picked up the shell, her torn fingertips stinging, but she didn't care. She turned the jagged edge toward the zip tie and started sawing. The shell was thick and strong and it didn't crumble.

Thank you, God!

She sawed, her fingers growing tired. Her hand slipped, and she sliced into her arm. Pain radiated through her. She felt the stickiness of blood. Remembered Trey's blood on her hands.

Please don't let this be a serious cut. I want to live. Want to be there for Trey. With Trey. Him and Bekah. A family. If You'll only let me. I'm no longer afraid of losing him. I love him and need him in my life.

288

Rejuvenated, she concentrated on her hand. The blood flow seemed to be slowing. She would rest for a few minutes and try again. She closed her eyes and heard male voices nearby, coming closer. She opened her eyes, mouthed help, but it was a muffled sound. She kicked her feet to make noise, the sand absorbing every sound.

"Velichko's not here," the man said. "Was a long shot."

Trey. Was that Trey? Had he come to find her?

"And no Eryn," he added, sounding so sad her heart split.

"Trey. Trey. I'm here," she called out to no avail. "Right here in the cave. Come look. Please. Please don't leave."

"We should get back to the compound and regroup," Gage said.

"Gage!" she tried to scream. "I'm here."

"You're right. Let's go." Trey's voice was so dejected. "I can check in with Piper again, and maybe she's thought of something else."

Eryn listened. Heard footsteps. Receding footsteps rustling through grass.

They'd been so close. Now they were gone. Gone!

No. Not this. They would check this place off their list and had no reason to come back here again.

Time rushed past, and Trey was nearly out of his mind with panic and worry. He paced the conference room floor waiting for Piper to return his call. The only way he could think to locate Eryn was to talk to Velichko's prison cellmate and maybe learn something about Velichko that only the cellmate knew. Piper was trying to get permission for Trey to have a conversation via the telephone, but an hour had passed without a word from her.

Hannah entered the room, carrying a basket. A tangy spice emanated from under the fabric covering, but even the idea of eating something left Trey ready to hurl.

"I figured by now you all must be tired of snacks and want some real food. So I made a breakfast casserole." Hannah set the basket on the table and came over to him. "How are you holding up?"

"Not good, and I can't even think of food."

"But you didn't have breakfast. You have to keep your strength up." She rested a hand on his arm. "Please try to eat. For Eryn, so when you *do* get word on how to find her, you'll have the energy to help her."

He appreciated Hannah's positive take on finding Eryn so he sat in the chair she pulled out, but honestly, he didn't know if he could eat.

She put a scoop of egg casserole and a golden-brown biscuit on a paper plate and handed it to him. The others sat, too, and dug in. He took a bite of the casserole. If Hannah made it, it had to be delicious, but it tasted like mush. Still, he forced himself to chew and swallow. To rinse and repeat until he consumed every bite. Took him a good thirty minutes to accomplish the task, but he did it.

His phone rang, and seeing Piper's name, he grabbed it from the table.

"Tell me you have permission," he snapped.

"Sorry, no."

His heart dropped.

"But I was able to talk to him."

"He tell you anything we can use?"

"Maybe, but it's a longshot."

"I don't care. We don't have anything else."

"As I mentioned, Velichko's father abused him. He told his cellmate that his dad worked nights so Velichko took refuge during the day in a cave near their house when he wasn't in school."

A spark of hope burgeoned in Trey's heart. "And you think he could've taken Eryn to this cave?"

"It's possible. At least it's not some place that we've checked."

Trey shot to his feet. "The house he sold. Was that his childhood home?"

"Yes."

"We'll check it out." Trey hung up and relayed the information to the team. "When we walked down to the beach, we must've been near that cave. Eryn could be in there, and we were right by her."

Riley looked up at the clock. "High tide's in less than an hour."

"Then let's move," Trey said already on his way to the door.

He could easily imagine Eryn in the cave, the water rushing in. She'd told him at the pool about her unease around water. She played if off as nothing much, but he could tell it ran deeper than she let on.

He imagined her in the cave. The water coming in. Lapping closer and closer. Hearing him and the guys talking outside when they'd taken a trip down to the beach. Then walking away.

His heart ached with the thought. She had to be terrified. Simply terrified. And he'd failed her in a way for which he might never be able to forgive himself.

≈

The thunderous roar of waves rushed into the cave. The water splashed against Eryn's chest, and a deep shiver shook her body. The water was cold. So cold, even in August. She knew if she didn't drown, once most of her body was submerged, she would die of hypothermia in less than an hour. But she didn't think that would likely happen as she could see the water line marks on the wall. The highest level was clear over her head even if she was standing. She would drown before hypothermia took her life.

Tears filled her eyes. She would pray again, but she'd been praying for hours, and she didn't know what else to say. Other than to ask to die as peacefully as possible. She'd held out hope for so long. Believing Trey and the team would come back to find her. They rarely failed in anything they did, but in this case, Velichko left them nothing to go on.

And why would they go looking in some cave on the beach? It didn't make sense. If she was at the compound helping them out, she would be searching for a building of some sort, not a cave.

She peered up at the rock above her head. It looked smooth from years of water rushing in and out. She had to admit God's amazing creation and power was evident in her little cave. And if He could create such an awesome sight, He could rescue her. If He wanted to.

Maybe He didn't want to. There was still time, and she should keep hoping. Believing. For Bekah's sake. Her precious child couldn't lose her mother, too. The loss would so devastate her. Maybe scar her for life.

Please, Father. For her. For my child. Let me live.

And what about Trey?

Yes, for Trey, too. I don't want him to know the pain I endured when losing Rich.

She held her breath and waited for something to happen. But the only thing that followed was the water creeping higher, wetting her shoulders.

Not long now.

She heard a sound outside the cave and hope blossomed again.

How many times had that happened today, and it turned out to be the waves crashing a bit harder?

Still, she listened. Were those footsteps?

"Hurry," a male voice said.

"Trey!" she screamed, but it came out muffled.

Was she hearing things, like being stranded in a desert and seeing a mirage, or was he really here?

She thrashed around in the water. At least as much as she was able. Her legs were stiff from the frigid water now, her arms cramped and inflexible. Her whole body ached with the cold.

A light shone into the cave from the ocean side, illuminating the space. It glistened off the water that now reached her chin.

"See anything?" Gage asked.

"No," Trey replied.

"I'm here! Here!" She pushed up to make herself taller. Barely an inch higher, but higher. "Trey. Please Trey. I'm here!"

"Maybe we were wrong," Gage said.

The light went out.

"No. No. Please keep looking. Go to the other side. Please!"

Waves rolled in, and she couldn't hear if they'd departed or not.

Salty water lapped into her mouth, and she choked. She lifted her head higher and coughed around the soggy rag.

Oh, dear God. Is this it? Is it the end?

27

"There could be another entrance," Trey said. "I'll head south. Riley you go north. And Gage west."

They split up, and Trey moved as fast as he could, sloshing through the water and over the slippery rocks to climb the steep berm. Prepared in case she was handcuffed, he held bolt cutters firmly in his hand and braced his injured arm against his body to lessen the pain.

Please don't let it be too late. Let me find Eryn.

Frantic now, he climbed higher. Spotted a hole in the rocks. Did it lead into the cave?

He barreled ahead. Reached the opening and knelt to turn on his light.

He barely took time to take in the details. All he needed to see was that she was alive with water lapping at her gagged mouth. "Eryn! Thank God I found you."

He turned and cupped his hands around his mouth against the wind.

"I've got Eryn!" he called out. "She *is* in the cave. Going in now."

He slipped into the cave. Into the cold water. How could she stand being submerged like that?

He had to get her out quickly before she couldn't breathe or hypothermia took her.

"I'm here, honey. Everything's going to be fine." He cooed in a soft voice as he waded over to her. "I have to pocket the flashlight to free your hands."

She peered up at him, her eyes big and terrified. He wanted to release the gag and hold her for a moment, but a wave crashed in and covered her face.

She tried to cough, but it was pitiful with the gag in place.

He shoved the flashlight in his pocket and reached down to find her hands. Salt water licked at his wounded arm, the pain nearly taking him down, but he couldn't fail her again. He felt a pair of handcuffs and slid his fingers down to the chain holding them together. He positioned the cutters in place. Metal firmly in the jaws, he let go with his hand to grasp the cutter and make the cut. Another wave crashed in before he was ready, tipping him over.

He tumbled into the water. Held firm on the cutters but came up coughing. Eryn was trying to cough, too. Anger surged through his body. At the man who put her here. At himself.

He planted his feet. Repeated his steps. Snapped the bolt. Dropped the cutters. Lifted Eryn from the water and saw zip ties float free, a deep gash in her wrist.

His anger swirled inside, and he lifted her into his arms. She moaned in pain. He ripped the gag free.

"You came," was all she said.

"I'm so sorry it took so long. Are you hurt anywhere?"

"I'm fine."

She wasn't fine, but he accepted that she didn't have a serious injury other than the cold threatening her body.

A wave hit them, and his leg muscles strained to keep them upright. He waited for it to subside and stepped toward the exit. "I'm going to slide you through. I know your arms are likely weak and the muscles stiff, but I'll need you to move free of the opening so I can get out, too." He looked deep into her shell-shocked eyes. "Can you do that for me, honey?"

"Yes." Her teeth chattered, and her whole body convulsed with the cold.

"Okay, here we go." He hated to let her go, but he carefully slid her out.

"My arms," she said. "I can't lift them."

"Give it a minute."

If she couldn't move soon, he would have to crawl out on top of her, but he didn't want to do that with the sharp rocks under her body.

"Eryn!" Gage called out, and Trey heard footsteps pounding closer.

"Help," she said. "I have to move so Trey can get out before the cave fills with water."

"Don't worry about me," he said. "I have plenty of time."

It was her he was worried about. The cold. The shock.

Gage bent down and lifted her away from the opening. Trey surged against the water and pushed out. Once on his feet, he took Eryn from Gage's arms.

"I'll get blankets ready," Gage said and he took off, calling out to Riley on the way.

"I thought I was going to die," Eryn whispered through blue lips.

"I wish I'd found you sooner. Better yet, that I'd never left you alone."

"Not your fault." She snuggled closer, her arms limp.

He moved as fast as he could toward the SUV without taking a tumble. At the vehicle, Gage had emergency blankets out, the heater running on high, and he was on the phone telling everyone at the compound that they'd located Eryn.

Trey settled into the backseat with Eryn on his lap and wrapped her in the blanket. Gage and Riley climbed in.

"To the ER. Fast," Trey called out.

"No! I want to go home. Have to go home. Must see Bekah. Now!"

"We should get you warmed up first."

"I'll be okay. Just take me home."

Trey didn't want to agree, but he also didn't want to cause her more anguish. "You heard her."

Gage nodded, but the look he gave Trey in the mirror said he didn't like it. Still, he got them moving, and once on the highway, he floored it.

"I was afraid I'd lost you," Trey whispered against her wet hair. "And I'd never have the chance to tell you that I love you."

She shifted to look at him. "You do?"

"Yes. Totally and completely."

"Me too," she said. "I mean, I love you, too."

His heart blazed like a roaring fire. He never expected this. Never believed she could change her mind. "When I thought I might lose you, I understood how you felt about not getting involved again. At least more than I did before."

"I'm ready now."

"Are you sure?"

"Honestly, no. Maybe I'm reacting to the near-death experience. But I want to try with you if you're willing to move forward without a commitment."

"Are you kidding?" He smiled. "Gage. Does that job offer still stand?"

∽

Eryn spent the rest of the drive snuggled against Trey's chest. His clothes were wet and cold, but the blanket covered them both, and the heat pouring from the vents had warmed her to the point where she stopped shivering.

Trey and Gage talked about the logistics of Trey starting on the Blackwell Tactical team, and Eryn only hoped she didn't end up breaking his heart. She loved him. That much was clear, but had she truly let go of her fear?

She hadn't done so well at trusting God in the cave. She'd cried out so many times. Doubted. Feared. But it all worked out in the end. She was safe. With the man she loved. What more could she ask for?

Maybe that Velichko was caught.

"I heard you mention Piper," she said to Trey. "How did you find her?"

"She left a message on your answering machine. She talked to Velichko's cellmate, and she was the one who gave us the lead on the cave."

"Glad I insisted on everyone having a landline," Gage said.

"No one is happier about that than me." Eryn smiled up at the mirror.

"I should call Piper and let her know you're okay." Trey shifted around to get out his phone. "Wait. No. I'll bet my phone is toast."

"I should be able to fix it for you, and we can call Piper the minute we get home."

"I like having my very own techie." He nuzzled her neck. "My very own woman to love."

She grinned at him and snuggled back against his chest until they pulled up to Gage's house. She pushed off Trey's lap and stifled a groan at the raging pain in her arm muscles. No matter. Once she had them wrapped around Bekah, she would forget all about the pain.

Trey held the door for her, and she stepped inside. Her mother and Hannah were sitting on the sofa. Bekah was playing on the carpet with Mia.

Eryn's mother shot to her feet and charged across the room. She swept Eryn into a hug. "Our prayers have been answered."

"Yes," Eryn said. "God sent Trey to my exact location."

Her mother pushed back. "You're all wet."

"A cave at the beach," was all she was willing to say near Bekah.

"Then you must've been very brave."

Eryn felt tears coming, so she looked away and called out to her daughter.

Bekah looked up. "Mommy, did you go swimming with your clothes on?"

"Something like that." Eryn knelt and held out her arms, the pain nearly taking them down.

Bekah came running. "I had the bestest day. I got to play with Mia and David all day. And Gammy and Hannah played, too. We swinged and played with Barkley. And built with Legos and played Candyland and Chutes and Ladders, and I won."

Eryn laughed with joy over having her chatterbox of a child in her arms and tightened her hold.

"You're squishing me, Mommy."

"Sorry. I just missed you so much."

"But you got to go swimming. We didn't." She pushed free and pouted. "Can we go swimming now?"

"I was thinking," Hannah said as she got up. "Bekah's had such a fun day here, why don't we make it an all-day event and have a sleepover?"

Bekah's eyes lit up. "Can I, Mommy?"

As much as Eryn would like to be near her child, a good soak in a hot bath and a long sleep was exactly what she needed tonight. And maybe some alone time with Trey, too. To talk about the future and what it held for them.

She kissed her daughter's cheek. "Of course, you can."

"Yay." Bekah went cheering back into the family room and dropped down on the carpet.

Eryn gave Hannah a thankful look and before she could manage to get up, Trey was there gently helping her. "You should get out of these wet clothes."

"You, too," she said.

"Then let's go," her mother said. "I hoped you'd be home for dinner so I made clam chowder in the crock pot."

Eryn was glad for her mother's nurturing, but she honestly wanted to send her home so she could be alone with Trey.

Hannah came over and gave Eryn a gentle hug. "I'm so glad to be able to hug you."

"Good news," Gage said. "Trey's going to start working for us in two weeks."

Hannah pulled back and gaped at Eryn. "I'll let you go tonight, but you *will* tell me all about this tomorrow."

"Yes, ma'am." Eryn raised her arm to salute, but the pain was still too great, and she let her arm drop.

Outside, they climbed into her mother's car. She shifted into drive. "I'll stay long enough to run you a bath, Eryn, and hear about what happened today, but then I'll leave the two of you to have dinner on your own. Especially since it sounds like I'm going to be seeing more of Trey."

She winked, and Eryn finally realized that Trey—her Trey, the man she loved—would be living at the compound. Excitement churned in her stomach and mixed with a hint of anxiety, but the excitement won out.

At her cabin, Trey held the door again and gave her a look that made her toes curl.

"Oh, my," her mother said and blushed as she rushed into the house. "I'll get that bath running."

"I better put that filter back in place." Trey laughed.

Eryn chuckled. "I'll call Piper while my mom runs the bath."

Eryn went to the landline phone and dialed.

"Eryn is that you?" Piper's anxious voice asked.

"Yes. Trey found me and I'm home."

"The cave?"

"The cave."

"I'm sorry, sweetie. I know how hard that must've been for you." As Eryn's good friend, Piper knew all about Eryn's fear of water.

"I'm just glad this's over, and I have you to thank for telling Trey where to look."

"Wish I could've done more and faster."

"You did plenty."

"You'll be happy to hear that Velichko's been apprehended at the airport. You'd think he would have been smarter than to take a plane."

Eryn shook her head. "Did he use his real name?"

"No. We're testing a new technology—sunglasses equipped with facial recognition technology cameras. It's linked to a central database that contains criminal records. The wearer can instantly view an individual's personal details. We thought this was a good application so the agents we tasked with manning the airport wore them."

"That sounds so cool," Eryn said. "You will, of course, let me try them out."

"You know it." Piper chuckled.

"Seriously, we'll have to get together soon so I can thank you properly."

"No thanks needed, but I'd love to see you. It's been too long."

Eryn promised to call, disconnected, and faced Trey. "They caught Velichko."

"Seriously? Already?"

Eryn nodded and explained. She crossed the room to Trey. "So everything worked out fine."

"And now, we can start talking about that future."

"Yeah," she said. "Right after this."

She raised up on tiptoes and pressed her lips against his. His were still cold but tasted deliciously sweet. Likely because Eryn now felt free to express her feelings for this amazing, wonderful, incredible man and knew he reciprocated those feelings.

"The bath is ready if—" Her mother's words fell off, and Eryn heard her back out of the room.

She loved her mother, but she wasn't going to call out and tell her it was okay to come into the room. Not until Eryn had her fill of kissing Trey.

EPILOGUE

Eryn lifted Kiera's veil over her face and smiled at the beautiful bride. Kiera's mother was being seated in the sanctuary, and Eryn felt a real responsibility to get Kiera to the altar on time. Eryn had been touched that Kiera had asked her to be in her wedding party along with Hannah and Maggie and was eager to have her new friend living at the compound with them. Maggie had a Christmas wedding planned, so she would be moving here, too. Eryn couldn't wait to have all the girl power at the compound.

"You look perfect," Eryn said to Kiera.

Kiera turned to look in the full-length mirror at the community church where the team members attended. She'd chosen an A-line princess dress with chiffon lace at the bodice and neck. Her auburn hair was swept up in a bun holding delicate lily of the valley silk flowers, and the veil was no more than a whisper of fabric covering her face.

"I do look good, don't I?" She giggled like a little child and turned. "It's love, I tell you. And the three of you seem to be infected with it, too."

Hannah chuckled. "If this is a sickness, I don't want to

ever get well."

Maggie smoothed the mesh skirt on her cute ice blue above-the-knee dress that matched Eryn's and Hannah's. It had a delicate grosgrain ribbon belt that divided the lace bodice and flirty skirt.

"Ditto that," Maggie said. "I wish we hadn't decided on the Christmas wedding. It seems so far away."

Far away was better than not at all. Eryn nipped on her lip. She and Trey declared their love not very long ago, but she'd expected him to pop the question by now, and he hadn't done so.

"He'll ask," Hannah said as if reading Eryn's mind.

Eryn felt hope burgeoning in her heart. "You think so?"

"I know so."

"I agree," Kiera said. "If you could only see the way he looks at you, you'd know it, too."

"And he loves Bekah. I hardly ever see one of them without the other."

Eryn thought about the last month, and their time together since he joined the team. Almost every moment of their down time, he played with Bekah. In fact, there were times she arranged a play date for Bekah with Mia and David so Eryn could have Trey all to herself.

"You could be right. I mean, he once said he couldn't work on the team if we weren't together, so I'd thought he meant married to me." She sighed. "I wish I was brave enough to ask him."

"You, not brave enough?" Kiera shook her head.

"Shocking!" Maggie clutched her chest in pretend shock.

Eryn laughed. "I don't want to put him on the spot."

"I wouldn't ask either," Hannah said. "Just enjoy your time together."

A knock sounded on the door.

"I'll get it," Eryn offered. She hurried to open it and found Kiera's twin brother Kevin waiting. He was one of Coop's groomsmen, and Eryn hoped there wasn't a problem. Eryn stepped back and Kevin entered.

"Wow, sis. You look great." He shook his head. "So you're really doing this, huh?"

"Yes."

"That's what I told Coop, too."

Kiera frowned. "Why? Why did you have to tell him that?"

"He's shaking like a leaf. Said he was afraid you'd have second thoughts and remember what a grump he can be and you wouldn't walk down that aisle."

Eryn could hardly imagine Coop shaking over anything, but she smiled at the thought.

A soft smile slid across Kiera's mouth. "He *can* be a grump, but he's my grump till death do us part."

"Then I'm here to tell you it's time to make that promise, and you should get out there before his knees lock up and he passes out cold." Kevin laughed.

Kiera hugged her brother. "Thanks for being in the wedding. I know you're not into this kind of thing."

"Hey, I'll do about anything for my favorite twin."

"Your only twin."

"Yeah, that, too." He grinned, looking so much like Kiera that Eryn had to shake her head at the resemblance. "See you at the altar."

Tugging on his tie, he bolted for the door.

Kiera turned toward them. "Okay, ladies, it's showtime."

Eryn hugged Kiera, as did Hannah and Maggie, and the three of them followed Kiera out the door. Hannah adjusted Kiera's train, and they strolled down the hallway to the sanctuary.

306

"I am so excited for this day," Hannah said. "Almost as excited as I was at my wedding to Gage."

The worship center door was open, and Kiera's dad stood waiting, nervously fidgeting with his tie like Kevin had done. White rose bouquets matching the bridal party bouquets and pale blue bows sat in stands at the end of the aisles, and a white runner covered the aisle. At the front stood Coop, Gage, Jackson, and Kevin. They wore basic black two-button tuxes with a white shirt and fine-lined striped black and white ties. Coop shifted on his feet, his face paler than normal, and his hands were clasped so tightly the fingers had turned white.

"Oh, my," Hannah said. "Gage looks so handsome. I know I should be commenting on Coop since it's his wedding, but I was too nervous on my wedding day to really appreciate Gage in a suit, but oh my." She fanned her face.

Eryn grinned, but thought she might be doing the same thing if she could see Trey. He had to look fine in a suit, too, but he arrived at the cabin after she left for the church so she hadn't seen him. He was sitting with her mother and Bekah. Bekah wanted to be in the wedding, but Kiera had chosen not to have a flower girl as she didn't want to hurt Mia or Bekah's feelings by picking one of them.

"Ready to do this, sweetheart?" Kiera's dad asked.

"Am I ever." A radiant smile captured her face, and Eryn could imagine it lighting up even more when she caught sight of her husband-to-be.

"Then let's signal the quartet." He raised his hand and waved at the string quartet to begin the music.

Maggie started down the aisle first, and Eryn followed at a distance. Alex and Riley had donned suits, too, and they sat in solidarity with their newest team member, Samantha Willis, who joined them two weeks ago as their forensic expert. They'd taken the row where Coop's family might have sat if he'd wanted them at his wedding. It made Eryn sad that he didn't want to include them, but she was glad he had his team family here supporting him.

When Maggie reached the front, she held out her hand to Jackson, who clung to it for a second, his eyes shining with love. These two had come through such a difficult past, and to see their happiness was priceless to Eryn.

Tears formed in her eyes, and she had to blink to keep them at bay. She kept her eyes forward until she reached the pew where her family sat. Her mother. Bekah. And Trey. He was family now, too. Just not officially.

Bekah wore a crisp white dress, her hair curled with a beaded white headband holding it back, and she was kneeling on Trey's lap, looking back at Eryn.

"Mommy," she said softly, her arms going around Trey's neck. He swiveled to look at her. His eyes widened in admiration.

She felt the sizzle of electricity flowing between them clear to her silver strappy sandals. He started to smile—slow, languid, luscious. It lit up his entire face, and she couldn't contain her responding smile. She almost forgot where she was and caught her toe in the runner. She nearly stumbled but righted herself and continued up the aisle.

She reached her position and turned to find him still watching her. She couldn't take her eyes from him, and knew then, without a doubt, if any man was worth stumbling over, he was the one.

Let him ask me, Father. Please let him ask.

Trey could barely force himself to stand and watch the bride come down the aisle because it meant turning away from Eryn. The icy blue color of her dress complimented her dark hair and tan skin that looked so silky smooth in the strapless dress. The skirt swirled around her knees and the high heels gave her legs a long sleek look. Gone was his fierce defender of the innocent, and a very soft and feminine woman stood before him.

He didn't know which he liked best, but man, he liked her. Loved her. Couldn't quit telling her, which is why he'd had to force himself to be more reserved the past month than he wanted to be. She still seemed a little skittish, and he didn't want to scare her off, but if he had his way about things he would be up at that altar waiting for her to marry him.

"Pretty," Bekah whispered bringing Trey's thought back to the wedding march. Kiera looked beautiful, and Coop was a lucky guy, but no one was as lucky as Trey. Looked like he would be settling down with Eryn and this precious little munchkin in her frilly little dress in his arms, too. Could he be any more blessed?

Kiera reached the front and everyone sat.

Sandra leaned over. "She's ready, you know. Just ask."

He didn't know how Sandra knew that, but he knew he got a big goofy grin on his face and patted the ring box in his pocket. He would wait until the end of the evening. Until the bride and groom had their special day. Until Bekah was tucked up in bed. Until he was under the stars at the outdoor reception with a starlight dance planned for later in the night.

He forced his mind to the wedding. To listen to the vows. But his gaze kept tracking to Eryn. He caught her eyes on him several times, and he suddenly wished it was dark already and they were alone under the stars.

When the music started playing and Kiera and Coop rushed down the aisle, Trey couldn't believe the ceremony was over. He watched Eryn pass by, her hand tucked in Kevin's arm, and a wave of jealousy washed over him. She wasn't interested in Kiera's brother, nor he in her, but the fact that she was touching him made Trey long for the same thing.

As did the way Maggie and Jackson held onto each other when they followed down the aisle. They would marry next, but maybe Trey could fit something in before Christmas. Nah, that wouldn't be fair to them. A January wedding might be nice, though.

After Kiera's family was escorted down the aisle, Trey looked at Bekah. "Are you ready to go see Mommy?"

She nodded and lifted her arms around his neck. "Carry."

Trey stood and settled her in his arms.

"I swear that girl has forgotten how to walk since she's had you in her life," Sandra said and smiled.

"I like riding," Bekah said. "And hugging." She tightened her hold on Trey's neck.

"Maybe a little less tight would be good," he squeaked out.

She relaxed her grip, and Trey looked ahead to see Eryn in the receiving line. She was on tiptoe looking over people until they locked eyes again, and she sighed contentedly.

"I told you she was ready," Sandra said.

"Yeah. Yeah, she is," he replied, his heart clipping along at racehorse speed.

Trey only hoped he could make it through the night without dragging her off to some secluded place to pop the question.

Eryn was flushed from the fun. Sharing the night with her Blackwell Tactical family was even more magical than it had been at Hannah and Gage's wedding because there were so many more "significant others" in the group. In fact, Alex and Riley looked a bit uncomfortable with all the love flowing around. She vowed to help them find someone special before the year was out. Not a challenge really as they were both great catches, but she knew they each had some resistance to long-term commitments. She would have to team up with Hannah to figure out what those issues were so the guys could find the light.

And then there was Samantha, Sam as she preferred to be called. Eryn didn't know her story, but she did know the very beautiful dark-headed Sam was single. Hmm, maybe Sam would be perfect for Alex or Riley. Time would tell.

Sandra stood and gestured at Trey who sat by their table, leaning back in his chair, his long legs out and crossed before him. He'd shed his suitcoat and rolled up the sleeves of his white shirt and loosened his tie, but Eryn would never forget the picture he made when she'd first spotted him in the church.

Tall, broad shoulders, trim waist, the suit tailored to accommodate his many muscles. Yeah, he was a fine-looking man. Her man.

"Looks like it's time to take little Miss Sleepyhead to bed," her mother said.

Bekah was sound asleep on his shoulder, and her arms hung limply over his side.

"I'll carry her to the car for you." He got up, and Eryn planted a kiss on her daughter's forehead.

"Thanks for taking her," Eryn told her mother and hugged her.

"Hey, I'd be a fool not to leave you under the stars with Trey tonight." She pulled back. "He's a keeper, you know."

"I know." She looked up at him.

"Be right back, and since I practiced all my dance moves with Bekah, I'm now prepared to dazzle you on your feet." He smiled at her.

She chuckled. "I'm ready to be dazzled."

She sat anxiously in her chair waiting for him to return. She loved how he naturally fit into the "dad" role. She could easily see him with the five children he wanted. She still wasn't sure if she was ready for that, but they could talk about it. Maybe negotiate the number down.

He soon returned, crossing the lawn with long-legged strides. She didn't wait for him to reach her but met him near the dance floor.

"You really did mean you wanted to dance, right?" she asked.

"Yes." He caught her hand in his and led her to the wooden platform with white glittery lights strung on poles surrounding it.

The floor was crowded with wedding guests, but he found a spot and drew her into his arms. The music was soft, slow, and romantic. She rested her head against his chest, and she couldn't feel more contented than she felt at this moment. But then the thought of children with him niggled its way into her mind, and she lifted her head to look at him.

"Do you still want five kids?" she asked.

His eyes widened. "Is that something that would be a deal breaker for you if we got married?"

This was the first time he used the word *married*, and her

heart almost stop beating. "No. But I'm not sure I'm ready to commit to that. It would be great to see how things went with each child and then plan accordingly."

He suddenly stopped moving. "Are you thinking about having children with me?"

She wanted to deny it as she was still feeling insecure, but she nodded.

A grin spread across his face, and he took her hand to lead her off the dance floor and into the dark. When they were out of sight of the guests, he turned to her. Stars sparkled overhead and a soft breeze blew in from the ocean. She couldn't imagine a more perfect moment, until he got down on his knee and pulled a ring box from his pocket.

She gasped. "You were planning this?"

"For weeks," he said. "I've had this ring in my pocket waiting for the perfect time."

He opened the box. Held it out. "I love you, Eryn. I don't care how many children we have, but I need you in my life. Bekah, too. Will you marry me?"

"Yes, yes, of course. Yes!"

He slid the ring on her finger and came to his feet. She admired the diamond solitaire with a wide white gold band. "This is perfect. I couldn't have chosen better myself."

"I have to admit, Hannah and your mom helped me."

He was so amazing to ask for help to make her happy, and she raised her arms up to clasp his neck. He lowered his head and their lips connected. His were warm and insistent and he kissed her for longer than she could imagine, leaving her breathless.

He lifted his head, and she stroked his cheek, happiness bursting inside of her. "I have to confess, I wondered why you hadn't asked sooner."

"I didn't want to scare you off."

"Scare me off? Never. I want to spend the rest of my life with you and have your children. Bekah will be so excited to hear that she might finally get a sibling."

He lifted Eryn and swung her around in a circle. "You have made me the happiest guy alive."

"Your family." she said, suddenly coming back to reality. "I haven't even met them."

"We'll take care of that right away, and I know they'll love you and Bekah as much as I do."

"Thank you." She hugged him hard. "For being the kind of man who can love another man's child. For making my daughter feel so special. So loved."

"I promise I couldn't love her more than any child we might have together." He smiled. "It might be too soon to mention this, but I'd like to adopt her."

Eryn had thought her heart couldn't be any fuller, but his statement proved that it could. "That would be wonderful."

"Now about a date for the wedding. If only Jackson and Maggie didn't have December all sewn up." A mischievous grin lit his eyes. "So January then?"

She laughed, and as she reached up to hug her soon-to-be husband, she offered a prayer of thanks to God for bringing this amazing man into her life, and for making her see that forever with the right guy was always worth the risk of loss. Always.

Want to read other books in the Cold Harbor Series? Read on for a sneak peek of the next book in the Cold Harbor Series!

Dear Reader:

Thank you so much for reading COLD CASE, book 4 in my Cold Harbor series featuring Blackwell Tactical. You'll be happy to hear that there are additional books in this series!

Book 1 - COLD TERROR
Book 2 - COLD TRUTH
Book 3 - COLD FURY
Book 4 - COLD CASE
BOOK 5 - COLD FEAR
BOOK 6 - COLD PURSUIT

I'd like to invite you to learn more about the books in my Cold Harbor series as they release and about my other books by signing up for my newsletter. You'll also receive a FREE sneak peek of my latest book. I love to interact with and hear from readers, so hop on over to the link below and let's connect.

https://www.susansleeman.com/connect/

Susan Sleeman

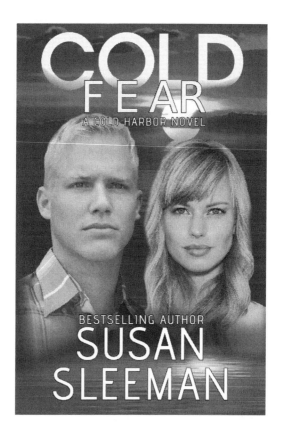

A shared past...

Riley Glen's former girlfriend, recording artist Leah Kent, is performing at a summer concert nearby and calls to tell him she's in danger and needs his help. After the concert, he discovers her bending over a woman's dead body, and the woman has Leah's name freshly tattooed on her wrist. Leah claims she just found the body and didn't have anything to do with the murder. When two other bodies are found, both boasting Leah's name in bright ink on their wrists, she comes under suspicion for the murders.

Riley jumps in to defend her from both an imminent arrest and a killer's deadly rage.

A new beginning?

Riley and Leah had once been a music team and deeply in love. But Riley's lifelong dream was to be a sniper, not a musician. He chose to follow his dream and has been successful in his career just as Leah has found success in hers. He still has feelings for Leah, but their lives are on vastly different courses. But when she begs for his help to clear her name and protect her, he agrees to do what he can. Riley soon discovers this killer is highly trained and vicious, and Leah won't survive another day unless Riley uses every skill he possesses to try to save her.

Coming soon!

ABOUT SUSAN

SUSAN SLEEMAN is a bestselling and award-winning author of more than 30 inspirational/Christian and clean read romantic suspense books. In addition to writing, Susan also hosts the website, TheSuspenseZone.com.

Susan currently lives in Oregon, but has had the pleasure of living in nine states. Her husband is a retired church music director and they have two beautiful daughters, a very special son-in-law, and an adorable grandson.

For more information visit:
www.susansleeman.com

Made in the USA
Columbia, SC
02 August 2018